
★

Someone leaned against me. I tried to shrug them off. The weight fell heavier on me. Then a feeling of dread settled over me. I turned, afraid to look.

The young woman with the Hawaiian shirt leaned against me, her hand at her throat, her gray eyes terror stricken.

"Oh, God!"

I grabbed for her, but couldn't get a firm grip. She slipped away, down my body, one hand at her throat, the other clinging to my pocket. I grabbed for her again. She tried to hold herself up, but she slipped through my fingers and slumped to the floor—the dark figure against the flickering, bloodred floor.

★

"...a quirky and savvy story..."
—*Rocky Mountain News*

Also available from Worldwide Mystery by
CHRISTINE T. JORGENSEN

A LOVE TO DIE FOR

you BET your LIFE

CHRISTINE T. JORGENSEN

W💿RLDWIDE.

TORONTO • NEW YORK • LONDON
AMSTERDAM • PARIS • SYDNEY • HAMBURG
STOCKHOLM • ATHENS • TOKYO • MILAN
MADRID • WARSAW • BUDAPEST • AUCKLAND

To my parents, Ruth and David, whose love
and patience endured; to my dearest friends,
Janie and Sylvia, who were first to aid and abet;
to my Jim, who believed in me.

YOU BET YOUR LIFE

A Worldwide Mystery/August 1997

This edition is reprinted by arrangement with
Walker and Company.

ISBN 0-373-26245-0

Printed in U.S.A.

ACKNOWLEDGMENTS

There are many people to whom I owe a debt of gratitude, but I especially need to acknowledge the invaluable support of the Rocky Mountain Fiction Writers, the generous help of the critique groups, and the special assistance and support of Christine Goff, Jim Cole, Janet Grill, and the Saturday mystery critique group, Lee Karr, Kay Bergstrom, Diane Mott Davidson, Leslie O'Kane, Peggy Swager and Dolores Johnson.

I would also like to acknowledge the contribution of my editor, Michael Seidman, whose salient comments have been instrumental in this book.

Finally, I would like to thank Central City, Colorado, for the many fine research opportunities afforded me.

ONE

I SAT AT the kitchen table in my seafoam shortie with late June's early morning sunshine pooling on the table and warming my skin under the aqua lace of my nightie. The nightie was one of my favorites...a creation I'd bought at Grace and Lilly's Little Nothings lingerie boutique before their top seamstress was murdered and I lost my best supply of gossamer excitement.

Stella the Stargazer:
　　You're dead meat. Because of you, my wife has decided she's sensitive and needs self-fulfillment. Do you know what that means? It means she left me and moved to Denver.
　　I've located her now, thanks to a buddy, and I'm going to bring her back. I don't care what it takes. But you're to blame, and I ain't forgetting it.
　　I'm everywhere. I'm everyone. And I'm waiting for the right time. Bitch! Pray you don't meet me.
　　　　　　　　　　　　Pissed Off and Ready to Kill.

My first reaction isn't always my best one. But Pissed Off and Ready to Kill spelled PORK.

I laughed. Or tried to.

I write an astrological column for the lovelorn in a weekly paper, the *Denver Daily Orion,* and it's going over well with readers who want advice on a variety of things. I answer each one of my letters personally, which takes a growing amount of my time, so I had brought some of the letters home the night before to try to catch up.

I don't even have to make up the letters myself anymore. And I love reading them.

But there are exceptions. This was one.

I dropped the envelope onto the tabletop and ran my fingers over the printing on the letter. Paranoia grew in me.

Maybe Pissed Off and Ready to Kill looked like a pig. I visualized dark, close-set eyes, beady and mean, large ears, curved forward at the top, and a receding jaw with spriggy stubble on his chin. Very ugly. I thought back to the last time I ate pork. Yesterday. In a bacon, lettuce, and tomato sandwich.

I reread the letter.

The line "I'm everywhere. I'm everyone" sent chills over my shoulders in little ripples. My amusement was fading fast.

My uncle Ralph lives on a farm in Iowa and raises pigs. He maintains that they're sly, mean and vengeful. Of course, in a bitter moment after one of his sons had run off, smashed the family car, and spent a night in jail, he also said "Pigs are smart—they eat their young." Ralph is not a patient man.

And angry pigs are not a laughing matter.

"I'm waiting for the right time." That implied he knew where I lived. I looked around my cozy, humble third-floor apartment.

I peeked out my window onto the sun-drowsy street below. Cars lined the curbs under mature, wide-spreading trees. I scrutinized each front seat for the dark menacing shape of a piglike watcher. The leaves of the silver maple tree outside my window pretty well blocked my line of sight. I had to squint at the far ones at the end of the block and stare hard. It made my eyes sting.

This was the first threatening letter I had ever received. I've had some weird ones before, but nothing like this. Nothing so angry. I think it was the line "You're dead meat" that bothered me the most.

I picked up the phone and punched in the numbers for Detective Lee Stokowski, who works homicide with the Denver Police Department, and was embarrassed to learn that he has a rep for possessing the best thighs in the department. I'd met him several months ago when he was investigating a murder. He'd been willing to listen to me then, at least at first. And he was fairly objective, given that the murder I reported was missing the weapon and the body.

While the phone was ringing, I turned the envelope over in my hand. There was no return address...but there was an Eden, Kansas, postmark.

Stokowski answered in a sleepy baritone voice. I thought I heard him slurp coffee in the background as I explained about the letter I'd just opened. I read it to him. He was silent for a few moments after I finished.

"I didn't know the *Daily Orion* had subscribers in Kansas. Do you know who he's referring to?" he asked.

"No. I get maybe twenty, thirty letters a week now. I can't keep all of them at the front of my memory."

"That many people write in?"

"And growing. Thirty-five so far this week."

"Who'd have thought there were that many screwed-up people who would admit it!"

"They're not screwed up, Stokowski."

"Do you have any idea who sent it?"

"Of course not!"

"Look, Stella, you know as well as I do that there are a certain number of weirdos and nutcases out there and you're in a business that just begs for trouble. So. You get a threatening letter. There's no name, no address, you don't know who he's talking about. There's nothing official I can do."

"And unofficially?"

"I could guard you all night long."

"Nothing else?"

"Stop eating ham and bacon." He hung up.

I refolded the letter, put it back in the envelope, and made out a manila file for it. I keep my correspondence.

There were several options before me.

I could ignore it, I could run away, I could hide in my apartment the rest of my life. I could go in disguise with

sunglasses and a red wig left over from Halloween, I could
hire bodyguards, or I could eat my way into twenty more
pounds and a completely new identity.

None of these carried much charm. I decided to think
about it tomorrow—it worked for Scarlett O'Hara. I call it
creative procrastination.

I refilled my coffee cup and grazed through the cup-
boards for comfort food—something to satisfy my gums.
It's sort of a food lullaby for my nerves. It has absolutely
nothing to do with hunger.

It was cinnamon toast that morning. Lots of butter. With
the load of anxiety I was carrying, I wouldn't live long
enough to have to worry about fat grams.

I brushed the toast crumbs off my chest. Another week
or two of this and I'd waddle.

I FIGURED IF Pissed Off and Ready to Kill was out there
loaded for bear, I could at least be a cute little corpse with
fantastic underwear.

I dressed for work with more than usual care.

I slipped on sandals and a swirly cotton skimmer dress
of turquoise, chartreuse, and fuchsia over the coolest undies
I owned, original Gracies in sheer lavender cotton.

Lingerie is a passion of mine. Unfortunately, I don't have
a lot of passions at the moment, not that I don't want them,
just that I'm between love scenes, so to speak, so I figure
I can indulge myself in this. Even though no one but
Fluffy—my pet chameleon—and I see them, I get a certain
special feeling. A sort of secret confidence. Not as good as
a bulletproof vest, but a whole lot more fun to wear.

I hoped it would help. There was a yawning pit of nerves
somewhere near my stomach, munching on what was left of
my calm.

It was only eight o'clock in the morning, and little heat
waves were shimmering off my living room's hardwood
floor. Perspiration gathered on my upper lip, and tiny beads
of the stuff ran in irritating trickles down my chest between

my breasts. Hot and humid is rare in Denver. So rare, in fact, that I don't own an air conditioner.

I moved Fluffy in his terrarium to the coolest spot in the apartment, beneath the Schefflera, the oldest living thing related to a plant in my abode. Fluffy got a painful squint in his eyes when he spotted my dress and hung upside down by one foot. A major display of anger. He hates fuchsia.

Fluffy isn't a genuine chameleon; he's actually a green anole, but I've always called them chameleons. He's about seven inches long from the tip of his snout to the end of his long skinny tail. He varies from bright chartreuse to rich brown depending on his mood or the thing he's trying to match. He likes to show off. He's a shy clown—though the time I lost him on a brown carpet wasn't funny.

I sprayed his home with distilled water—it doesn't leave mineral spots on the glass sides of the terrarium—and told him I was leaving.

And finally I realized I was stalling. I was nervous about going outside. PORK was affecting me and my life, and I wasn't even thinking about him.

I glanced in the mirror. What I needed was a change in appearance.

I bunched my straight brown hair in a knot on the top of my head and clamped it down with some flowered combs to keep it out of the way. Then I wound a chartreuse scarf loosely around the whole thing to create the illusion of thick and wonderfully wild hair.

Next I pulled out a pair of bent sunglasses missing one lens, punched out the remaining lens, and stuck those on my face. I figured this outfit would startle almost anyone, and that would give me time to make it to the car. It was parked pretty close to the back door.

I tried it out on Fluffy. He jumped to the top of the small tree in the corner of his home and put a little hand over one of his eyes.

I was set.

In the past my apartment has been invaded, and I'm still

a little sensitive to it, so I put a piece of paper in the door when I closed it, down close to the bottom where it wouldn't be noticed but would fall to the floor if someone opened the door.

The stairs in my apartment building are heavily carpeted, to keep down the creaking as well as to look nice. I crept down them, peering through the banister to see if anyone lurked below. No one was there.

At the back door I crouched so I wouldn't be my usual height, pushed the door open, poked my head out about midway on the door, and scanned both directions. Nothing.

Then I heard a gasp. I turned.

She was in curlers and a duster. "My Gawd!" she screamed. "We've got gypsies. Harold! Bring the Mace." It was Mrs. Busby from the first-floor-east unit. I ran for my car.

THIS WAS THE hottest summer on record in Denver for years, and there wasn't an air conditioner or fan left on the store shelves anywhere in town. For me, the only source of cool was the office.

I don't even have air-conditioning in my car. And if I did, I couldn't afford the gas to sit in it and run it all the time anyway. I drove to the office, sweating. Unfortunately, my eyebrow pencil ran in the heat.

The *Daily Orion* occupies most of an old redbrick building a couple blocks south of Speer Boulevard on Pennsylvania Street. Paint is peeling on the trim, and the windows need a good polish. But it has a patina of integrity, and it looks comfortable, as if it expects to be around for another half century. I love it.

I left a little trail of sweat beads on the pavement from the car to the entrance of the office and pulled open the door. A wash of cool air flooded my face and arms. I was alive, and I was safe.

Zelda—actually Sally Ann Miller, our receptionist—sat at her desk, intent on the book in front of her. We call her Zelda because she looks like the kind of worldly-wise, gum-chewing glamour woman that runs the joint. And she does.

Today Zelda's hair was a tangled blond mane tumbling down one side of her face onto her soft, rounded shoulders. She wore a décolleté dress that sculpted her attributes along with vivid lipstick that matched her fingernails. Her whole appearance was familiar, but I couldn't place it.

She barely lifted a hand to acknowledge me. She was well into her sticks of gum and the book, chewing as she read. When she reads, little if anything disturbs her concentration.

"Hey, Zelda! How's it going?"

"Shhh!" Her eyes traveled rapidly across the printed lines of the page. I sidled past the little chair and table used for waiting clients and peered over Zelda's shoulder.

She jerked away, slapping the book facedown on the desk top. "If it's one thing I can't stand, it's a hovering secondhand reader. Buy your own thrills." She uses a gravelly voice on purpose so everyone will give her respect, but she doesn't need to. She would get it anyway, just naturally.

I noticed the cover of the book and felt my eyes widen.

It was Zelda. Or rather, Zelda looked just like the cover of her book—a buxom blond heroine with a bodice to envy, passionate hair, and a hero with muscle-ripping abdominals.

"I never trust a man with better hair than I have," I said.

She finally noticed me. "Jesus, Mary, and Joseph! What in the world happened to you? It's not even Halloween!"

I tried to brush off her shock. "I just thought a change would be interesting."

"Your eyebrows are running down to your chin!"

I pulled the glasses frames from my face and scrubbed at my cheeks.

"What? Are you getting tired of being a lovelorn columnist?"

"No, why?"

"I know! That's it! You used to earn good money as an accountant, and now you don't earn enough to feed that lizard, and you're starving to death, and it's made you nuts!''

I gathered the shreds of my dignity, picked up my stack of mail, and went to my desk in the far corner of the newsroom.

Even though there are no walls, or even any tape on the floor to mark where the walls might be, it is my office—a battered old wooden desk and a telephone, all to myself. It didn't matter that there were a few dangling wires, the occasional electrical dimming, I loved the smell of old paper that permeated the room. I patted the worn old oak of the desk top.

Telephone to his ear, Jason Paul sat at his desk, his back to me and his long legs stretched out in front of him. Jason is one of the reporters for the paper. There are two. The other one also sells ads.

I placed the letters on my desk and fanned them to decide which to open first. Part of the fun of reading them is selecting the envelope—it's like opening presents.

I picked a plain white envelope, slitting it open with a neat little pearl-handled letter opener that my mother gave me in celebration of what she hoped would be a great career. She worries about me still. It's nice, actually.

The letter was written on plain white notepaper in a distinctly feminine hand.

June 24

Dear Stella,
    You haven't herd from me for a while. Have U! It's your old friend, Big Dick. And it is. Believe U me. I keep waiting to get an answer from U. Plese rite.

Yours
Big Dick (its big enough to share!)

I tossed the letter on my desk, reminding myself that it was only a letter and it couldn't actually touch me, but I still felt like I should wash my hands and my eyeballs.

Jason cradled his telephone receiver and swiveled in his chair, an antique oak desk chair that he found in the storage room. It's his pride and joy. He looked at my hair, his head tilted to the side.

"Is this a new style, Stella?"

"How do you like it?" I patted my coiffure. It was fun watching him swallow and work at an answer. His melt-your-heart brown eyes clouded with the effort. "Well—" he said.

Jason is somewhere in the neighborhood of twenty-six years old, with rumpled golden-brown hair and the irrepressible appeal of Caesar, my beloved childhood pet golden retriever. One big difference though: Jason doesn't drool on my knee, and Caesar did. Especially when I munched oatmeal cookies.

His pained expression dissolved and he jumped to his feet. "You're on another *case!*" He grinned, a broad, infectious grin. "My God! Another *case!*" He grabbed my arms and pulled me out of my seat, hugging me to him. He was surprisingly strong. And he smelled good. I had never noticed that before.

"Stella, this is so great." He whirled me around the room once, then stopped at his desk, finally loosening his grip and holding me out at arm's length. "Stella?"

It took me a moment to answer. I was a little overwhelmed, and I wasn't sure what was going on inside me. He's very attractive, if you like them young and handsome. I've been trying to ignore him. Since my last boyfriend, I no longer trust my taste in men. Jason was suddenly a little too attractive.

"No, Jason, I don't have another *case.* And if you'll remember, that other case wasn't all that much fun. I got a Big Dick letter, that's all."

"It's making you dress funny. And you have strange streaks of dark stuff on your cheeks."

"It's melted eyebrow pencil. Besides, it probably makes my face look thinner."

When I first started at the paper, Jason's primary assignment was writing up parades and obituaries, but he's been working seriously since then.

I'd like to think it's because of me; actually, he's taken his job seriously ever since he got a byline on a human-interest story about a woman named Cleota Banks, published in one of the big daily Denver papers—one that prints real news, as it happens, as opposed to the *Daily Orion,* which publishes weekly, happy news, all the news we wish would happen.

After his byline story I gave him a nameplate for his desk. "Jason Paul, Reporter." He's very proud of it.

Jason winked his brown eyes at me with a veteran reporter's world-weary suavity. He strolled over to my desk and slouched cynically against the pillar that holds the building up off my head. I hoped it wouldn't break under the weight of his new sophistication.

"You get a lot of those crank letters now, don't you?"

"Not so many. One earlier this morning and this one. I thought he'd quit."

He frowned. "It's a pretty high price for fame." He pulled his lanky frame away from his slouching post and stretched.

I started to pick up the letter to throw it away, then changed my mind. I lifted the letter and envelope, using my thumb and one finger only, carried them to the file cabinet where I had a file marked "Scuzballs," and dropped them in. When I'd received the second of these, I'd decided to save them—just in case.

I looked at the remaining letters. One seemed to stand out. As soon as I picked up the still-sealed envelope my fingertips began to tingle, and I felt a cool mist sweep over my forehead, like a freezer door had opened right in front of me. The room grew dim, and I couldn't seem to see. A faint metallic taste filled my mouth.

I felt slightly dizzy, breathed a little harder, and felt the sides of my face and my mouth grow cold. The light dimmed.

Then the room turned bloodred, and before me against a flickering background, holding her throat, stood a woman reaching out to me. A very dead woman.

TWO

I STRAINED TO SEE MORE, to catch the features on the face. It didn't occur to me to wonder how I knew that she was dead. It was just one of those things I knew.

The vision began to fade. I clutched the letter tighter to try to expand on what I could see. The metallic taste grew stronger, bitter. Then abruptly it all disappeared. I found myself still seated at my desk, breathing like I'd run a fast mile, the envelope clenched in my fist.

Jason was staring at me quizzically. "You always wrinkle up your letters like that?"

"Always. Testing the quality of the paper."

He wasn't convinced, but he didn't say anything. I don't know how to explain these weird little spells I get, and the few times I've tried to explain them to someone I've only gotten into deep trouble, so I really don't talk about them.

For years I've had the ability to "see" little things, like when as a child I "saw" Brandon Milholland behind the hedge throwing road apples at old Mrs. Simpson's cat. The cat was as mean as they come and deserved it, so I didn't tell on him.

As I grew older, I came to see much more ominous things, usually accompanied by a fainting feeling, like now.

Fingers shaking, I smoothed out the now somewhat crumpled envelope and drew out a pretty gray letter with little blue geese flapping their way across the top of the page.

The letter was written in a series of very distinctive loops and dashes.

June 26

Dear Stella the Stargazer,

I took your advice. I wrote my mother's spirit a letter and it helped! She spoke to me from heaven and told me to avenge her murder. So, I'm coming to Colorado. I'll contact you as soon as I get there. Thanks. I don't know where I'd be if it weren't for you.

Sincerely,
Yvonne Talmadge

I turned the envelope over in my hand. A Wichita, Kansas, postmark. I remembered the PORK letter had also been from Kansas. My brain began to throb, the way it does when I think I've done something awful. "Oh, Lord."

Jason was watching me closely. "So, what's up?"

"I'm just wondering if this letter is connected to one I got from Pissed Off and Ready to Kill."

"My God, Stella! Are you getting real threats?"

"Well, I don't know whether it's real or crank."

"Is this one a crank?" Jason nodded at the letter in front of me.

"Oh no, I don't think so." I turned the crumpled letter over in my hands. There was only the faintest tingle in my fingers.

I examined the envelope again. "Is Eden, Kansas, anywhere near Wichita?"

Jason leaned over my shoulder to read. "Never heard of it."

I breasted the letter so he couldn't see it. My tongue felt thick and clumsy when I spoke. "This is personal correspondence. It's not public information. The people who write to me believe in me. I can't just handle it like it was—stuff. It's not right."

"Yeah, I guess. You looked so funny when you picked it up, I thought it was a threat. Like you knew who wrote it. Or you'd seen it before."

I shivered. "There *is* a previous letter from Yvonne. I remember generally because of its eloquent pain. Her mother...died."

I slipped Yvonne's letter under the pad of my desk and went to the file cabinet, where all my letters are in alphabetical order.

Jason watched me with great interest as I pulled Yvonne's first letter and the copy of my reply to her from the manila folder.

"You've only been at this for four months, Stella. In a year you won't have enough room for all those letters."

"Not to worry. I'll think of something." I sat down and reread her first letter.

June 2

Dear Stella,

I've been struggling with a huge problem and I can't seem to solve it or forget it. I'm a Gemini, and I've read that Geminis sometimes have trouble making up their minds about what to do. Sometimes I get so down I think it isn't worth going on.

Eight years ago I had a terrible fight with my mother just before she was murdered, and I can't get over it. I can still see her face when I slammed out of the house that night. What do you suggest? I've *got* to do something.

Please don't write back that you think I'm nuts. I'm not.

Sincerely,
Yvonne Talmadge

I remembered thinking when I read it the first time that the letter was so nicely written, cogent, and succinct that I believed her. Beneath her letter was my reply.

June 4

Dear Yvonne,

It sounds as though you have never successfully resolved your feelings about your mother's death, maybe because you weren't able to talk to her and make peace with her before she died.

If there is any way for you to resolve that, it will help you to feel closure. Perhaps by writing a letter to her, even though she isn't here to read it, you can spell out in a personal way your thoughts and feelings, which might help you let go. And who of us knows about the afterlife completely? Perhaps her spirit will hear your thoughts.

Sincerely,
Stella the Stargazer

At the time I had felt my reply was inadequate, particularly given the distress in her letter. It still seemed inadequate. Besides, I hadn't even responded to her implicit question about Geminis.

But how did this connect to her letter today? I hadn't said a word about confrontation. I try very hard not to recommend extreme action. You never know what people will do.

I swallowed. How had my innocuous suggestion turned into a voice from heaven demanding vengeance?

Jason had settled a hip on the corner of his desk and was scrutinizing me.

"What?"

"It's because you were on television after that murder. Now everyone thinks you can see the future. You're going to get a lot of this upsetting mail, you know. You can't take it all so seriously, Stella."

I stuffed the letters back into the file and replaced it in the cabinet. The room seemed to be warmer, and I was beginning to sweat again. My stomach growled. Stress tends to bring out the eater in me, but it was barely ten in the morning. I sighed, pulled all the rest of the letters together in a stack, and sat down. I wasn't eager to open any more letters. All I could think of was my mother's little saying, "Trouble travels in threes."

Jason went back to his desk and started telephoning again. He hadn't mentioned what he was working on, but

I overheard him inquiring about a job. I had my mouth open to ask him about it, but my own phone rang.

It was Meredith, my best friend, calling about our vacation.

"Yes, we're leaving on schedule, day after tomorrow, Friday morning, July second, for Silverado. All's fixed."

"Thank goodness," she said. "Now work out our horoscopes. And concentrate on winning lots of money."

"Meredith, aren't you taking this too far? This is a vacation."

"Silverado's a gambling town," Meredith said. "You might win a fortune. Remember Little Nothings and your lingerie bill—how much do you owe now?"

"I have my savings account." I didn't actually have a savings account anymore, but I wasn't going to tell her that. There are two things I don't discuss with anyone, my bed count and my bank account. Of course, it makes it real tough to get a loan.

She paused a minute. When she spoke again, her voice was very serious. "Stella, you took a great big risk when you changed jobs, and it worked great. Don't start getting rigid now. Now's the *time* to take risks. Step up to life. Just work out our horoscopes—promise? It's time for the Big Risk."

I reminded myself that she didn't know about my letter from Pissed Off and Ready to Kill. I didn't know whether she was talking about her love life or my career life, but she's my best friend, so I swallowed my irritation. I didn't want to tell her about PORK, because she might decide we shouldn't go. "Stella, are you all right? You sound a little absent, if you know what I mean."

I glanced around the room to make sure no one was listening in, then cupped my hand over my mouth to muffle my words. Meredith and Detective Stokowski were the only people in the world who knew about my spells. I wanted to keep it that way. "Meredith, I had one of my spells this morning."

"Oh, Lord! Was it a funny one or a...bad one?"

"I saw a dead woman."

"Oh, Stella. Oh no." She hesitated for a long moment. "You need to get out of town. Maybe you can outrun it. You've never tried that before. Can you leave a day early?"

"It might work—at least for a little while. All right, I'll see if I can leave a day earlier. But you know how hard it is for me to get time off. Mr. Gerster is a real tough guy when it comes to that."

"Do that. And don't worry about anything. And don't forget the love aspects in those horoscopes. I need a crusher, something really wonderful, dazzling."

"Well, horoscopes don't bring them, they just tell you whether it's a good opportunity." I try to discourage Meredith a little because she sometimes goes overboard on romance. But as much as anyone, I wanted to find that wonderful soul-filling love that wraps me up in a cocoon of warm, fuzzy excitement.

I went to the front office where Zelda was reading and fanning herself. "Zelda, I need to see Mr. Gerster."

Her nose wiggled just a bit, like she was sniffing out news. If Jason had as good a nose for news as Zelda, he'd be working on the *New York Times*. "So what's up?" she asked. "You look frazzled. Colorful, but frazzled."

"It's one of those days. Just swirling in the toilet bowl of life."

"Well, Gerster won't help. He's in a snit."

"How can you tell?" Mr. Gerster is not an emotive man, actually very like Fluffy that way.

"He's in some kind of a mood. Menopause, I think," Zelda grinned wickedly. "Jason was in earlier to ask about getting a fax and a portable phone and *he* came out with his ears slicked back. And you know how Mr. G. likes Jason. *I'm* not calling him." She dismissed me with a wave of her bloodred fingernails and went back to her book.

I thought about that for a moment. Maybe that was why Jason was calling about another job—he wanted a fax. He does tend to love electronics and all the paraphernalia of living in the twentieth century, and Gerster regards all those things as gadgets. I realized I hoped Jason wouldn't leave. Then I realized I don't know why he stays here in the first place. He's good enough to go with real *news*papers.

Zelda looked up. "So are you putting down roots or something?"

"C'mon, Zelda. Call him and tell him I have an appointment with him." Zelda can persuade him to do almost anything...if she wants to.

"Why?"

I swallowed, thinking fast. "I'm in a jam," I confessed.

She laughed. "You're always in a jam, kiddo. That's part of your charm—that and your horoscope."

"You get me in to see him, I'll do you a big, hot, bone-crushing love horoscope."

"A deal." Zelda picked up the telephone receiver and punched in the numbers. "H'llo, Mr. Gerster? Do you remember your appointment with Stella? She's been waiting." Her gum chewing slowed, then stopped with a pop. She cradled the receiver, a look of surprise on her face. "I'll be damned. He's going out. He'll see you tomorrow."

I worked first on my correspondence and then on the horoscopes I'd promised Zelda and Meredith.

I take my horoscopes like some people take their religion, straight, but I wasn't sure how Zelda would take hers. It wasn't positive for romance. Not even for the rest of the week.

Her stars indicated that she was in some kind of romantic slush pile somewhere in the astrological universe. The best thing she could do would be to get a whole stack of romance novels and live vicariously until the stars repositioned.

"Are you sure you got it right?" she asked when I read it out to her. "I've had more loveless nights than a skunk at a tea party. I don't know why you couldn't have lied a little. What's a friend for if they won't spare you a little grief for a while?" Disgusted, she flung her nail file into her top drawer along with six little bottles of nail polish and a collection of lipsticks worthy of a department store.

"Well, I'll get that cute Detective Stokowski's tight thighs into my living room this weekend if I have to create a crime, dammit!"

On the whole, Zelda's horoscope was better than Meredith's, where romance was a black hole, only slightly better than her financial picture, which was a screaming disaster. On a scale of ten, this was a minus seventeen.

I'm a sort of recovering Virgo whose aspects stumbled in the last leap year. At least that's how *I* explain it. I decided several months ago that I'd never, ever fit the compulsive Virgo, however hard I tried—and I tried, believe me.

I had just decided that my horoscope could be called a horrorscope when my phone rang, startling me out of my wits.

"Stella. Edie here. Listen, there's an emergency. You've got to help."

Edie Lorton is not a woman ordinarily given to hysteria. I've known her since my days at the accounting firm, my former job, and she is a steady, warm, essentially practical person with a phenomenal memory. This was a radical departure for her. "What is it?"

"Amy. She's going to get married."

"Amy Wilson is a thirty-five-year-old woman with a fully functioning head on her shoulders. Why is this any disaster?"

"It's the mistake of a lifetime, I tell you. You know the trouble my friend Angie has had. Her husband is a complete sleaze, totally dangerous. She ran from him, and now he's tracking her."

"How does Angie's disastrous marriage relate to Amy?"

"Don't you see? Angie only married because she thought she had to be married, and look at her."

"Edie, lots of people get married and live happily ever after. I mean, it is an acceptable, legal institution, not to mention an expected state for women of a certain age…even today."

"Don't you see? Amy is marrying this man just because

she thinks it's her last chance. She wrote off to some *love columnist* who told her to do it.''

Love columnist? *Love columnist?* ''Well, who is this guy she wants to marry? Maybe he's not so bad.''

''Hell if I know. Somebody she met at some church function.''

''Church function? Oh, that's different. Then for sure he's unsuitable.''

''Don't start with me, Stella. *You're* the love columnist who told her to go for it. You're responsible. When this turns out to be as bad as Angie's mess, you'll be sorry.''

''I'm sorry already.'' Deep down inside I had a feeling this was trouble number three.

THREE

IT'S HARD TO MAINTAIN an attitude of fear. It requires constant vigilance and reinforcement. Even then it begins to seem a lot less real after a while.

So I circled my apartment building only three times and drove through the alley twice, examining each parked car and Dumpster before I parked and skulked into the back door of the building. Fortunately, I didn't run into Mrs. Busby again.

I felt relieved and a little silly when I found the little piece of paper still snug in the crack of the door.

At six o'clock I was in my apartment, sweltering. A hot breeze blew through the open window, and rays of late-afternoon sun slanted in, shimmering on my hardwood floor with the shadows of the leaves of the silver maple trees lining the street outside.

I had double-locked my door and jammed a chair under the knob, and I had a can of hair spray at the ready. I'm sure it wouldn't have stopped a determined assassin, but it would at least slow him down.

A huge buzzard fly circled overhead, but I was too hot to catch it for Fluffy.

I was in front of my refrigerator in a bra and panties with a minifan on inside the fridge, blowing out at my thirtyish sweating body.

I didn't have to worry about my food spoiling; I'd already eaten the little that had been in there.

My lovelorn correspondence was spread on the kitchen table at my side, the envelopes fanned over the surface of the table like cards at a casino table. I stared at them. The phone rang.

I pulled it over to me by the extra-long cord and lifted it to my sweaty ear.

Edie Lorton. Again.

"Stella, I need you. I'm calling because we need a fourth for bridge tonight. Amy and Bill are coming over, and Angie can't play tonight, and this is all your fault anyway, so you have to come."

"Angie?" A little chill ran over my arms and across the back of my neck. I pictured her intense face, her private, watchful eyes. In the year since she arrived at Edie's I had never seen her relax. She is a prime candidate for stress-related death. "What's the matter with Angie?"

"Uh, some kind of heart thing. Angina, I think. Look, Angie will be fine. It's Amy who needs help. She's stuck to Bill like she's afraid he'll disappear. I want to try to talk some sense into her."

"Well, good luck. _I_ don't believe in meddling in other people's lives." Even as I said it, I looked to the ceiling to see if lightning was going to strike me.

Edie snorted. "You! You're responsible for all this."

"I am not!"

"Air-conditioning, candy, and the chance to right a wrong."

One of the beads of sweat along my forehead reached critical mass. It rolled down my temple, gathering speed, and raced in front of my ear before I caught it with a swipe of a towel.

I thought of my horoscope—"tonight lie low." "I'm hot, and I'm stuck to the chair with a glue of sweat. If I get up I'll rip all the skin off the backs of my thighs. Of course I'd lose weight that way, so there's something to be said for it."

"I really need you—"

Another annoying bead of sweat trailed down my side, tickling and itching. I looked at my refrigerator with the miserable little fan. What was I going to do if I stayed there—perspire and ponder the letter from Pissed Off and

Ready to Kill? "Give me twenty minutes." I sighed and hung up.

I slipped on sandals, a T-shirt, and shorts that immediately plastered themselves to my skin, and dragged myself downstairs. The building manager was at the front door, checking the lock.

"Problems?" I asked.

"This morning Mrs. Busby chased a gypsy out of the lobby. Called the police, too."

"She didn't!"

"That gypsy was huddled at the back door—can't have that here."

"I don't think that was a gypsy," I said. I wasn't sure how to explain this.

"Well, if it wasn't a gypsy, then it was a homeless. Can't have it."

"What if it was just someone leaving?"

"If it was one of the people here, causing trouble, there'll be big trouble. Eviction-level trouble. I ain't going to put up with these things." He leaned toward me, his dark eyes glittering with suspicion. "I don't like to have Mrs. Busby upset, got it?"

I was real glad I hadn't put on my lensless sunglasses or the paisley scarf over my head. I nodded and went to my mailbox at the back of the lobby, waiting until he was out of sight before I wound the scarf around my head, slapped on the frames, and crouched to open the door.

I peered around. Nothing.

Then I heard a gasp, turned, and saw Mrs. Busby. I bolted from the building and crammed myself into my car. I could still hear her screaming when I pulled away.

Edie lives just east of City Park in Park Hill, an older residential area with families who stroll down sidewalks in the evening and children who play on lawns, laugh and shout, and leave Big Wheels on sidewalks. Edie's block is a mixture of bungalows, mansions, and graceful silver maples. Even the remaining elm trees are stately in their struggle against Dutch elm disease.

Everyone on her street has a garage, so there were only three cars along the curb. That cut down the surveillance time for me. I only circled the block twice before I pulled over and stepped from my car into the full evening heat.

Next door a dog barked from the fenced backyard, rousing the dog across the street, who barked along with him. Edie must've been watching for me, or else she heard the canine chorus. She stepped out on her broad porch just as I started up her walk. "Welcome to Bark Hill," she called.

Her house is a comfortable bungalow with deep eaves and oak ceiling beams and potted ferns. It fits with Edie's stout earth-mother persona—bean sprouts, short brown hair, and negative-heel sandals. She has a tendency to like animals much more than people, unless the people are a project of hers.

The house and Edie are a kind of Park Hill refuge association. Almost any day of the year she has a lost animal or a stray needing a home. Her latest human rescue, Angie Sayers, her old college roommate, is on her way to becoming the longest project Edie has ever had; she has been hiding out from her ex-husband, who thinks she is still his property, for almost a year.

I scuttled up the sidewalk, my back feeling vulnerable.

Edie pulled me to the front door, then into her wide living room, which is decorated like a garden in muted floral prints with a rich green carpet. It is one of the most comfortable and inviting rooms I've ever been in—and now it was definitely at odds with Edie's mood.

I nodded at Amy, who smiled at me from beneath her head of dark hair tied at the nape of her neck with a droopy black bow.

Amy is somewhere in her mid-thirties, with big brown doll's eyes, the longest eyelashes I have ever seen except on a cow, and a nervous habit of running her tongue over her front teeth, like they are itchy and need scratching. When her smile faded I noticed how thin her face was, and then how thin she had grown. She could turn sideways and get lost in the sunshine. I thought love would have plumped her up. I started to say something, but Edie pinched my elbow like she knew what I was thinking and said heavily, "Stella, meet Amy's fiancé, Bill Orloff."

Bill was a man barely clinging to his early forties who had probably been quite good-looking twenty pounds ago. His clothes were polo-snob casual and matched his sun-streaked hair, but his glasses were dime-store issue and looked like he'd sat on them recently, because they rode loosely on his nose.

I nodded and said something polite and suitably inane. Bill extended a hand. "Now don't you all call me Mr. Orloff. Just call me Bill," he said and pumped my hand earnestly. His glasses slipped winningly down his nose, and he pushed them up with his forefinger. They slipped back down immediately.

He leaned toward me in a disarming way. "We all appreciate you all agreein' to play with us tonight. We're so disappointed Angie couldn't come. For a while we all thought we might not be able to play, so we all thank you so much."

He used the word "all" so much I almost looked around the room for more people. He had a softly southern accent and a way of leaning slightly toward me as he spoke, as if he were used to speaking confidentially. It made him seem older than he was, and a little saintly.

"Bill is a retired minister, and he hasn't quite recovered from it yet," Edie said. "Stella, I've been telling them about how you can see the future. And tonight you're going to *see* it—and you're going to tell Amy and Bill what disasters you see."

"But I *don't* see the future. I just read astrological signs."

She looked at me hard for a moment, her eyes boring into mine. "Amy, if you can separate from Bill...I know it's hard, but—" She shot a look at me, then turned to Bill. "Bill, would you mind? There's a tray of refreshments in the kitchen. Could you get them? I want to have a quick word with Amy—women's talk, you know."

He rose a little hesitantly, then left.

Edie waited until he had cleared the room, then leaned forward, her voice lowered but intense. "Now, Amy. Stella and I want—"

Amy broke in. "Oh, Edie. You're so cynical." Amy's tongue snaked over her front teeth. "I don't want to hear any more. Bill and I are engaged. He's going to give me a ring any day." Amy turned to me. "All Edie talks about is battered women and family violence—"

"My point was that a woman can want marriage too much." Edie planted her hands solidly on her hips. "You can pay too high a price for marriage. Look at Angie. Her marriage was hell, and she was nearly killed. This is the twentieth century. Women don't have to accept the old indentured-servitude role of Wife anymore just to be successful."

"Well, don't preach at me. I'm hardly losing myself—"

"Oh, for God's sake, Amy." Edie turned to me. Now they both glared at me. "Talk to her, Stella. You know about relationships that turn sour and cost too much. Tell her. In fact, read her horoscope, it'll probably tell her."

I barely opened my mouth.

Amy started up again. "I don't need to hear sour, ugly things from anyone, Edie Lorton. I think marriage is the most important institution this country has ever had."

"I'm not arguing about marriage. I'm saying that relationships have to be built over time to get to know each other. Neither you nor Bill have known the other very long. And relationships aren't easy."

"Love is easy. And there isn't anything worse than being single all my life." Amy's tongue darted over her teeth again.

"Bullshit. There's a whole lot worse things than being single," Edie said, her voice weary. I wondered what had made her so leery of love. After all, *she* hadn't gone out with Rick the Ick—*I* had.

I stepped between them. "Look, Amy. You've got a sizable estate. Draw up a decent prenuptial agreement. That way you'll have some protection if things don't work out."

"Spoken like a true accountant, Stella. I don't know why you ever left that job. You calculate better than anyone I know."

"A prenuptial agreement is just a reasonable caution." Glancing up, I saw Bill enter the room, a tray of drinks rattling in his hands. "Gee, Bill. I hope you're feeling real comfortable. Come on, Edie. I thought we were going to play bridge."

Bill forced a smile. "Well, it's real nice to know that Amy has such dedicated friends. *Protective* friends. That's a rare thing in this world. And you don't have to worry about her with me. I'm the kind of guy that takes care of the little woman."

The little woman, my ass! I began to see what Edie was complaining about. I felt my lips twitch. *He* thought I was smiling.

Edie smirked, pulled out her chair, threw herself into it, and picked up the cards to deal. We sat down. The candy dishes on the corners of the table are my personal favorite part of bridge. "What did you say happened to Angie?" I asked.

Edie hesitated, as if she'd dealt a card wrong, then answered. "Angie has angina—can't play tonight. Are you still going to Silverado this weekend, Jane? Stella, I mean."

"How'd you know—?" I frowned, then realized Edie had made a neat change of topic.

"I'm the one who told you about the Owl and the Pussy Cat Inn. We're all going up this weekend, too. The bridge group—David, Jeena, me, Bill, and Amy. We're all staying at the same inn."

I had forgotten. "At least I'll have some friendly faces, people I can trust, around me." I wished I hadn't said it as soon as the words were out.

The expression on Edie's face was pure shock. "Whatever do you mean?"

I tried to cover up and laughed, but it sounded feeble.

"It's nothing, Edie. I just got a nasty little note in the mail, and it has me on edge, that's all. You know what that's like—another excuse to eat." I reached for the crystal bowl to my right.

"Oh my!" Amy patted the bow at the back of her neck. "That makes me shiver right now."

FOUR

LATER THAT EVENING as I left Edie's house, I peered down the street, scanning for suspicious cars with people lurking in the front seat. Then, driving home, I stared so hard in my rearview mirror for cars following me that I nearly hit a stoplight pole at a corner.

I circled my apartment building twice before I parked in my space, right under the light at the back of my building. Then I recognized the couple who lived—and fought—in the apartment above mine. They were approaching the back door.

I jumped from the car, locked it, and raced up behind them, entering on their heels. Literally.

I stepped on her heel and ran her stocking. Fortunately, it wasn't Mrs. Busby. It was at that point that I decided I was overreacting. Of course, it was much easier to decide that once I was safe inside.

I double-locked my door, wedged the windows so they wouldn't open wider than four inches, and put Fluffy in a safe place.

Although I was tired, I wasn't sleepy, so I poured a glass of skim milk and rummaged through the letters I'd brought home to work on. One envelope was pale lavender and smelled faintly of violets. I pulled the letter out.

June 27

Dear Stella,

I'm a Gemini dating a Scorpio man. We've been going out for several months, and I like him, but I've begun to wonder what he does for a living. He always has money, sleeps all day, and only goes out late at night. He also carries a ski mask in his car.

When I asked him, he said he's a bank robber.

What do you think of someone with a sense of humor like that? We're planning to marry in September. I hate to change the date.

A puzzled Gemini in Lyons

It took me five minutes to answer. It would have taken less time, but my first six letters were too sarcastic to send to her.

June 30

Dear Gemini in Lyons,

What makes you think he's joking? Sounds to me like he's an honest hardworking robber in need of a quick squeeze.

Sounds like you want that marriage too much. Pay attention to your Gemini self. Those doubts are a sign you shouldn't tie the knot with this guy—it could take you to jail.

You can screen men by asking how they like their mothers. If he doesn't like his mother, drop him like a hot rock.

If he says "Who?" run for your life.

Stella

It wasn't a very sensitive approach to the problem, but it was the best I could muster under the circumstances. All the time I was working on it, I kept going back to Edie's vehement objection to Amy's marrying Bill. Maybe there was something she knew and I didn't.

Or maybe Edie had spoken from sad experiences of her own. It can be very hard to separate our own experience from that of others.

It could have been me, speaking from mine.

There had been a time when I'd wanted a relationship too badly and had given up too much for it. I had very nearly ended up a hollow soul, feeding myself endless stale love crumbs. Maybe that was why letters like this one stirred me on a visceral level and made it almost impossible for me to do anything less than urge her to get out of the relationship.

When I finished the letters, my eyes were gritty, and I peeled off my underwear. My lavender Gracies and I had made it through the day.

As I dropped them into the laundry basket I wondered if I would ever find another who could make such pretty things and sent a little thought to the woman who had stitched them, wherever she was. She, too, had wanted love too much.

I finally fell into bed and a troubled sleep.

I DON'T KNOW what woke me, maybe a cat howling or scavenging in the trash cans in the alley, but the hoot of a railroad train floated faintly in on the very-early-morning breeze. That sound always stirs all my lonely spots.

My mind slipped from one thought fragment to another. I thought about Amy and how she so clearly trusted Bill. I snuggled up to my body pillow, pulling it into the curves of my body, and wondered if I'd ever find a man I could trust, whose love would fill the hollows of my loneliness.

At least I had a job I loved, which was going well. And then I thought of Jason and the telephone call I'd overheard. I hoped he wasn't seriously looking for another job. I'd miss him more than I wanted to think about.

My eyelids opened just enough to see the threads of first dawn light leak into my bedroom window. The early-morning breeze had already died down, and not a breath stirred through the open window. I couldn't seem to fall back to sleep, so I finally decided to avoid the heat and exercise early. Since the lowest crime rate is between four and six in the morning, I figured anyone after me would be either asleep or too tired to catch me. If I really have to, I can run pretty fast.

I put Fluffy into his little harness and pinned him to my one pocket T-shirt. I'm a pretty intrepid power-walker, and even with the harness to pin him to me, Fluffy has to cling with all twenty of his little toenails.

Fluffy has amazing toes.

Early as it was, I was sweating by the time I reached the BonBon Bakery and bought cinnamon buns. Of course, I only stopped at the BonBon for Fluffy. He loves cinnamon. I can tell because he turns green and breathes heavily when I go in.

Later, showered, buffed, puffed, and polished, I left my place wearing a fuchsia cotton tank top and a skirt of gold, magenta, and cherry swirls. I peered out the back door. There were no sleepy-eyed porcine men.

By the time I got to the office I decided I could happily leave town a day early. I slipped in the door and waved to Zelda.

She barely raised her eyes from her book. Her hair was piled on top of her head with spit curls in tendrils along her cheeks, à la Scarlett O'Hara. She had added a beauty mark on her cheek.

She frowned, then shoveled her gum to a cheek. "Close the damn door. What d'ya think, we got air-conditioning?"

"Ease up. We're friends, remember?" I found my hands raised in front of my chest, just as Mr. Gerster used to do with me.

A patch of angry red skin on her neck caught my gaze. It was too big for a love bite. Besides, she wasn't dating any vampires.

She caught me looking at it. "Eczema. It's this damned heat." She looked at me closer, like she'd spotted a wart on the end of my nose. "You don't look so good, Stella. Maybe you ought to take off early."

This when I even had on makeup. "Is Mr. Gerster in?"

"When is he not?" She picked up the phone and punched in the numbers to his office. "Stella's here for her appointment," she announced. "Of course she has an appointment. It's right here in your book." She put the phone down and scribbled my name in his appointment book. "Go right in," she said, and resumed reading.

Mr. Gerster looked up over the rim of a pair of half glasses and adjusted his bow tie.

"I wanted to clear my vacation time with you, Mr. Gerster."

"Vacation? What vacation?" He looked like he thought I'd lost my mind. "When?"

"Today." He couldn't possibly do without me.

He waved his hands. "Go."

"But I want to go today, instead of tomorrow."

"Fine."

"But my column—"

"I presume you'll be inside the borders of our great country?"

I nodded.

"Mail it."

So much for being indispensable.

I EXPLAINED TO Zelda and Jason that Mr. Gerster had finally agreed he could spare me. "So Meredith and I are leaving as soon as I can pack Fluffy and some clothes."

She looked at me. "At least you've got something neat to do. With your ESP you could win a fortune at the slot machines or blackjack in Silverado. And on your pay, you've gotta need the bucks."

Jason's eyes narrowed suspiciously. "I didn't know you really had ESP. Is that how you get all those news leads?"

"No. I don't have ESP."

"I don't believe you."

Zelda reached for her purse. "If I give you twenty bucks, will you win me some cash?"

Jason's head was tilted quizzically to the side. "I think it's more than a simple vacation, isn't it? I think you're really going on a case."

I WAS *NOT* GOING on a case.

I was simply running away.

We took Meredith's car. I told her it was because hers

had air-conditioning and was the more roadworthy, as in only five years old with the original tires. Actually, I wanted to leave mine in plain sight at the apartment so PORK would think I was there.

We left the city in the late-afternoon rush hour, and by the time we reached the foothills I'd begun to feel a sense of relief. No more tight chest, no more rapid breathing, and no worries about being stalked by a gun-toting pig—for at least a few days. And in spite of all my protestations, I was really hoping to win some money.

I was L.R. Lacking Rent. I had approximately one hundred sixteen dollars and twenty-two cents left. And that was after I'd searched the crevices of the couch and found seventy-eight cents.

I'd recently been notified that I was to receive an inheritance that would solve at least my financial problems, but the money wasn't available to me yet. Wouldn't be for maybe six months. So for right now I was *nada*.

Meredith was so excited she'd forgotten to ask about her horoscope. I was relieved. It was such a downer I didn't want to tell her about it.

Once past the foothills we drove up the winding canyon road, a clear, rock-filled stream tumbling on one side, and rock, Engleman spruce, and subalpine meadows on the other. A sign at the Last Chance Mine said eight thousand feet altitude. A mile and a half farther the road curved around an outcropping of rock, then burst into Silverado's main street.

Decked out for the Fourth of July, Silverado was the epitome of an old mining town-turned-gambling spa on a flag-waving holiday, except that the streets were filled with modern-day visitors wearing shorts and T-shirts.

"God, I am so ready for this vacation," Meredith said. "I just love Silverado. It's like a step back in time as soon as you enter. Honky-tonk music, the clatter of coins, and the smell—it's just like the old boomtown must've been. So romantic. Think of it—money, romance. Hey, how did my horoscope come out?"

The sun flashed on her chestnut hair, and her brown eyes were glowing. Meredith can be intense, and she tends to go overboard, especially on romance, so I was cautious about encouraging her. At the same time, I didn't want to ruin her mood. I hedged. "Your horoscope said romance wasn't good. You should focus on finance instead."

"I can tell by your expression, Stella. It was a lousy horoscope." Her head dropped, the sun seemed to shine less brightly. I felt like I had just told her that her gold nugget was pyrite.

She changed the subject, trying to shrug off her disappointment. "I read that one of the buildings is haunted by an old-time gambler."

"Probably rats in the attic."

"No, he was supposed to be a good guy. Shot to death for winning."

"I was joking, Meredith."

"Well, wait till you get inside. Just pull the handles and watch the little cherries line up. You'll be hooked."

"Sounds like *you* are, at least."

"Well, not hooked. But I sure like it. Drop those coins in the slots and wait for them to spill out the bottom."

I looked at her face. A smile played across her lips, and her eyes shone with anticipation. "What if you lose?"

"Oh, I never do. I'm a lucky person. I can feel a win coming on. You'll see."

We pulled up in front of the Owl and the Pussy Cat Inn, a Victorian house complete with turret and gingerbread painted in contrasting colors of teal, green, and burgundy and a huge, glowering spruce on one side. In its heyday it had been a mansion to write home about. It was still beautiful today.

Meredith stepped from the car and breathed in deeply. "It's perfect. It looks like something from *Jane Eyre*. Now all we need is a romance." She looked at me pointedly.

"Meredith, let's just hope there aren't any madwomen in the attic."

My room was at the front corner of the house and in-

cluded the little square turret, so I had windows in front
and on the side. The town was built up the side of the
mountain in a series of terraces, and the inn perched halfway up the main street.

The night air was clear and clean and smelled of pine
from the giant blue spruce on the other side of the inn. It
was the biggest spruce I'd seen at that altitude. The lower
limbs had been trimmed from the trunk to let in a little
light; otherwise it was a dense, sullen tree with light sage-
blue tips on its branches. I was glad my room didn't look
into it. I'd have felt haunted.

The sheer window curtains billowed, and I heard the
strains of music, laughter, and slot-machine clatter from the
casinos floating in on the breeze.

I moved to the side window and leaned out. With a
stretch I could see to the back corner of the inn, where a
footpath led up through a meadow past the last row of
homes. I could see straight down below onto the rooftops
of Silverado. Anyone with vertigo would be dead up here.

The telephone rang. "Hi, Stel." It was Jason.

"Jason, I've got to go. Meredith is waiting for me. We're
going to the Golden Fleece Casino." I wandered to the
window and looked down on the bright lights of the town
again, soaking up the carnival atmosphere.

"Yeah, well, the Golden Fleece lives up to its name. It's
famous for fleecing people. And you don't have all that
much gold to fleece."

"Jason, did you have something to say, or did you just
call to breathe over the wire?" I rubbed my calf where it
ached from the climb up from the parking lot in front of
the inn and from the registration desk to the room.

"Just be careful, kid. Trouble follows you." He sounded
as though he was talking through ice cubes, as if he was
trying to imitate Humphrey Bogart or sound older.

"Cut it out, Jason."

"Stel—all kidding aside, please be careful."

"What's the matter?"

"I was thinking about your letters. I just don't want anything bad to happen to you."

"Why's that?" I held my breath, not really wanting to hear anything romantic because it would put me in a quandary—he's too young, too immature, too exciting, I'm too old and cynical—but if it wasn't at least suggestive of romance, I'd be disappointed. Talk about a double bind!

There was the slightest hesitation before he answered. "Just because."

After I hung up, I slipped into my electric pink jumpsuit with streaks of orange, blue, and electric green all over. I love it, but it's not one of Fluffy's favorite outfits; I can tell by the way he blinks. I think it's because he has so much trouble trying to match himself to it.

Fluffy was on the dresser top in his travel cage, happy to be out of the heat. Just to show how happy he was, he'd turned a twiggy brown color to match the branch he was sitting on.

I went down the polished oaken staircase to the wide, paneled foyer. The only concession to modern life was the registration desk and its up-to-date telephone console, complete with glowing green digital numbers. Even that was tucked away as much as possible, almost under the staircase, so the full Victorian effect was in place. And almost overwhelming.

Meredith was already there, wearing tennies and an iridescent orange jogging suit with sunbursts of gold front and back. "So you'll be able to find me in the crowd," she explained.

She practically jogged in her excitement to get down the hill and into the casino and had to wait for me to catch up at the corner. "There's a blood rush of excitement just hearing those bells and whistles, isn't there?"

"It's the altitude. The thin air makes you dizzy."

"No, it isn't. It's the anticipation. You never know what'll happen. Whether you'll win a fortune and change your life forever, or lose it all."

"This is limited stakes, remember, so it won't be mil-

lions. The top is five thousand.'' I had a tingling feeling
all over my skin. If I could win a jackpot, my rent problems
would be over.

"You have to do dollars, three at a time, to really win."
Meredith reached the door of the casino and dove inside.

I stopped a minute on the threshold of this fantastic carnival world. People of all sizes, shapes, and ages filled the
aisles, and the room overflowed with flashing lights and
raucous bells, whistles, sirens, and coins clanking into
metal troughs. I felt a surge of something like overwhelming gastroenteritis.

Some of the crowd were laughing and partying, but most
of them were solely intent on the machines before them.
Like automatons, they fed coins into the maws of the machines, their gazes glued to the red, yellow, and blue spinning figures.

I spotted Amy smiling happily into Bill's face at the far
end of the room. He looked older than the thirty-nine years
that Amy maintained he was. He wiped his forehead and
neck with a snowy white handkerchief, as if he were having
a hot flash. I figured the gambling was a little hard on a
minister, retired or not.

Underneath the cacophony of the casino I heard the
steady pulse of my heartbeat in my ears.

I don't know whether it was the altitude, or the bells and
whistles, or the constant clank of coins, or the flashing
lights, but something made my blood pound and my head
feel light. My skin tingled and grew ominously cool.

From the coin-changing booth, Meredith motioned me to
join her. I started to take a step, but the room was growing
monochromatic gray.

I reached for the cool metal of the side of a slot machine
to steady myself. The woman feeding coins into the machine frowned at me, said something I was glad I didn't
hear. She tried to shoo me away, but I felt too unsteady to
let go. I draped myself against the machine for stability.

My forehead and cheeks felt cold. A metallic taste filled

my mouth. My ears rang, and the room began to grow dim
before my eyes. I was having one of my spells.

A form took shape before my eyes, a figure dimly outlined against a background of dark red. Light pulsed around
the room like circling blue-and-red police-car strobes. An
intense, compelling excitement filled my head, followed instantly by a sharp, cold flash of fear.

I began to shake.

It was the figure against the bright red background again:
the dead woman I'd seen before I opened Yvonne Talmadge's letter.

FIVE

I COULDN'T SEE her face, but I *knew* that it was a woman, crumpled in a painful, unnatural way. I thought if I could see enough to understand it, maybe I could prevent whatever was happening.

I strained to see, to force more detail into the picture, but the vision broke up and the sensations were gone. All that was left was a bitter metallic taste in my mouth, bewilderment, and a deep sense of foreboding.

Since childhood, when I discovered I had this "sense," I've tried to understand it. When I was ten I "knew" that Quincy Halverson had stolen Aunt Tillie's black lace underwear from the clothesline. It was as though I'd seen it, only I hadn't. I looked at Quincy, into his bland blue eyes, and saw his thought, I guess.

In my teens I tried to elicit these spells at times. After all, they were innocuous and sometimes hilarious. I figured it would be fun to be able to read minds. But the spells remained totally unpredictable.

It has only been lately, after years of having simple little visions, that I suddenly began to receive violent, dread-inducing scenes. That's how I think of it now, as receiving thoughts or picturing what someone else sees.

I have wondered if they were prompted by stress or guilt for a thousand sins I might have committed. Years of skipping church and using profanity weighed heavily on me.

A hand gripped my elbow, shook it lightly. "You need to sit down." Her voice was warm, unexpectedly comforting and insistent. She led me to a stool in front of a slot machine, where she pushed me gently onto the seat. "Put your head down, you look awful."

I glanced up briefly, not recognizing her, but the movement of my head made me feel more dizzy. I put my head down again and my gaze slid to the side of the room, looking for an open space, some place away from the teeming people, noise, and lights. I noticed the carpeting.

It was red.

"Are you all right?"

I shook my head. "A little motion sickness. I never was any good on a boat," I muttered. I had no intention of explaining my spells to a complete stranger, however helpful she was.

I looked at her more closely. She had clear gray eyes that I trusted immediately, framed by a bush of shoulder-length auburn hair. She wore a wild Hawaiian shirt that Fluffy would have loved, tucked into a pair of skintight black jeans, and on her shoulder she carried a bright canvas bag with yellow birds on it.

"I know you! You're Stella the Stargazer, aren't you? I saw you on television a couple of months ago. I—are you all right? You look—" She stopped midsentence and looked hard at me, until I felt even more uncomfortable than before.

"There's not enough air—"

"Put your head down," she said. She moved next to me, braced my body with hers, and put her hand on the back of my neck to stabilize me. "Look at the floor and breathe steadily—not too fast."

Deep, slow breathing helped. I felt air puffing in my face. She was fanning me with a paper napkin. "You don't know me, but I—"

"Stel! You going to be all right?" It was Meredith. She bent down and peered comically into my face.

This was too embarrassing. I tried to joke. "I'm fine, just looking for a quarter I thought I saw." I straightened up slowly. The room swayed a bit, then settled down and stayed put. I blinked.

"For heaven's sake, Stella, are you okay?" Edie Lorton stood before me, her feet firmly planted in her negative-heel sandals and hands on her stout hips. "You look like you saw a damn ghost.'' She turned around, looking for someone. ''Bill and Amy are here somewhere. Oh, here they come.''

The woman who had helped me shifted and pulled away. I reached for her. ''Thanks, thank you. I might have embarrassed myself to death if you hadn't been there.''

''Well,'' she grinned. ''I was wondering how on earth I'd find—'' Then she was bumped to the side by David McClintock shouldering his way through the crowd.

''Watch it, buddy!'' said an irritated gambler.

''Put a cork in it,'' David said. He was another one of the old bridge group—certainly not my personal favorite. He had a long face, sharp features, and a thatch of reddish hair that slanted carelessly across his forehead. He'd have been a good-looking guy if he'd had a hint of humor. He usually hung around with a woman named Jeena Gay.

He pushed in front of the auburn-haired woman who had helped me. ''So. What's happening?''

At this point just about everyone I knew, plus a few I didn't know, crowded around. It was pretty embarrassing.

''Please, I'm fine. I just got out of breath. I'll just sit here for a minute.'' I looked around for the woman in the Hawaiian shirt. She was gone.

Meredith posted herself at my side, her brows knitted in a concerned frown. ''What happened? One of your spells?''

I nodded briefly. ''Nothing to worry about.''

With Meredith next to me, I sat for a few minutes on the stool and breathed slowly. The crowd drifted away, drawn back to the slots. My head cleared. I *was* fine, but I hoped the woman would come back so I could thank her. ''Meredith, I think I'll just wander back to the inn for an early night.''

''Oh no! You can't do that. I don't mind waiting, you'll feel better any minute. We can gamble a little, and then we'll both go back early.'' She peered into my face. ''What you need is a Coke, or something to drink.'' She waved at a hostess carrying a tray of soft drinks.

The hostess wound over to us to take Meredith's order.

"These will do." Meredith grabbed two colas from her tray.

"Hey, those are for someone else."

I took the cola Meredith shoved into my hands. "I'm diabetic. I'll go into a coma and die if I don't get sugar."

The waitress scuttled away.

"Drink it," Meredith said. "You'll feel better. I don't want you wandering around the streets of Silverado on your own. Stay for a little while, at least, then we can still make it an early night."

I capitulated, and followed Meredith to the change booth where I changed bills for nickels, in spite of Zelda's advice. I went straight to a nickel slot machine along the wall.

Meredith pounced on an unoccupied quarter machine behind me. She put a hand on it so no one would come along and take it, then turned to me again. "You drank the soda?"

"Yes."

"You sure you're all right now?"

"Fine. Now stop. It must've been the altitude. I must have hurried too fast coming down the mountain from the hotel to here."

"I knew the cola would help. That and chicken soup, but they don't serve chicken soup. If doctors would stick to cola, chicken soup, and the occasional aspirin, we'd all live to be a hundred and twenty."

"Meredith, quit it. I'm fine."

Meredith shrugged, pushed her hair back, and turned to the slot machine.

Thirty minutes later I was down to my last six nickels. I thought about Zelda, played it big, and put in three nickels at a time. Red cherries lined up. Nickels poured out of that machine, hundreds of them. Meredith handed me a plastic bowl to hold them.

At the change booth I changed the nickels for silver dollars. Meredith got another roll of quarters, and we set out. I was now up by sixty-five dollars.

Maybe Zelda was right. Maybe I had a certain *touch* that

told me when to play. I held my chin just a fraction higher.
It could mean another new career—that would finance my
astrological lovelorn column writing.

The noise level in the casino had risen even higher. I
saw Bill and Amy in the corner of the room, Bill's face
shiny and bobbing encouragement. He stood quite close to
Amy, watching the crowd, as she dropped one coin at a
time into the machine. And there beyond them stood the
woman I'd been looking for. I started to wave to her, but
a cocktail waitress carrying a tray stepped in front of me,
offering a soda. I took one. In the minute it took to accept
it and look back, the woman was gone.

When I reached Amy, her cheeks were flushed and she
was scooping up a small handful of quarters from the slot-
machine trough. There was more than a hint of tension in
the air. I felt kind of sorry for Bill; he was trying so hard
to have a good time, and his glasses were slipping down
his nose at a record rate.

"How did you do?" I asked him.

"The Lord giveth and the Lord taketh away..." He
smiled and pushed his glasses back up on his nose. Min-
isterial humor.

"Bill, you're such a joker. I'm through with this," Amy
said and handed her bowl to Bill. Her tongue flickered over
her teeth. She shifted her hip into his side and tucked a
hand around his elbow, a possessive little gesture that you
see between two people who know each other intimately.
It was a message aimed at me: "See, *I* can climb right into
him, so keep your hands off." She didn't need to worry.

Bill frowned and thrust the bowl back at her. "You don't
want to stop now, Amy, the night is young."

"Yes, I do. My feet hurt. All I'm doing is giving my
money away." Amy's tongue searched over her teeth.

"Well, it's not all that much. You can afford it. You
need to blossom more, Amy. We've got the whole rest of
the night."

"We *sure* don't want to hurry home too fast," came her
soft retort. Just as she said it, there was one of those rare

pauses in the carnival racket of the casino, and her words carried. Amy pinked with embarrassment and busied herself with her teeth at the slot machine while I felt distinctly as if I'd witnessed a telling incident in the love life of Amy and Bill. My sympathies were with Bill, stuffy or not.

I glanced around and discovered, by the look on her face, that Meredith had also overheard. Then David reeled up, a glass in his hand and a crooked grin on his face. "Well, Bill, all the babes making moves on you tonight?"

"Had a few drinks, David?"

"I saw that redhead. Talking into your ear." David leered at Bill with a taunting look.

Amy went stiff as a ramrod and jerked the slot-machine handle so hard the machine rattled.

Bill pressed his lips together until they were almost white, and his chin quivered. He glared at the drink in David's hand and looked for all the world like he was ready to kill. Or at least slap the glass away from him.

I held my breath.

David laughed and lurched off toward a waitress. The crisis seemed averted.

I stopped before a slot machine with shocking pink sevens at the top. They matched my jumpsuit. It had to be a winning combination. I stroked the top and sides of it, like it was Fluffy needing a little encouragement.

I fed dollars into it.

My fingertips tingled ever so slightly. I squinted at the cherries and the bars, willing them to line up, and pulled the handle down, hesitating ever so slightly halfway down. I was getting into this gambling thing.

Three dollars at a time means your funds go pretty fast. A few dollars trickled out into the trough, but nothing to get excited about. I felt discouraged.

Meredith was behind me again, cheerfully putting quarters into a machine that was chugging them back out at about an even rate.

I fed another set of three into my machine. It spewed out twenty dollars. That was a little better. I fed in another twelve, three at a time. Three came back. Chicken feed. So where was the jackpot? At this rate I'd have fed all my winnings back in before we left for the evening.

I put in another set and pulled the handle. It went down. I heard a squeal behind me and turned. Coins were spewing out of Meredith's machine.

"I got fifty dollars worth!" She grabbed her bowl and scooped them up.

"Are you even with what you lost now?"

"Almost."

It was incredibly noisy. A siren and bells were clanging overhead. I fed in three more coins and pulled on the handle. It wouldn't move.

"Damn! Isn't that just like it!" I pulled again. It didn't budge. I looked at the woman to my left. She stared back, then pointed to the top of my machine. There was a yellow light flashing. "Did *I* break it? Oh, damn. The damn thing's broken!"

She shook her head in disgust. "You got a jackpot." She swore inelegantly and left.

"Hey, Meredith! I won." Meredith couldn't hear me. The noise was deafening, and people seemed to be jostling me from every side. I looked around. I thought I saw the woman who had helped me and waved, but then David's tall frame blocked my view. His face was ruddy and scowling. He glanced at the flashing lights, then at me sourly, and left.

"What happens now? What do I do?" It didn't seem real. And no coins were coming from the machine.

"They'll come to you. Just wait," someone answered.

Just then a young man appeared, wearing a black tuxedo and carrying a clipboard. He checked the machine, wrote down some numbers, then smiled and shook my hand. "Congratulations!" He reached over and fastened on me a pin with "Golden Fleece Casino" printed on it and a picture of a studly young man holding a sword and a hank of yellow hair. Just what I'd been wanting—but in real life. "Do you want your winnings in cash or check or credit?"

"How much did I win?"

He looked momentarily surprised, then pointed to the top of the garish machine. "Five thousand dollars."

"A check." When the chips are down, I can make a decision.

Bill, Amy, Edie, and Jeena appeared as if summoned by some magic wand, led by David.

Amy patted me on the arm and murmured things I couldn't hear while Bill's head bobbed behind her. David's lips wouldn't let him smile. He looked like Fluffy when he discovers he's been fooled into eating hamburger.

The young man returned, gave me a check with a flourish, reset the machine, and left. I stared at the check, then held it up for the group to see.

People were crowded round even more now, as though being close to a winner somehow confers luck. I felt claustrophobic. Someone pushed heavily against me from behind, but I couldn't see who. I held my ground. No one was going to push me away from my magic machine.

I folded the check and tucked it into my bra—close to my heart—then fed one last set of dollars into the machine, just for good luck. I pulled the handle and looked down at the trough, to see if coins would rain down. The carpeting caught my eye.

The same bloodred color that I'd seen in my spell. Light from overhead made throbbing, flickering patterns. My heart slowed, then began a tattoo in my chest. I felt my mouth go dry, and my breath roared in my ears.

Someone leaned against me. I tried to shrug them off. The weight fell heavier on me. Then a feeling of dread settled over me. I turned, afraid to look.

The young woman with the Hawaiian shirt leaned against me, her hand at her throat, her gray eyes terror-stricken.

"Oh, God!"

I grabbed for her but couldn't get a firm grip. She slipped away, down my body, one hand at her throat, the other clinging to my pocket. I grabbed for her again. She tried to hold herself up, but she slipped through my fingers and slumped to the floor—the dark figure against the flickering, bloodred floor.

almost feel her strength ebbing. "Where's the ambulance?" I shouted.

The casino security guard appeared. "Ambulance is on its way. Stay calm. People have heart attacks up here more often than you'd think."

"Heart attack! Not people this age, surely," I protested. "And heart attacks don't look like seizures." I stared across the room. People avoided my gaze and turned away, busying themselves putting coins into the slot machines.

"It happens more often than you think," the guard said, as though that would explain it. "People get so excited, they don't watch themselves and they overdo."

"Overdo?" I looked for a sign of colossal stupidity, like a missing head or a single eye in the center of his forehead, but he was all there in every way.

I raised my voice a little, thinking it might convince him to take my concerns seriously. "She's too young. None of this makes any sense. People have seizures all the time. They don't die from them."

His eyes shifted irritably. "Look, if you're a doctor, say so. Otherwise, forget it."

"I'm not a doctor. I'm—" I felt frustrated, outraged, as if I was a child given a brush-off by an impatient adult.

"Yes?" He scrutinized me. "You play one on TV?"

"I'm...a columnist."

"A writer! Oh, I see. And a clairvoyant, no doubt." What a wit.

After what seemed a lifetime, two men appeared with a stretcher and a heavy black bag. They shuffled us aside and took over, their hands moving competently.

I began to feel more confident and hopeful. The young woman's tremors had subsided, and her color was better, rosier. Her lips remained blue, but her neck and cheeks were pinking up. The rest of her face and body flushed cherry red, even her arms. At least she was getting enough oxygen, I thought.

The two men worked quickly, muttering unintelligible syllables to each other.

I was dimly aware of Edie and Amy standing behind me. Bill crowded in next to me and shoved the woman's purse into my arms. "You better hold on to it, so it doesn't get lost," he said.

I slipped the straps over my shoulder. Meredith grasped my arm and we stood in a mute circle—unable to leave, unable to help, just trying to will her into consciousness.

It was hard to breathe, and I shivered, chilled, although the air was warm and stuffy. The carnival atmosphere I had enjoyed before had soured, and my head was pounding dully. By now she should be returning to consciousness.

The paramedics tensed. Their movements were orchestrated, their energy concentrated, all on her and each ragged breath. "We're losing her."

They couldn't be. She was flushed now. Healthy. She looked so warm.

The paramedics glanced at each other, telegraphing some grim message. "Let's get her to the ambulance," one said.

They lifted her onto the stretcher, wrapped her with a blanket, and snugged up the straps in rapid, economical movements.

"She's gone," someone murmured.

"She can't be," I whispered. A grapefruit-size lump formed in my throat. I seemed to be propelled forward and reached for her hand.

"Get back, don't touch her!" The voice belonged to a tall law officer with a thatch of brown hair that escaped his cap and fell handsomely over his forehead. His brass name-plate identified him as Sheriff Bob Samson. He marched toward us, his arms outstretched, herding us back and away from the stretcher.

"Back up. Everybody. Give them room to work." Sheriff Samson glanced at the fallen woman, winced, and pushed us back farther. "What's the status?"

One medic made a barely perceptible shake of his head. "We've gotta get her out of here—to the hospital."

The sheriff hesitated, seeming to read his unspoken words. Then he turned his attention back to us, all business.

"You," the sheriff said to those of us nearby. "I need your names, and I'd like to talk to you in a minute. But just step back for a second. Let the men through."

The medics raised the stretcher, locking the legs in place, then rolled the stretcher toward the door. I followed.

She couldn't leave so suddenly, so completely. It had to be a mistake. Surely she'd waken any minute.

The crowd separated to make way for them. It reminded me of a painting of Moses parting the Red Sea. I slipped out in their wake.

I felt drawn by a need to be there for her and torn by both disbelief and conviction. She mustn't be dead, and yet...I knew she was, and I felt bereft, as though something very precious had been stripped from me.

There had to be an explanation—something that would tell me that there was a reason.

I pushed my way out of the casino. The ambulance was still at curbside, the back door ajar. They were pumping at her chest. One of the medics was on a radiophone. I could hear the radio voice but couldn't make sense of the words. I wanted to shout "Don't give up on her," but I could feel it was useless.

Before I could speak, the two paramedics fell silent, heads down, their hands momentarily quiet in defeat. A heavy sigh rose from them—perhaps from me too—as if her soul had taken wing, flown up and away. One of them, I didn't know which, cursed softly. She had gone.

"What happened? Why did she die?" I asked.

The blond emergency technician looked at me awkwardly. "You need to step back, miss. We have to take her to the hospital."

One of them stayed with her, working, and the other climbed quickly into the driver's seat. The ambulance roared to life.

"Things like this don't just happen!" I said.

The paramedic shrugged, then slammed the door. I watched the ambulance pull away, then turned back to the casino, numb.

INSIDE, I SHOULDERED my way into the crowd until I was next to the sheriff.

"Do you know her?"

"There should be some identification in her purse. She carried a large bright striped bag with birds on it."

"The one you're carrying?"

"Sorry. I forgot," I said and pulled the straps from my shoulder. There were splashes of damp brown stuff on it, and a little dust bunny dangled from the corner fold. I dropped the whole thing, bag and dust bunny, into his outstretched hands.

He fished in the bag, pulled out a wallet, and flipped it open. I peered over his shoulder. Her picture looked back at me, her fine eyes crinkling in a smile.

Yvonne Talmadge. Wichita, Kansas.

I sucked in my breath and felt my pulse quicken. For a sickening moment the four-year-old child deep inside me who believed in magical thinking took over. Could I have caused...? Then I shook myself back into the rational world.

I glanced back at the license for her birth date and street address. 299 Redline Street, *Wichita*. Only twenty-seven years old. Too young to have a heart attack from excitement. Yvonne had come to Colorado to confront someone. Who?

The sheriff realized I was reading over his shoulder and sheltered the license with his long-fingered hand. "You were standing right next to her."

"I didn't know it at the time. It's so crowded in here, I was standing next to a whole lot of people. I didn't see her until I turned around." Maybe if I had turned around sooner, spoken to her sooner...

"You ever see her before?" He wrote something down, then looked at me, his eyes narrowed into disbelieving slits.

His suspicion of me was almost palpable. I glimpsed myself sitting on a slab bed in a cold, gray cell, shivering under an itchy blanket. I realized I had to convince him I was a mere innocent bystander.

I shrugged, shook my head, and raised my hands, turning the palms out. All the body-language signs I could think of to convince him of my innocence. "No, honest!"

He tapped his pencil against the notepad, then rubbed his chin. "Doesn't seem like the usual overexertion collapse."

"The usual? Do people die like this very often?"

"Well, once in a while. People don't watch the altitude, drink too much, and get too excited. Cardiopulmonary arrest."

"She had a seizure, not a heart attack."

He scrutinized my face with a peculiar light in his eyes until I became acutely uncomfortable. He wanted something and was willing to wait until I gave it to him.

To tell him I'd had a vision of this would put me on his list of candidates for a rubber cell, so I hedged a bit. "Well," I replied. "I never met her, but—but she's written to me."

His eyelids lowered a fraction. "And...?"

"I write an astrological column for the lovelorn, and she's written two letters to me. She believed that her mother had been murdered and was very troubled about proving it. We were supposed to meet in Denver. The meeting here this evening is purely coincidental."

"Coincidental." Suspicion was written across his face. "And the second letter was about..."

"The second letter was very brief. She thanked me for my reply and said she was going to confront someone."

"Did she say who she was going to confront?"

"No. Just that she'd call me for a meeting." Edie, Meredith, Bill, and Amy inched forward, trying to listen. Edie was so curious she was leaning forward; Meredith was right behind.

The sheriff's gaze darted around the room, lighting first on Edie and Meredith, then on Bill and Amy, feigning nonchalance but deliberately staying close enough to hear. He made an arc toward them with his pencil. "Are these your friends?"

"Yeah," I said and waved to them. Bill flinched.

"Do they know her?"

"You'll have to ask them."

"I thought they were your friends."

"They are. We don't live in each other's pockets."

The sheriff's pencil drummed against his little notebook in a tattoo of suspicion, then he seemed to come to some decision. He asked for my full name and address, here and in Denver. After that he abruptly turned to Edie, Meredith, Bill, and Amy and finally David, who had returned, leading Jeena by the hand, to ask them their names and addresses. Then he left. Not so much as a goodbye or so long.

The crowds had begun to thin out. My nose itched. My eyes were leaky. I rummaged in my purchase for a tissue. Most of the time they multiply like rabbits until I'm carrying a bag full of disgusting crumpled wads. Tonight I couldn't find a single one.

I still had a handful of quarters, which I dumped into my pocket. The slot machines had lost their allure.

Edie dropped the last of her coins into the machine and pulled the handle. Two dollars plunked into the trough. "God, this can drain the cash right out of your hands in no time," she muttered. "You know, I can't get the picture of that poor woman's face out of my mind. So strange..." She finished the sentence with a shudder. "You just never know when your time's going to come, do you? One minute you're on top of the world, thinking about nothing. The next, you're on a slippery slope, headed for the pit."

The image of a yawning black hole was too much. I giggled. Too much tension and too much tragedy, and I laugh. I felt like pond scum, of course, but that only made it worse.

"I don't see what's so funny," Amy said.

"Nothing. Absolutely nothing," I said, barely in control.

"Oh my," Amy sniffled decoratively.

I've always wanted to be able to sniffle that way. Some women have that talent, and it's one I've envied for years. Even mirror practice didn't help. When I sniffle it sounds like a major mucus-management problem.

Amy moved closer to Bill and fanned herself. "This is too much. I feel a little sick."

"Yeah, it's hot in here," Bill said. They melted into the crowd. It occurred to me that for a minister, he wasn't very comfortable with death—or with tearful women.

Even Edie looked a little disgusted with me and headed for the door. Meredith and I followed.

Outside the air was surprisingly and pleasantly cool; a sweater would have been welcome. I pulled my elbows in close to my sides for warmth and shoved my hands into the pockets of my jumpsuit. There, if I'd only looked earlier, was a napkin.

"Meredith, you and Edie go on and gamble some more. I'm going back to the inn." I glanced pointedly at my watch. It was nine-thirty. If I hurried, maybe I could get there before the manager retired and put the check in the inn's safe.

Edie's brow furrowed until her gaze was piercing and uncomfortable. "Maybe we should go with you."

"Edie's right. You shouldn't be out by yourself," Meredith said. "Besides, you've got that check on you."

"It's only three blocks—what can happen? I'm going straight there." I waved toward the inn.

The more Edie protested, the more I wanted to be far away from her. Finally, we agreed. Edie went off toward Porcupine Pete's to join up with some of her bridge group. Meredith and I started up the road toward the inn.

I sneezed three times and pulled the napkin out of my pocket. I opened it and started to wipe my nose.

Then I saw the writing on it.

"Oh, my God. Look at this!" I whispered. I sheltered the napkin in my hand and read.

I have to talk to you. Don't tell *anyone*.
    Call me at 771-2323. *ASAP*

—Yvonne.

SEVEN

THE COLD FINGERS of a mountain breeze ran across my neck and face. It was eerie, as though Yvonne was reaching out to me through the mists of her death. "Meredith. She was trying to tell me something."

Meredith shuddered, then jammed a fist onto her hip. It's an annoying gesture, but she only uses it when she's really upset. She says it centers her. "Stella, you absolutely can't get involved. It's too dangerous." Then she cocked her head suspiciously. "You didn't take that from her purse, did you?"

"Hey! I didn't! I found it. In my pocket. It's not my fault." My tongue went thick and dry, like it was wearing a fur coat.

The temperature had dropped at least to the fifties, and a stiff breeze made it seem much chillier.

"Stella," Meredith whispered. "You've got to call that sheriff." She started to shake, but I thought it was more from the cold air than fright. I shoved the note back into my pocket and shivered with her.

Meredith was right. I had to call the sheriff, tell him about this note. Whoever she was supposed to meet here in Silverado may have killed her. I was certain now that it was murder. She might have been in the casino to gamble, but she'd written the message *after* seeing the people surrounding me. And for the most part, they had been the bridge group.

"Stella! Earth to Stella!" Meredith was peering into my face.

"Meredith, do you remember the way she clutched at her throat, the seizures, how blue her lips were? And her purse had cola spilled on it. I think Yvonne was poisoned."

I looked down at the knees of my jumpsuit. They were damp where I'd knelt on the floor next to Yvonne. "I'll bet there's poison right here!" I pulled them away from my knees, just in case the poison could go through my skin.

Meredith glanced down at her pants. They were dry. "Let's get back to the inn. Now!" She started to jog up the road.

Silverado is a two-main-street town, laid out in a crooked cross. One street runs along the cleavage between two mountains; the second runs across the shoulders of the mountains. Most of the town is built along these two cross-roads. The remaining buildings, mostly Victorian homes converted into bed-and-breakfast inns, crawl up the side of the mountain along narrow lanes dotted with pine and spruce trees.

We jogged only a block before I had to slow to a walk. It's not that I'm out of shape, it's that the air is thinner up here. I told Meredith I was looking for pine cones for a Christmas wreath. She's a good friend. She laughed, but she didn't say anything.

We left the illusion of the safety of light and crowds, skirting the discreet yellow pools from the street lamps, preferring the dark arms of the pine trees across the street. We passed the Opera House, where ushers in the garden collected intermission litter to the strains of *La Bohème*. I was breathing hard in the chilly, pine-scented air.

By the time I reached the shortcut steps that led from this street to the upper road, my thighs and butt muscles were burning from the ascent. With one foot on the bottom stone step, I halted, gasping for oxygen. "This place is a cardiologist's paradise."

"You should work out more," Meredith said. "You'd be in better shape."

"The pain lets me know I'm alive." I rested my forehead on the cold metal of the handrail, pretending to look for pine cones.

"Stella," Meredith whispered. "It's too dark up there." Her whispering made it seem even more spooky.

"Yeah, but it saves a long, dark walk up the road."

"You can't see the top. You don't know what's up there."

Sometimes I get cranky when I'm getting scared. "Oh, stop! I do too know what's up there. The road. Now come on."

I forced myself to talk out loud and sound completely matter-of-fact, but I went up the stairs as fast as I could.

"Stella, do you feel someone's eyes on us?" Meredith's voice was hoarse and shaky.

"No." I lied. I was catching her nervousness.

"Then why are you running?"

"I'm not running. I'm exercising."

"You're breathing like a horse."

"It's the altitude." I stumbled on the uneven surface of the steps and grabbed the handrail. By the time I came to the top, I was wheezing. I stopped so fast Meredith bumped into me. I was positive someone was watching.

"Hello?" I called. My voice echoed in the empty streets.

"Who's there?" Meredith asked. No answer.

"I heard something. Footsteps," Meredith croaked. Meredith's worse than I am under this kind of pressure.

"I can't hear over the pounding of my heart. It's our imagination. Forget it," I said. We hurried along the road, feet crunching on the gravel edge.

The inn's porch lights shone bright and welcoming. Even the dim light of the turret windows of my second-floor room glowed warm, soft, and cheerful. I'd left a small light on to keep Fluffy company in the night. We raced up the porch steps, flung open the door, and leaped inside into immediate relief—and the safe scent of lemon furniture polish, with a hint of soapy perfume, the kind Amy wore.

The reception desk in the corner of the foyer was dark, and the little desk light out; only the green luminescent glow of the telephone console lit the area. Mrs. Johnson, the inn's owner and manager, was off duty, and a small hand-lettered notice was propped on the desk.

MANAGER MAY BE REACHED FOR EMERGEN-
CIES AT 771-4032.

BREAKFAST IS SERVED BETWEEN 7 A.M.
AND 10 A.M.

"You need to put your check away. D'you think Mrs.
Johnson's awake? We could knock on her door and see,"
Meredith said.

"Right, then she'll be awake for sure."

There were only the sounds of an old house, slumbering
in the dark. My nose wrinkled. The soapy scent was
stronger. I wondered if Amy was in the darkened front
room. Maybe stacking the bridge decks. Or exploring Bill's
assets. I listened intently, then waved to Meredith. "It'll be
fine. Come on."

I led the way upstairs to our rooms. "At least the only
people staying in the inn are the bridge group. They're not
likely to steal a check."

At the top of the stairs Meredith headed for her room. I
hesitated. "Meredith," I whispered. "D'you want to find
out where that number is?"

"No! I'm going to sleep. And you should too. You've
done enough for one day. This is supposed to be a vacation."

"Please?"

She ignored me and let herself into her room. I heard her
set her chain lock in place.

As soon as I was in my room with the door locked behind me I felt more comfortable—and wide awake. Fluffy,
barely breathing, eyes half closed, was perched on a twig
in his travel case on the table. A very contented chameleon,
he looked like a short, thin cigar with legs and a long, thin
tail. He'd matched himself to the twig almost exactly, very
proud of his color job.

I picked up the telephone and punched in the numbers
for the sheriff's office. A woman's cigarette-roughened
voice told me he wasn't there.

"Please tell him I have a—" I paused. The line echoed

hollowly, reminding me that someone could listen in. "Ah, something pertaining to the woman who died tonight in the casino." I gave her my name, spelling it slowly.

After she said goodbye I waited for the telltale click of a third receiver, confirming someone had listened in. I was nearly ready to hang up when I thought I heard it, faint and far away.

I hung up and watched a moth circling the lamp on the bedside table. He fluttered and flapped around the bulb, every once in a while plinking into it. Then he would flop and dart away, starting the futile circle again, each time as energetically as the first. Maybe it was nature's way of pointing out to me the futility of action, or perhaps the need for perseverance. I resolved the question.

I caught him, took him to Fluffy's little travel cage, and threw him in for Fluffy to stalk. Fluffy's beady little eyes were flat and sleepy.

I threw myself on the bed.

YVONNE TALMADGE, a young woman from Wichita, Kansas, with a big problem, had come to Colorado to meet someone, presumably about her mother's murder. And she was at the Golden Fleece Casino, presumably to meet someone. Virtually anyone. I remembered the splashes of brown liquid on her purse. Most likely she was poisoned then by a cola drink. Because...she knew something or had something—and might tell.

Yvonne had recognized me because I'd been on the television and in the newspapers after I helped to pinpoint the murderer of a friend of mine. And she was in the casino...to meet her murderer. If I'd talked to her I might know who that was.

I drew in a long breath. The murderer wouldn't know Yvonne hadn't told me anything. In fact, the killer probably would think she had.

I rolled from the bed, pulled the note from my pocket, and flattened it out on the top of my dresser to examine it.

It was a plain white cocktail napkin except for the front

fold, which was emblazoned with the name of the casino and the same picture that was on my pin—the studly young man holding the gaudy yellow hank of hair.

She had used a fine-tip ballpoint pen and scrawled in feathery loops and sharp spikes. The periods were almost dashes, and the napkin had been torn a little where she'd underlined the ''anyone'' and the ''ASAP.'' The number written on the napkin was probably that of the place she was staying.

I dialed. A tired female voice answered, ''Golden Eagle Motel.''

''May I have Yvonne Talmadge's room number?''

''We can't give out room numbers.'' I could hear her turning pages, like she was leafing through a magazine.

''Well, uh, I'm her sister, and I'm supposed to meet her there.''

''I don't have it that you're staying here with her. She didn't sign for two people.''

''I'm just picking her up.''

''Well, we're at 221 Pine. I'll connect you, but I can't give you her number.''

I let the phone ring four times before I replaced the receiver.

Fluffy sprang off his twig, taking huge, heavy breaths so that his little ribs went way in and out. Then he flicked his tail. The moth fluttered around the top of his cage, but he ignored it. I bent to talk to him. He likes that. It's his version of a bedtime story.

I started to get undressed and dumped my leftover quarters from my pocket onto the table with a jangle, kicked off my sandals, and unbuttoned my jumpsuit.

That's when I saw the key among the change.

It wasn't mine. It was an ordinary silvery key with a worn, round head.

I turned it over in my fingers. Possibly a car door key, or a room or padlock key. I thought of all the times I'd bumped into and been bumped into...when could she have brushed my pocket and slipped the key inside? It was almost as though Yvonne were still trying to tell me something.

The scene flashed before me again.

Yvonne tottering when I turned. Her eyes wide, her right hand clutching to her throat as if it burned. Her left hand...where? I couldn't remember. Then she fell hard against me, grabbing me as she fell, her left hand catching on my pocket as she slid to the floor. That was it. That had to be when she had slipped the napkin and the key into my pocket.

I called Samson again. And heard his operator tell me she would tell him I called again, in a tone of voice that said she thought I was a flaming weirdo.

I thought about calling Detective Stokowski in Denver. I closed my eyes and heard him talking. "Put them in a safe place, and call Samson in the morning. You've got nothing solid to go on." And then he'd lecture me on the trouble I was causing. I wondered if Zelda had lured him into her living room.

The napkin and the key were Yvonne's last desperate attempt to tell me something. If there was anything else, it would be in her motel room. By morning the killer might have cleared the place out. If not already.

I checked my watch and considered the situation. It was nearly midnight. It was spooky out there. I didn't have her room number. I picked up the phone and dialed Meredith's room. She answered in a sleep-clogged voice.

"Meredith, I located the place where Yvonne is—was staying. The Golden Eagle."

"For God's sake. Have you lost your mind?"

"Let's go there."

"No."

"Yvonne would want us to."

"No, she wouldn't. I can hear her right now. Don't go there, call the sheriff instead, and stay safely at home."

"I did. He wasn't in. He's not going to do anything until morning. Besides, he doesn't even think there's anything wrong. You know the statistics on catching criminals indicate a significant drop in the rate of solving the crime after twenty-four hours. It's already almost two hours since Yvonne collapsed.''

"And almost one hour since I went to bed."

"Meredith—"

"It's not safe, Stella. Now cut it out."

"We can get up there and back in no time."

"No. And you're not to go either." She hung up.

I rebuttoned my jumpsuit, pulled on socks and tennies, and grabbed a sweater. It's cool in the mountains at night, and I didn't know how long I might be out.

Before I left, I checked on Fluffy. The tip of a moth's wing stuck out of his stoic little lips. He blinked with pride. I think he just catches them to be macho, because moths are so dry it takes him forever to swallow them.

Downstairs was dark and empty and smelled like oak and lemon. A quick peek showed me that the parlor was empty, but a faint soapy smell lingered in the air, and the love-seat cushions felt warm to the touch. I decided I was paranoid. There was no telephone in the room, so anyone sitting here would hear nothing.

The front door was locked after midnight. I let myself out as quietly as possible.

The night air was crispy-cool, laced with a faint smell of wood smoke and pine trees. Wispy clouds floated over a half-moon, making the night eerie and alive with the flickering light. Like Halloween. I pulled my sweater tight around my neck and glanced up at the moon to see if a witch was flying across it.

As soon as I slipped away from the porch light, I felt my neck prickle. I turned up my collar and sneaked from shadow to shadow, ducking beneath dark pine boughs and trying to avoid stumbling in the ruts at the side of the road.

There were no shortcut steps to the next level, only the narrow, winding road, and my muscles were aching by the time I reached the Golden Eagle, three levels up the mountain.

The motel faced out, looking down on the town: an office, brightly lit by a No Vacancy sign in the window, and six connected units each with a picture window next to the door and a porch lamp between them—except for the last unit, where the lamp was out. For some reason it reminded me of jack-o'-lantern teeth.

The Golden Eagle looked as though it had shared too many nights with too many people and was tired of human beings. I was beginning to feel the same way.

In front of each unit was a carefully parked car. I could see a Wyoming license plate on the first, but the others were obscured. The windows in the first three units were dark. Unit four had a light glowing dimly through the curtained picture window, as if occupants were out but expected. Unit five was brightly lit, with an occasional movement of shadows in front of the closed curtains. The one on the end, six, was dark.

My stomach growled. I wanted a chocolate bar.

The only way to avoid exposure from the light of the office was to creep below the retaining wall of the parking area, along the mountainside. At that point the sparse grass was long, tough, and very slippery. It grew in toe-tangling clumps, interspersed with a thin layer of dirt and gravel that clung to the sloping bedrock.

I was opposite the second and third units when a shadow crossed the window of unit five. I jerked and pitched to the side. My uphill weight-bearing foot suddenly slipped. For three heart-stopping feet I skidded, amid loose gravel and dirt, clattering down the mountainside in a mini-rockslide.

My arms flew out, raking the air for any solid hold. My other foot flew up. I landed hard on my rump, sliding farther in the moving scree. I slipped maybe three feet before my fingers closed on a ridge of solid boulder. More loose rocks and dirt clattered down the mountainside. I held statue-still and listened, over the sounds of my panting, for the sound of a door opening.

Nothing.

Ten feet in front of me, the retaining wall was markedly lower where a huge rock outcropping shored up the parking area. The boulder overhung the mountain, and I couldn't get around it. I had to move out where I'd be exposed.

I pulled myself together and inched forward.

By craning my neck I discovered that I was even with the fourth unit and well out of the lights cast by the manager's office. I climbed to the parking area, shook myself off, and strolled casually to the third unit, to look like I belonged should anyone notice me.

Clouds crossed the moon, casting the night in and out of eerie shadows. I stole along the cars, checking the license plates. Those in front of units two and three had Colorado license plates. I moved to the next one in front of unit four—Utah. There was no car in front of unit five, but the light inside was on and television voices leaked out through the window.

I scuttled past the glowing, curtain-covered window of unit five to the last car, a dusty Ford Escort. It had Kansas license plates.

A grinning stuffed-toy cat with wide phosphorescent eyes and suction cups on his paws was splayed against the window like he was on a torture rack. I peered inside the car. The backseat was clean and empty.

In the front a diet cola can stood on the dashboard, and a battered box of tissues and a map of Colorado lay on the passenger seat. On the floor in front of the passenger seat I saw two crumpled Snickers wrappers and an empty corn curl bag. *That* was a diet I could relate to.

There was a Wichita, Kansas, sticker on the driver's side of the windshield.

I dug the key out of my pocket and tried it in the car door. It didn't fit.

I moved to the trunk of the car and shoved the key into the lock. A thrill ran along my shoulders and arms. I lifted the lid. The inside was clean and bare except for a collapsible umbrella and a worn blanket. I felt beneath the blanket. Nothing.

Out of the corner of my eye I caught a sudden shadow at the window of unit five. Voices sounded and the doorknob rattled lightly, as if someone might be getting ready to leave.

I was standing in just enough light to be clearly visible from any number of vantage points. A duck, sitting or dead. Neither one was very good. And I still had to get back to the inn, three haunted blocks away. Without a weapon.

Impulsively I grabbed the umbrella and swiped at the places where I remembered touching the trunk. I lowered the lid to within three inches, then slammed it. The noise echoed in the quiet.

Suddenly a hundred eyes seemed to follow me, measuring my every move. I remembered the feeling when I was a child, playing Kick-the-Can in the twilight of early summer nights. Sneaking through the soft, humid scents of evergreen bushes and damp grass, we'd slither around the bushes, skulking little shadows, except for an occasional snuffle or grunt. There was a suffocating thrill of excitement in the threat of being caught before reaching home base.

But this was different. This wasn't a game.

Voices in unit five dropped. A wedge of light shone out. I crouched behind the car, ran around the front end, then dashed to the recess of the doorway to unit six.

The voices resumed, louder now, as if the door was cracked. I sucked in a desperate breath. The breeze lifted my hair, sending a chill over my scalp.

I leaned heavily against the door, listening to the rise and fall of the voices. I had to hide. I gripped the doorknob behind me, turned it. The door fell open. I stepped inside.

Warm, stuffy air poured past me into the cool night. I blinked to accustom my eyes to the dark of the unit.

Please don't let there be someone sleeping in here.

And if there was, what would I say? Sorry, I got the wrong bed? Party, anyone? Don't shoot!

My eyelids were tight from staring, and my eyeballs stung. I still couldn't see if anyone lay in the bed.

The door of the next unit suddenly rattled and swung wide. Light spilled out from the open door, and a shadow fell across the narrow sidewalk. A voice, hushed but furious, whispered, "Dammit, you can't do these things! I'll be right back."

I pushed the door closed, latching it silently. Then I flattened myself against the wall and held my breath until I saw little stars in front of my eyes from lack of oxygen. Every sensory cell in my body was tense and alert. I listened so hard my ears hurt. If anyone had touched me at that moment, I'd have shot through the roof like a missile.

Carefully, I pushed the curtain aside. A faint glow of light illuminated the room. The bed was empty. Thank God.

Then I peeked out the window. No one in view. Only the voices speaking in barely whispered tones, sharp and angry. It sounded like two female voices, although one was low and so quiet I could barely hear.

"But...the police..."

"Stay inside and don't go out again!" Then more sibilant sounds of whispered consonants, none of which I could hear adequately, primarily because my brain was screaming at me. The police! I'd forgotten about them. It wouldn't be long before they figured out where Yvonne was staying...they'd be here...I had to get out of here.

My hand gripped the doorknob. Then I heard the scrape of shoes against cement...coming closer.

I jumped back, threw myself to the floor, screwed my eyes shut to keep from getting dust in them, and scooted beneath the double bed. It smelled like one thousand and five years of dust. The footsteps stopped at the door.

I lifted the edge of the bedskirt just enough to see out— and saw the little collapsible umbrella lying half out and half under the bed. Twelve inches of telltale umbrella. I started to reach for it.

The door swung open. A flashlight flicked on and played around the room as if the person sensed my presence. I breathed through my mouth, in tiny silent respirations.

How would strangers in the next unit know the police would be coming?

All I could see were feet and ankles. Thick, sturdy ankles

swathed in pink socks, standing in old white Reebok tennies, women's tennies, worn down on the sides. One shoe
had a bright blue shoelace, the other one, orange. Broncos
football team colors.

My burglar was a female Broncos fan.

I heard the shoes walk to the bathroom. I grabbed the
umbrella, pulled it in under the bed with me, handy if I
needed it for a weapon.

I heard a rattling noise in the bathroom as though she
had put down a handful of marbles, then something soft.
Then the footsteps returned. At the door I thought I recognized them.

The light flicked off, the door opened, the shoes went
out, and the door shut softly.

As soon as I heard the crunch of gravel against tarmac
I pulled myself out from underneath the bed, stepped to the
window, and peered out. In the weak light of the cloud-
wisp-covered moon I saw a familiar, sturdy figure crunch
across the narrow parking lot to the far end, then strike off
across the mountainside.

Edie...!

I sucked in a gigantic breath of air. I thought Edie was
at Porcupine Pete's. Why was she coming here? To leave
things in the bathroom? And for that matter, was this
Yvonne's room, or someone else's?

EIGHT

I HAD VERY LITTLE TIME. The police were supposed to get here any minute. I felt along the wall with my hand for the light switch. My fingers were curled around the toggle when my brain slipped into gear and I stopped. The light would make me a terrific target.

My eyes were almost accustomed to the dark, so I reached a little farther and pulled on the drapery cord. The curtains parted, admitting a trickle of light from outside. I'd never appreciated how hard burglary is.

The room was tidy and probably beige. I couldn't be sure of the color, only that the room was devoid of character and contained little to identify its occupant.

I hurried to the bathroom, closed the door, and flipped the light switch. My eyes stung with the flood of light, and it took a moment to adjust. Blinking, I gazed around.

A makeup case sagged forlornly on the countertop, with brushes and dabs of purple eye shadow spilling onto the white-and-gold-flecked Formica surface. A pair of inexpensive gold-colored earrings lay beside the makeup case. A strand of pearls lay next to them. Pearls. That was what I had heard Edie place on the counter.

I turned to the shower, shoved the curtain aside. A bright yellow sample-size bottle of shampoo stood in the corner of the tub. The waste-paper basket held only crumpled tissues.

No men's clothing, no men's cosmetics. Only one cosmetic bag. She was traveling alone.

I stepped into the closet area, pulling the door behind me until there was only a crack of light shining out.

My heart was pounding in my ears. It was so loud I could barely hear any other noise. I had to hurry, but the faster I tried to move, the slower I seemed to go. I sincerely hoped it was Yvonne's room. It would be so difficult to explain this to an offended stranger. But even more difficult to explain to the police.

A suit bag hung from the rod. No name tag. There were three dresses and a jacket, size ten, bearing what department stores advertise as a "famous women's designer label."

I stooped, feeling for luggage beneath the clothing. A new, inexpensive suitcase stood beneath them, next to the wall. A tag dangled from the handle.

"Yvonne Talmadge, Wichita, KA." No street address, just Wichita, Kansas. I laid the umbrella on the floor and opened the suitcase.

The lingerie and T-shirts were in tidy piles, but had the distinct look of having been rifled through. Of course I noticed the lingerie. Traditional, white, and utilitarian. Nothing outrageous. Or interesting, for that matter. Still, there is something very intimate about lingerie. I poked along the corners and peeked in the lid pocket. Nothing. I wiped it all over and closed it gently.

I suddenly wondered if she had friends back in Kansas who would miss her, people who would describe her fondly and cry at her funeral. I sincerely hoped so. I felt furious that someone had killed her. Her death seemed like a metaphor for something profound, but I didn't know what it was.

It was a terrible, bleak moment.

There was a thump from the other side of the wall. Ominously close. I flipped off the bathroom light, wiped the switch, and raced back to the bedroom.

The bedside stand contained only a pristine Gideon's Bible. I riffed through it, on the off chance that it might be the one place no one ever looked. Nothing. I wiped it with a tissue to smear any prints and replaced it carefully.

The picture frame over the bed was fastened tight to the wall. Nothing hidden behind there.

Another thump. I scurried to the door and took one last

look. The umbrella! I raced to the closet, grabbed the umbrella, and raced back to the door. I wiped off the light switch at the side of the door and stepped out, pulling the door shut.

The path that Edie had taken down the side of the mountain was almost certainly shorter and quicker, but more exposed and vulnerable.

Sticking to the shadows, I slipped along the dark sides of parked cars, still clutching the umbrella, and ran across in front of the lobby lights to the comfort of the dark street. My ears were hyperalert to any odd noise that would identify a lurking presence.

Crickets sang in the grasses. I listened for a change in their chorus. Whenever they stopped droning, I stopped walking and huddled against a car, or wall, or the darkest place near to me, until they took up their chorus again.

The entire last block I sprinted, completely convinced someone was following me. Clutching the umbrella, bent low, weaving, I raced to the bottom of the wide porch steps of the inn, which I took in twos. I grasped the doorknob, twisted, and pulled.

It was locked. Of course.

I fumbled blindly in my pocket for the keys to the inn, desperate and gasping for breath, each second expecting a bullet to pierce my back.

My fingers shook, and sweat broke out across my forehead. Finally I felt the key with my fingers, pulled it out, and shoved it into the lock. It turned easily.

I lunged over the threshold, shut and locked the door behind me. The foyer was dark and empty, lit only by the green glow of the telephone console. I darted to the window, pulled the lacy curtains just far enough apart to see, and peered out beyond the circle of the porch light to the old thick-trunked blue spruce at the side of the house, just off the road I had come down.

My lungs were screaming, and I was beginning to feel like a complete fool when the moon burst from behind a cloud and streamed light across the little yard. A two-legged shadow detached itself from the trunk of the big tree at the side of the house.

I raced to the back of the inn, through the kitchen to the back door. Silently opened it and listened. The crunch of footsteps echoed faintly on the air.

I sneaked out on the porch and over to the railing, leaning out as far as I dared, holding the umbrella like a club, ready to swing. The shadow moved into the light, walking slowly, thoughtfully, head down. It was a woman. I could tell by the hips and legs. Fascinated, I watched as she walked seemingly unaware of my gaze. Then she stepped into a patch of moonlight.

Angie Sayers...looking haunted and ghostly in a light blouse that lifted on the night breeze. I squinted, looked again, hardly believing my eyes. Angie, who supposedly had angina, was making double time up a mountain road. Why on earth would she follow me? And why would Angie be at the Golden Eagle instead of at the inn?

I went to my room and, juggling the umbrella, nervously fumbled my room key into the keyhole. Inside, I pushed the doorknob lock, hooked the chain lock, and shoved a chair beneath the doorknob. Then I grabbed the umbrella, knelt to the floor, and peeked beneath the bed. Nothing.

I crossed to the bathroom—formerly a closet—pushed the door open, and searched the reflection of the shower in the mirror on the wall opposite the bath. I even stretched my arm around the door and pulled the shower curtain back to make sure no one was there.

Fluffy was in his cage on the dresser top, vivid green, the color of excitement, and his little ribs were pumping in and out as though he'd run a mile.

"Anybody here, fella?"

He blinked, then closed his eyes.

I pulled open the dresser drawers. My undies were the same, but my red-and-purple teddy was crumpled up as though someone had tried to look beneath it. I shuddered, then smoothed it, shut the drawer, and pulled it open again, hurriedly. The teddy was crumpled again.

Finally I threw myself on the bed and tried to think.

A television played somewhere, and water was running in the room next to me—Edie's room. She was still awake. But that meant she wasn't still out following Angie following me, unless she had left the water running as a decoy...or she had someone else in that room with her.

Then I thought about the back stairs and the back door to the inn. And made a mental note to check tomorrow to see if the front door key also fit the back door.

My gaze fell on the door of the big pine wardrobe. It was ajar. I yanked the door open. Nothing. I prodded the clothes with the umbrella. Nothing.

The umbrella. My heart beat faster. I reached for the phone and called Meredith. "Don't ask why, just come over here."

I sat slowly on the edge of the bed and began to examine the umbrella. It had been the only thing in the trunk of the car, except for an old blanket. I unsnapped the strap that held it shut and shook it out. A knock sounded.

I padded to the door. "Meredith?"

"It's me. Open up."

I pulled the chair away, unlocked the deadbolt, unchained the door, and let her in, yawning, wrapped in a blanket, hair tumbling to her shoulders. "Meredith, look at this."

I shook the umbrella to get her attention. It was an ordinary collapsible umbrella, about a foot long. The kind that springs open when you press the spring button on the side. It had a long, thick plastic handle, curved for easier gripping, that looked out of place.

"Have you lost your mind? You went to Yvonne's motel room? You brought Yvonne's umbrella here?"

I turned the umbrella in my hands, feeling its shaft, noting the odd bulge of the plastic grip. I twisted it sharply, like the lid of a jar. It turned, grudgingly.

"Stella, do you hear me? You can get charged with something for this. You could end up in jail, again."

"For opening an umbrella in a hotel room?"

"You're incorrigible."

I twisted the grip of the umbrella. "My mother calls me cute."

"Your mother is going to have to hire an attorney for her cute daughter."

It took three turns before I could pull the grip off the metal shaft. There was nothing visible inside the handle or the shaft. I stuck my little finger in the end of it and felt paper. Finally I took the umbrella by the top and swung it. Centrifugal force brought out a slim sheaf of newspaper.

"Look, Meredith!" Barely able to breathe, I smoothed the little roll of newsprint on the dresser top, beneath the light. It was heavily creased from repeated folding, and worn from handling.

"Oh my God, Stella. Now you're making me an accessory to your crime."

"Nonsense. Just lie about it."

It was an obituary and picture of a Margaret Prescott. The picture showed a woman younger in appearance than her stated fifty-five years of age, wearing a dark dress, pearls, and pearl earrings, with her hands folded serenely in front of her, sporting a large, dark engagement ring.

"Look, Meredith, do you see? Her eyes. They're so like Yvonne's that no one could miss the family resemblance. The black-and-white paper doesn't show the color of her hair, but I'm willing to bet it was auburn."

"And I'm willing to bet you'll be in big trouble." She curled up on the bed and pulled the blanket around her feet.

"Meredith, you have no idea what you missed."

"The opportunity to go to jail?"

I ignored the remark.

"What were you thinking?"

A coil of anxiety twisted in my stomach. "Well, it was scary out there, and I just grabbed the umbrella for a weapon. See, it's one of those that flaps open when you press the button. If I'd been accosted then I could point the umbrella at him, press the button, and presto! He'd be blinded by the exploding umbrella."

"Seven years' bad luck! Close that thing."

I searched the obituary for more information, but there was very little. Margaret had been born May 14. There was a slight prominence, a stubborn line in her jaw, fitting for a Taurus, the bull, but I might have been reading it into the picture.

She was survived by her husband, Stephen Douglas Prescott, and one daughter, Yvonne Talmadge.

"Why would Yvonne hide this?" I asked. When she didn't answer, I looked at Meredith. She was sound asleep.

Meredith roused herself enough to stumble back to her room and set her chain lock. I pushed the feeble doorknob lock and set the chain on my door. Then I shoved a chair back tight beneath the doorknob.

I slipped the paper into the Gideon's Bible to keep it flat, and replaced the umbrella handle the way I found it. Even with the night-light on and the umbrella stuffed by my side where I could grab it if I needed it for protection, it was hard to relax and sleep.

Now that the excitement of finding the article in the umbrella had worn off, I was just a little nervous about how I would tell the sheriff. Every time I closed my eyes I saw myself explaining. And explaining.

I'd left my trusty, loving body pillow back in Denver, and the umbrella I tried to wind myself around was scant comfort. Finally, toward dawn, I slept soundly.

IT WAS EIGHT-FIFTEEN Friday morning. The umbrella was digging a hole in my side. I woke from a dream in which my pillow had become a person that looked remarkably like Jason. Meredith was pounding on my door. I rolled over, pulled the umbrella from my side, and called to her that I'd make it to breakfast after a shower.

The common sense of morning sunshine streaming in the windows made the menace, terror, and adrenaline of last night seem unreal. My rationale for taking the umbrella now sounded extremely feeble, even to me. It was going to be more than a little awkward explaining it to the sheriff.

All of the events of last night flooded over me—
Yvonne's murder, Edie's bizarre comings and goings, and
my visit to Yvonne's motel unit. Edie was up to her armpits
in this mess. And now so was I, right up to my pierced
ears.

I dragged myself out of bed, surveyed the sleep smudges
under my eyes and my rumpled hair, and debated whether
I should try to spruce up or make myself look worse in the
hopes the sheriff would think I was a terrified, contrite little
wimp.

From my turret windows I saw the main street of town,
where the casinos were already reopening. A boy was
sweeping the sidewalk clean of the detritus of last night's
revels. If only I could sweep last night away as easily.

Up the mountain toward the Golden Eagle Motel, sunshine bounced innocently off the light green and gold
meadow grass. A mule deer picked its way out from behind
a scrubby pine, head lifted, sniffing the breeze. He looked
straight in my direction, then bounded away. I wondered if
he smelled my fear.

I figured the best thing to do was to face the sheriff as
soon as possible. Maybe when I gave him the key and the
note, he'd be pleased enough with the clue that he'd forget
to be furious.

Especially if I promised not to interfere any more.

I took a deep breath, then looked up the telephone number for the sheriff's office again in the bedside directory
and dialed. My stomach coiled.

A tired voice came on the line. Sheriff Samson wasn't
in yet.

A reprieve. "Please have him call me as soon as possible. It's very important," I said, virtuously gave my name
and number, and hung up.

All through the shower I pondered, What next?

After blowing my hair dry, upside-down for the maximum fluffability since I have quite straight brown hair, I
donned a purple, red, blue, and brown jungle-print shirt
with jeans.

I picked up my jumpsuit from the floor and looked at the smear of dirt on the right leg where I'd slid down the mountain in the dark. I shook it and ran my hands over the front, smoothing out the wrinkles, brushing dust from the pocket where Yvonne had shoved the napkin and the key.

My fingers caught on a corner that was torn away. The stitching must have given way when she slumped to the floor. Hot tears filled my eyes. I folded it and laid it gently on the floor of the wardrobe.

I knew I could not possibly sit back and wait for someone to take care of everything. And I knew I'd better be damned careful.

I took a safety pin—I carry a supply—and pinned the key and note to the backside of the chintz curtains, where it wouldn't show through, then laid the umbrella in the front of the top drawer of my dresser. The jackpot check I folded and put in my bra.

Fluffy jumped off his twig, begging for an outing. He gets terribly bored if he doesn't get an outing now and again. I can tell when he's depressed or bored, because he becomes withdrawn and closes his eyes. Meredith says Fluffy is just catatonic, but then she isn't very sensitive to his expression. It takes a little time to get close to a lizard.

I put him into his harness and pinned it to my shirt.

I was almost across the room, with my hand on the doorknob, when the phone rang. I snatched it up, thinking it might be the sheriff, but it was Jason. He'd heard about the death at the casino.

"Are you concerned about me, or are you just calling for the story?" I asked.

"You, of course—but you *were* there, weren't you?"

I admitted I was but held on to the story, making him work for each detail I gave him. I like to think I'm teaching him to be a good interviewer.

"Dammit, Stella, you're hogging the story."

"It's my story."

"You don't write news, you write a lovelorn column. If

you're going to be this way, I'll come up and get it myself.''

"You can't. There's no room. Not anywhere in Silverado." I hung up. We enjoy a very professional relationship.

Edie's door rattled open and shut. I peeked out. Edie,
her hair spiky and damp, crossed the hall and knocked on
Jeena's door.

The door burst open and Jeena, decked out in fuchsia
polka dots and looking terminally perky, emerged. The sunlight pouring in through the window shone through Edie's
short hair, creating a halo effect over her head. For an instant it looked as though the two of them were entering the
kingdom of light as they headed downstairs; then they
turned the corner and disappeared from sight.

I waited, listening to the sounds from downstairs in the
dining room, the clank of flatware against china, the scrape
of chairs against the hardwood flooring. I figured I had
fifteen minutes at best, and probably less, to search their
rooms for the obvious—correspondence from Yvonne, or
poison.

I grabbed my mileage-plus plastic card from my wallet—
I didn't want to scramble a charge card I might need later—
and padded to Edie's door, listened again carefully for footsteps, then slid the card into the doorjamb. The lock popped
open on the third push. I shivered a little at the lack of
security and stepped inside.

Like the whole of the inn, the room was decorated in a
tiny pastel-flowered print reminiscent of Victorian times. It
was a cozy room, with a single window and a simple oak
dresser against the wall. I pushed the door almost closed,
crossed to the dresser, and made a quick search of her top
drawer. Her purse was tucked in the second drawer. I fished
through it. Nothing except the usual tissues, lipstick, gum,
keys, wallet, letters. I riffled through the papers in a hurry.
Nothing from Kansas, nothing from Yvonne, nothing at all
out of the ordinary.

Her wallet held an assortment of gold credit cards, a
Denver Public Library card, a museum of Natural History

membership, and her social security card. The item of interest, though, was a picture of Edie—with David, in front of the Museum of Natural History, arms around each other, laughing, intimate and happy.

I stared at it a moment with surprise. I hadn't imagined Edie with David. I wondered what had come between them, and if she still cared for him.

She'd been almost bitter when she talked about love with Amy and Bill.

There was no date on the picture. I looked at it again, carefully—at the smile on her face, the sun shining on her shoulder-length hair. I'd known her for over a year, and all that time her hair had been short.

I repositioned her purse in the drawer exactly the way I'd found it. Then I checked the bathroom. The shower and the basin were still damp, with droplets of water clinging to the porcelain surfaces. The medicine cabinet was empty. In her cosmetic bag I found generic aspirin, toothbrush, toothpaste, facial moisturizer, and witch-hazel astringent. Nasty, but not poisonous.

I pulled the door closed behind me and sneaked up to Jeena's door. It was locked, too. Nobody trusted anybody in this group.

Downstairs there were more voices, footsteps, and the scrape of chairs. A door slammed on the floor above, and footsteps rang out on the stairs, coming toward me. A pair of men's loafers appeared. I shoved the plastic card hard into the doorjamb, flattened myself against the door, wrenched the card down, and popped the lock. I was getting good at it.

I heard the feet pause on the landing, then walk to Jeena's door.

I held my breath. There was a knock. I stepped back against the wall. *Please don't come in.* Another knock.

A hesitant step, then a creak of the floor. He walked to the stairs and clattered down them. I let out my breath and looked around. I didn't have much time.

Jeena's bed was rumpled, her nightie dropped on the

floor, and her purse was thrown onto her bed, dumped conveniently out as though she'd been looking for something in a hurry. I stirred the spilled contents, then riffled through her wallet. She had a single credit card, a driver's license, fifty-nine dollars cash, and several receipts from liquor stores. She had a penchant for cheap vodka. She had a bottle of it in the bathroom, along with a prescription of Zoloft, an antidepressant, prescribed by a local physician and obtained at McClintock's Super Pharmacy. McClintock. As in David McClintock.

There weren't any other drugs.

No suspicious packets of white powder, no unusual cosmetics, no tiny vials with crystals in them.

I was on my way out of the room when I caught sight of a book poking out from under her pillow. I pulled it out. It was a journal, of the kind you can buy in a stationery store, blank pages, pretty cloth cover. I opened it and paged through, scanning until my eye bumped on "Yvonne." The date was June 19, a week before she wrote me: *Yvonne's coming to Silverado. Memories hurt. I cried for an hour.*

There was no other mention of Yvonne.

Her last entry made my heart sad: *It's my 650th day since discharge, and I'm still alive.*

I closed it and pushed it back under her pillow. I hoped she took her Zoloft that morning.

My hand was on the doorknob when I heard footsteps in the hallway. Keys jingled outside the door. I froze.

Suddenly, there was a muffled sound of something being dropped and a soft "Damn!"

Footsteps retreated. I peeked out and saw Mrs. Johnson disappearing into a large closet at the far end of the hallway. I leaped from the room and hit the stairs at a run, clutching the bannister and stepping lightly on the sides of the stairs to avoid creaks. Stella, Cat Burglar of Silverado. Hardly the kind of thing you can put on a résumé.

My conscience was smarting a little.

Downstairs at the desk I stopped to collect my wits and asked the clerk if there were any vacancies in town.

"Are you kidding? This is the Fourth of July weekend! Rooms have been booked for months. We're full, and so is every other unit in town." With one exception; but I didn't mention it.

His telephone console bleeped and lit up with little neon numbers across the top. "Excuse me, miss," he said and lifted the receiver. "I'm sorry, we don't have room service." I went in to breakfast grinning. No rooms. Let Jason suck on that lemon.

The dining room was large and comfortable, with oak ceiling molding and small-print wallpaper in soft coral tones. The breakfast offerings were attractively laid out on a buffet along the far wall. Most of the people at the inn had finished eating, and card tables were already set up to play bridge on the sunny glassed-in porch.

My stomach rumbled at the smell of fresh muffins and coffee. I debated the possibility of arsenic in the apple-spice topping, then took a muffin anyway, along with scrambled eggs and bacon.

Meredith was nowhere to be seen. David, Edie, Amy, and someone I didn't know were solemnly playing bridge at one of the tables on the porch. David was looking very collegiate in a plaid short-sleeved shirt and chinos. Amy was wearing lavender slacks and a matching lavender cotton sweater. Edie wore lightweight cotton-knit slacks and top in an earthy hue of green. The blousy top had ornate sequin-covered leaves sewn on the shoulders and neckline.

I dropped a napkin strategically so I could check out their shoes. Amy had on a pair of strappy white sandals, and her toes were purple with cold. Looked pretty bad with her slut-red toenail polish. David wore loafers—so he had been knocking on Jeena's door. I wondered how Edie would feel about that. Edie wore tennies, one lace orange, the other blue.

"You lose something?" David asked.

"Shoe fetish," I answered. Amy dropped one of her cards.

JEENA WAS in the dining room hunkered over her coffee, both elbows on the table, grasping the cup with both hands and inhaling the steaming liquid like it was an emergency transfusion. She is tall and athletically built, slim, almost lanky for a woman. She was wearing white slacks and a white camp shirt with a white-and-navy tennis sweater draped over her shoulders, the sleeves tied in front. She looked ready to swing a tennis racket, except that her hands shook as she held the coffee cup to her face. She had light brown hair, cut short to curl softly around her face, emphasizing large eyes of an unusual shade of pale crystalline blue. Iceberg blue.

When I was growing up the neighbors had a wirehaired terrier with eyes of the same blue. He was almost a nice dog, until he chewed through the back screen door the day our toy collie went into heat. I didn't mourn the day he had an epileptic fit and dropped dead.

Nearly a year ago I'd met Jeena through Edie, who invited me to play with the bridge group. I didn't last long with them, but I remembered Jeena and her pale crystalline-blue eyes.

I slid into the chair across from her, where I could watch her face without being too obvious, and began to eat. "Hey, Jeena, seen Meredith?"

She eyed me like I was something green and slimy that she'd found at the back of the fridge. "She went to the casinos."

"Angie playing bridge?"

Jeena sucked on her coffee, watching me, like she was trying to read my face. "Angie's not here. We came without eight. Edie said you and Meredith might sub, but I figure we'll just play four at a time. Screw bridge."

"I thought I saw her last night."

Jeena's eyes darted to the left. "She stayed in Denver."

She was lying and very nervous. I twisted around, but there wasn't anyone there. "You feeling better?" I asked.

"Better than what?"

"Better than yesterday—at the casino. You seemed so upset."

"Upset?" Jeena's lips thinned in her rounded face.

Fluffy moved in my pocket. I had forgotten about him. His head showed at the edge of the pocket; he was trying to decide what color—red, blue, purple, or brown—he wanted to match. I hoped he'd settle for the brown and just blend in quietly. Jeena's mood didn't bode well for vacationing lizards—or blundering astrologists.

The bridge players were snapping their cards in the next room. I decided to change to a safer topic. "Looks like Edie and David are having quite a time as partners."

"Well, she better keep her hands—" Jeena blurted. My face must have reflected my surprise, because she immediately laughed with embarrassment and tried to pass it off as a joke "—to herself," she finished, glancing around uncomfortably.

I smiled, but it wasn't funny. Jeena looked like she needed some firm boundaries around her. Like walls, maybe rubber ones.

I suggested we go to the sitting room in the front. I pulled the door shut after us.

"You and David are pretty good friends, I take it."

"Yes. Edie's just playing a few rounds with him—that's all." I wasn't sure which one of us she was trying to convince. She leaned suddenly over the table toward me. "You know that Amy is going to marry Bill."

"I heard something about that."

"She's planned her wedding twice before, but it never comes off. This time she's determined." Jeena nodded in Bill's direction. "He doesn't know what he's in for. Nice guy. Used to be a salesman, you know."

"I thought he was a minister."

"Well, I don't know about that. Lived in Texas before he came here."

"Oh, that's nice."

"Well, not so's you'd notice."

The conversation was taking such decidedly peculiar

turns I figured I might as well broach the big topic. "I thought you knew Yvonne."

Jeena's face bleached to an interesting shade of beige. "What makes you think that?"

I shrugged. "I thought you called out her name." Actually she had wailed, but it was worth trying to get her to admit it.

"No! I didn't. I made a mistake. She just looked like somebody. But it wasn't her. It couldn't be. She's still in Kansas. It's not Yvonne! Can't be." She frowned and bit her lip.

"Jeena, I saw her driver's license. It *was* Yvonne. I'm sorry." I tried to reach across to pat her hand, but she yanked it away and jammed it in her lap. Her eyes screwed shut as though she was trying to shut out the bad news. Finally, she opened them and looked at me, her face a blank mask.

"You two were friends once—a long time ago."

She nodded slowly, rubbing her temples with her fingers. "A long time ago. It's hard...to remember, sometimes. We were roommates. She came just before I left."

"You knew each other very well...then."

She rubbed her head harder. So hard I was afraid her skin would break. "It's hard to know people there," she said. She closed her eyes.

I wanted to get her talking again. "Where, Jeena?"

Jeena looked up abruptly, her lower lip wet and drooping like a child about to cry. Her chin quivered. "At the hospital." Twin streams of tears streaked down her cheeks.

"What was the name of the hospital, Jeena?"

"Whispering Pines."

"Jeena, I know this is difficult, but do you remember whether Yvonne had any visitors while she was there?" I handed her a napkin to use as a tissue.

Jeena snuffled into the napkin for a few minutes, then raised her face, blotting her eyes. "There was one guy, maybe in his thirties, who she liked. She always looked forward to him, but she hated her stepfather."

"What did her stepfather look like?"

She looked puzzled briefly, then shook her head. "I never saw him, but the nurses said he was really something. Dark hair, slim. Not very old, maybe forty...not as old as Yvonne's mother. He'd come once a week, on Saturday afternoons. Sometimes Yvonne would be so upset she'd throw up. She finally refused to see him anymore."

Jeena rubbed her knee with her hand, digging her thumb into the flesh along her thigh. Fine creases appeared at the edges of her eyes, giving her the appearance of an older woman, one suffering from far too many life experiences. She was only thirty-seven, and now she looked sixty.

"Why was she there?"

Jeena looked at me, her eyes large and vague, like she was looking back into a painful place in her life, instead of me. It took her several moments to reply. "She killed her mother."

NINE

THERE WAS a barely muffled gasp from the other side of the dining room door. I got up and pulled it open. Amy was standing at the side, her hand to her mouth, her eyes wide.

"What are you doing?" I asked.

Jeena rushed past me. I heard her footsteps thumping up the stairs, heading for her room.

"I didn't mean to—" Amy rubbed her hand nervously on her lavender slacks.

"You just happened to have grown roots at the very spot and couldn't help overhearing—what?"

"I won't tell. Honest. I only meant to—"

"Talk to me, Amy. Explain."

"I'm sorry."

"Huh! Where were you and Bill all the time? Last night up to now?"

Amy's face bunched up. "We were together, that's where we were. As if it's any of your business." She turned and stormed away.

It was time for another cup of coffee. Edie was ahead of me at the coffee urn; when she turned toward me her face was devoid of expression. I couldn't tell whether she'd overheard any of my conversation with Jeena or not.

"Sounds like you and Jeena were getting into it. You might want to walk softly around her. She was pretty upset yesterday."

I nodded, more to keep peace than because I agreed. I wanted Edie to talk about last night, but I didn't know quite how to begin. "How're you doing at the cards today?"

David drifted up at that moment, stretching. "Edie's got a photographic memory. Makes it easier for her."

"So," I said, "you could remember where people are when something happens?"

She looked at me thoughtfully and raised an eyebrow.

"Yesterday, when Yvonne collapsed at the casino?"

She looked at me for a very long moment, then her gaze shifted away to a point over my left shoulder. There was a subtle change in her expression. I turned to see what it was that she was looking at, but there was no one there. She glanced back at me. "Yes. I suppose I could remember, if I tried." She walked away. I followed.

"So who was next to Yvonne, then, besides me?"

"I don't remember."

"I think you do."

She glanced quickly around the room, then leaned close to me. "Just mind your own business. You could get hurt."

"Is that a threat, Edie?"

"No. It's a warning. You don't know what you're getting into."

"And you? You put strings of pearls into a dead woman's motel room, and you know what you're doing?"

Edie froze. The cup of scalding coffee slipped from her fingers and crashed to the floor.

For a long, long time Edie stared at me. The she turned away and took a towel from the end of the buffet, sopped up most of the coffee, and gathered up the pieces of coffee cup.

I waited until she laid them on a tray. "So what about it, Edie? Didn't you know that was Yvonne's unit?"

She looked at me without answering. I could have been a thousand miles away, or an alien speaking another language.

"Why is Angie in unit five at the Golden Eagle?"

"You don't know she is."

"I'm right, though."

She shook her head angrily. "You'll end up getting someone killed."

I'd have given a lot for a really smart remark just then,

but I was so astonished all I did was watch her storm up the stairs and listen to the echo of her angry footsteps.

I had just started to cross the foyer after her when Sheriff Samson's tall, lean frame came through the front door, his hair falling attractively across his tanned forehead. He looked like a model for a cigarette advertisement, handsome, roughly tanned, and western, right down to his hat and the .44 Magnum holstered on his belt.

He brushed his hair off his forehead, replaced his hat, and stopped before me. "I was coming to see you," he said. He didn't sound rough and western. He sounded annoyed, but he wasn't a man given to facial expression. Through the window, morning sun glinted off the stubble on his chin. He looked like he hadn't slept the night before.

"Good. I'm glad you came. I've got some things for you. They're up in my room." I led the way, unlocked the door, and stopped.

I glanced around my room at the bed and felt the muscles at the base of my neck tighten.

The bed had been made up with fresh sheets, I could tell by the fold creases in the pillowcases, but it was messed up. The covers were rumpled as though they'd been pulled back, then thrown together. Someone had been fishing in the light fixture. I turned to the sheriff.

"My room has been mugged."

He didn't say anything, he didn't even blink.

I crossed to the curtain. Empty. The key wasn't there.

The eggs in my stomach congealed.

"They've been stolen," I said. The chances that whoever it was who entered had been actually looking for my jackpot check were zero to nothing. I shivered. It wasn't a safe position to be in.

"They?"

"The key and the note she gave me."

His jaw muscles clenched, like he might chew through nails. He drew a little pad from his breast pocket and began making notes. "You didn't mention them last night." His voice was stiff, and he looked like he'd just discovered half a worm in his apple.

I climbed down from the bed and yanked open the top drawer of the dresser. "The umbrella is gone, too. And my scarf, along with my favorite teddy, a new one in aqua-and-pink paisley. Maybe—" I yanked open the bedside drawer and drew out the Gideon's Bible. I flipped through it. The newspaper article dropped out and floated to the floor.

"Here, at least they didn't take this." Triumphant, I grabbed the newspaper and handed it to him.

He took it from me with grim suspicion in his eyes. "She gave you a newspaper article, too?" Sarcasm isn't a strong enough word to describe his tone of voice. I decided I'd be a lot better off if I didn't volunteer any information, but I did mention that I tried to call him a couple of times...after I discovered the key and note.

He read the article, making notes.

I went to the wardrobe and found my jumpsuit folded neatly, but not the way I had left it. A few of my other clothes were rearranged. Nothing else seemed to be missing.

Someone had violated my space. It felt very creepy. For a long and very uncomfortable period while the sheriff was writing, I thought about Edie and Jeena and how I had entered their rooms. I hoped they wouldn't notice, and if they did, I hoped it wouldn't throw Jeena into a paranoid tailspin.

There was a noise outside my door. Perhaps Amy, standing on the other side of the door, listening...again.

Stepping lightly, I crossed the room, yanked open the door, and found the innkeeper's large tabby cat washing his paws.

The sheriff eyed me suspiciously.

"I'm terribly allergic." The words flew out of my mouth. It wasn't true, of course, but I felt unbelievably foolish.

"Scat!" I said to the cat, who merely looked at me and

blinked. He had supremely mean, yellow eyes—the kind that say, "I'll eat your lizard if I get a chance."

The sheriff folded the article and pocketed his notepad. "Let's go downtown," he said, and moved toward the door.

"We can talk here."

"No, it should be at headquarters. Let's make it official."

"This is fine."

He looked around, his gaze darting over the room, then he turned to me. "Downtown."

We walked in silence to his squad car—a Chevy Citation, the last of the breed—and he drove to his office.

TEN

POLICE HEADQUARTERS WAS in a small square building set right on the street. Hanging from the window was a window box of incongruously cheerful flowers, red geraniums, button marigolds, and deep blue ageratum. I took a long last look at the free world and followed him inside. He led the way behind the long counter that separated the complaining public from the officers and the dispatcher.

A lingering odor of Pine Sol and burnt coffee pervaded the office, different from the stark smells of the central Denver police building. But of course, they didn't have as many criminal bodies pass through their doors, or else they had a cleaner class of criminals.

The sheriff's office was on the right—small, cream-colored, cramped, and totally utilitarian, right down to the single straight-backed oak side chair. He closed the door and adjusted the blinds so that he could see out. And the office staff could see in.

"Now," he said once we were seated. He tilted his head so that he was looking at me on the slant, and drew a notepad out from underneath a stack of thick manila folders. "Start at the beginning."

I knew that I could refuse to talk to him. I could insist that he charge me or release me, but that didn't seem the best way to go—if I wanted to remain free in this world. I started at the beginning, with Yvonne's death.

"All the way here thoughts were flying through my head, and I tried to make sense out of them."

"Go on."

"This is the way I see it. A young woman recognizes me at the casino and later dies suddenly next to me. Later I find a note from her and a key in my pocket. The note asks me to meet her, so I go to her place, knock, find the door open, and enter. I check and confirm that it was her unit, then I leave."

"And you don't take anything out of there?"

"Absolutely not. Not one thing out of there."

He drew in a deep breath, his eyes shadowed beneath heavy brows so that I couldn't read the expression in them. The feeling I got from him, though, was not warm and fuzzy. "And you didn't search the place?"

"No. I looked in the bathroom to see if there was anything that she left for me, like a note or something with my name on it."

"Like jewels or money, something like that?"

"Of course not." I leaned forward. "*My* room was searched, and things were taken. When can *I* fill out a complaint? When are you going to investigate?"

"When I'm certain there was a crime committed in your room." He looked at me steadily, his gaze boring twin holes in my eyes. It was like one of those staring contests you get into as a kid. The first one to blink loses. He blinked first, but my eyes burned something fierce.

"Someone went through it while I was at breakfast! It had to be someone at the inn. It doesn't seem likely to me that the inn staff would have been bribed to do it. It isn't outside the realm of possibility. Just unlikely."

He looked at me, then made a note on his notepad. "Now talk to me about the key."

"I found the key on my dresser top among the quarters I took out of my pocket—the same pocket where I found the note."

"So now, what was in the note?"

"I don't know what's in it now. What it said was 'I have to talk to you. Don't tell *anyone*. Call me at 771-2323. *ASAP*. Yvonne.'"

He wrote it all down. "So you knew where she was staying?"

"I found out by calling the number."

"You entered that unit without knowing...?"

"I was pretty certain."

"Pretty certain. Why?" He was struggling to contain himself.

"There was a car in front with Kansas license plates. And a stuffed-toy cat stretched out and stuck to the back window with suction cups, you know the kind."

"Tell me about the car."

"You found the car, didn't you? It was right there in front of unit six. With a stuffed cat stuck to the back window." I didn't want to tell him about the fact that the key fit the trunk. The ooze of his doubt weighed on me.

"There was no car."

"It was right in front of the unit."

"Make? Model?"

"Ford Escort. Dark."

"And the key?"

"It turned out to be the key to the trunk of the car."

"You opened it and looked through it?"

"But when I opened it last night, there wasn't anything in there. It was the cleanest trunk I've ever seen." What had seemed so reasonable last night looked a lot less so now. My cheeks began to burn. "Well, I thought someone was following me—"

"And did you go through her motel room?"

"Well, I was standing there in front of the door when I was startled and just jumped inside. You know how that is."

"No. I don't. Especially if the door is locked."

"It wasn't. It was open."

"You didn't steal the key from the motel lobby and then go to the unit and unlock the door and then ransack the place?"

"I did not touch a thing. I heard someone coming out of the unit next door, and since Yvonne's door was open, I went inside. Then since I was there, I peeked around."

"And did you by any chance recognize this person?"

"It was...Edie Lorton, one of the bridge group."

"She had two rooms reserved for herself?" he asked. He

sat up straighter and made a note on the pad in front of him.

"She was visiting a woman in unit five. I didn't see her. I didn't know who it was."

"Too bad." He made another note. "And then you wiped most of your fingerprints off the doorknob, right?"

"I didn't add or subtract anything, I didn't take anything, I just looked around. I confirmed it was Yvonne's room by reading the tag on her suitcase. I looked for a letter or note or something that would tell me why she wanted to see me. She wrote to me saying she wanted to see me about a problem she had, that she wanted to see me when she got to Denver—after she met someone here."

He leaned back in his chair, tipping it onto its back legs so he could rock ever so slightly. "Tell me why she wrote to you."

"She wanted help. She couldn't get it from the authorities in Kansas, and she thought I might be able to. She shoved a note in my pocket and a—" I stopped, lost my nerve.

He looked up, calm, prepared for whatever I had to offer. "And?"

I shifted in my chair. It was hard, and my rear was becoming paralyzed. "I figure she was meeting someone at the casino. She recognized me by accident, talked to me, and now the killer thinks that I know something."

He rubbed his chin, hard, so that each little whisker seemed to snap against his fingers.

I explained again that I had tried to call him, last night and this morning. Then I tried to explain how I'd decided to go to the Golden Eagle. It didn't sound very convincing.

I explained and explained and explained.

He studied my face as though he would find the truth if he just looked hard enough. He must not have found it because he dropped his gaze to a pad on his desk and then made more little notes.

He didn't say anything for a long time. He stared at his notes, tapping his index finger against the wooden top on his desk. When he finally did lift his head and look me in the eyes, I caught my breath.

"You're in a heap of trouble, lady. You've interfered in a murder investigation, and you've withheld evidence. I could charge you with obstructing justice. But this is nothing compared to the other trouble you've got on your hands." He laid his hands flat on the desk and pushed himself up.

"Well, it seems pretty obvious—whoever arranged to meet her here is the killer. All you have to do is find out who she planned to meet."

"That's how I figure it, too." He pulled a glassine envelope toward him, which contained a folded sheet of paper. It was so quiet in that room my ears began to ring, and I could feel my heart thumping in my chest.

"Do you know what this is?" he asked, waggling the envelope at me. "This was in her purse, the one you had on your shoulder. It's a letter from you to her. Do you remember the line, 'Call me. We'll set a time to meet'? Seems to me you're the person I'm looking for."

ELEVEN

"MEREDITH, TAKE A BREAK from the slots. Let's get lunch, I need to talk to you."

"You're in trouble again, aren't you?"

"Of course not. The sheriff let me go, but he *was* making some really ugly notes."

Meredith lifted her gaze from the spinning wheels of the Magic Splendor machine she was playing. "I'm winning, Stella. I'm really on a roll. Stella, I need this win, a whole lot."

I should have listened to her, but I was still too focused on my own troubles.

"Great. Now's the time to stop, then. It preserves your lucky karma."

She looked at me suspiciously. "You sense some losses coming, don't you?"

"No. When did you eat last?"

"Your Sense is warning me, isn't it?" Meredith over-subscribes to the notion I can foretell the future.

"Meredith. I can't see ahead. At least never when I need to. Not when it would be helpful. What I need is you to listen to me." She looked at me, pulled the handle one more time, and saw all the winning numbers spin past. She sighed and scooped up two plastic bowls of coins.

We found lunch in the buffet bar of the casino. Meredith selected naked lettuce and two broccoli florets. Her lunch looked like a rabbit's leftovers. I opted for a turkey sandwich.

"You don't have any vegetables," she pointed out.

I picked up a packet of mustard. "There. Vegetable."

We found a table for two in the corner next to two women in Spandex and little else.

She nibbled on a lettuce leaf while I told her about my interview with the sheriff.

"I'm being set up as his chief suspect, Meredith."

Meredith is my best friend, so she sympathized for five minutes and then told me I was doing it to myself.

"And why, you ask?"

"I didn't ask—" I protested.

"Because you didn't tell him about the note, because you entered Yvonne's motel room, searched it, and stole her umbrella, and then couldn't find the evidence you said you had? Seems to me you've screwed yourself. You aren't eating."

I looked at the slim thighs of the Spandexed sylphs as they got up from their table and left the buffet room. I shook my head.

"Well, you could wear Spandex, too, if you'd go back to the gym and work out a little. You're not fat. You're just out of shape." Meredith's a little short on sympathy when it comes to fitness.

"Soon," I promised. "Listen to me, Meredith. That note in Yvonne's purse wasn't from me. It's a forgery, or from someone else."

"You saw it?"

"No! I know what I wrote to her, and I never wrote saying 'Call me and we'll meet.' Or anything like that. Now, talk to me. What strikes you, out of all this?" I poked at my sandwich. Maybe if I just ate the meat out of the middle.

Meredith bit off two buds from a broccoli floret and savored them as she thought. "I'm not convinced that it's murder. I think you're overreacting."

"You've got to be kidding. It's murder. And I'm being framed. I'm damned lucky he didn't throw me in jail."

"Evidence?"

"Yvonne came to Colorado to clear up something about her mother's murder. So, the reason for Yvonne's murder was to prevent her disclosure...or whatever it was. Someone wrote to her arranging a meeting here. She died of poison. She was frightened enough to put a note and the key to the trunk of her car in my pocket. *And* she had that article stuffed in the handle of her umbrella.''

"Maybe Yvonne just put the article in there to hold the handle in place. She wrote to you wanting to meet you, and then she had a heart attack at the casino by accident." She bit the end off a carrot stick and munched. "Besides, who'd be nuts enough to murder someone in a room full of people? That place was packed. A full house. Fourth of July always is. Witnesses everywhere. How could you control what happens? It would take a fool to murder someone in a crowd like that."

"A fool...or someone very clever." I looked at her. An errant sunbeam glinted off her chestnut hair and lit her face. Her phrase, "an accidental group," struck me. There aren't accidental groups—people come together on purpose or for a purpose. The only accidental groups are in research. Her question interrupted my train of thought.

"What do you mean, clever?"

"Look, Meredith. Turn it inside out. Look at what's predictable. A full house. Lots of noise. No one can hear. Lots of witnesses—who can all also be suspects. Too many people. No one pays attention. High altitude. Excitement. People faint under these conditions, so there's the assumption that it would be an accidental death."

Meredith frowned and nibbled. "But not everyone is anonymous. You never know who you're going to run into. In fact, I ran into one of the most bizarre characters. I never expected *him* to be *here*. Of course, I should have. But that's another story." She brushed the thought away with her hand. "I mean, if you were going to murder someone, would you want witnesses? Especially witnesses you know, right there?"

"Remember this. The murderer knows that Yvonne contacted me, and knows I went to Yvonne's room, and followed me home and searched my room this morning and stole the key, the note, the umbrella, my silver earrings, and my aqua teddy—"

"Not the aqua paisley!"

I nodded.

"Damn!"

"The killer was at the casino *and* the inn, and none of us saw anyone strange, so most likely it's someone from the bridge group—right?"

She nodded slowly.

"The sheriff thinks it's me. I know it isn't. The only good thing in this whole scenario is that Pissed Off and Ready to Kill isn't here. That would be the last straw."

"I think you should get out of here."

"It'll only make me look guilty as hell."

"You'll be alive."

"And in jail...for something I didn't do."

"I don't know how you do this. No one else has these problems." She looked sad for a moment and shoved her lettuce around on her plate. "Well, at least one thing's going right. I'm winning at the slots. Now let's get down to the important stuff. Is that sheriff married?"

SUNLIGHT POURED from a bright blue sky, piercing the darkest shadows of the pine trees, glinting off windows and mica flakes in the road, but barely piercing my gloom. A dark doom cloud hovered just above me, ready to rain disaster at any moment.

These were people that I knew and liked...mostly. But one had probably murdered Yvonne.

I power-walked up the shortcut steps to the Owl and the Pussy Cat Inn, holding on to the railing. My feet were leaden and stumbling on the uneven steps, and my rear end was absolutely burning by the time I got even halfway up the steps. But it wasn't half as bad as the buzzing in my head at the bizarre fact that I suspected that one of my friends was a killer. And I was once again looking guilty because I was there. The handy fall guy.

Nothing to do with the fact that I have a special way of blundering into things.

If I fled to Denver, I'd look positively guilty to the sheriff. If I stayed and did nothing, I could be convicted.

Near the top of the steps, my thighs afire, my toe caught and I stumbled. This particular step was higher than the others and had a scalloped spot in it. I pitched forward and landed on my knees.

I'd have gone over the edge, but for the railing. On either side of the steps there was a twenty-foot drop to a cement pad where the homes had been cut into the hillside.

I brushed the grit off my stinging knee. This was at least the second time I'd come up these stairs, and I was still staggering on them. They were a real hazard.

I didn't feel secure until I was into my room, door locked. And even there it wasn't a really safe feeling. The room seemed almost to smell different from before, and I felt curiously vulnerable, with no sure way to protect myself.

I went to the turret windows and looked out toward the mountaintop, breathing in the cool air. A series of mini-flashes of light caught my eye, glinting from a bulky green-colored figure with a stolid gait. It was Edie, marching up the path in the direction of the Golden Eagle Motel, swinging her arms, looking neither left nor right, and with each step sunlight glinted off the decorative sequined leaves on the shoulders of her top.

Suddenly, as I watched her, she halted, turned, looked back right at me, her brow casting a shadow over her eyes, a dark streak that sliced her face. It was an eerie glimpse; then she turned away and resumed her march up the path.

My stomach churned at the idea she was a killer. It was a very lonely moment.

I glanced down at Fluffy, clinging to the edge of my shirt pocket, his little harness secure around his chest. I unpinned him, gently returning him to his travel cage, and was about to feed him a wax worm when I heard the telltale buzz of a fly.

I stalked the fly until I caught it, shook it to make it dizzy, and tossed it in the travel cage. Fluffy was ecstatic,

I could tell. He was breathing hard. It's nice when you can be happy with a simple meal. I think I even envied him the seeming safety of his cage.

It occurred to me that a backup plan would be a good idea. Aside from my hair spray, there was little for protection, and nowhere to hide except under the bed—not an especially desirable hideout.

I went to the door, opened it, and peered down the hallway. Halfway down the hall was a door I hadn't noticed before. I crept over to it and twisted the doorknob, and it opened noiselessly, as if recently oiled.

It was a cleaning-supply closet with an upright vacuum cleaner, several dust mops, a bucket and mop still wet from use, and, stacked in the far corner, three large boxes of toilet tissue. Perfect. I took the short duster with the thick wooden handle and the bottle of toilet cleaner.

IT WAS ONE-FIFTEEN when I locked my room and headed downstairs. The oak banister was cool under my hand, and the scent of lemon oil sharp and heavy. The quaint Victorian decor was beginning to wear on me. I realized I really didn't want to die in a place with that much chintz.

It seemed to me I'd have marginally better odds if I was at least a moving, sleuthing target. Although I wasn't quite sure what I was going to do, I was prepared to do something.

I can be completely frightened, terrorized, for some of the time, but after a while it seems to wear off—the way my nose gets used to a really bad smell about the time I think I can't stand it anymore.

From the hallway I saw that the bridge table was folded and leaning against the wall. I snagged a handful of mints from a dish and strolled toward the sound of voices at the far end of the sunporch.

A breeze blew through the open double-glazed windows at the side of the sunporch, carrying with it the whirr of hummingbirds darting through the lower branches of the spruce outside. The room was prettily done up in a green-

and-white garden motif, with a large false aurelia tree in
the corner soaking up sunlight. Edie, David, Jeena, Bill,
and Amy were framed at the other end of the porch.

Edie perched on the edge of a chair, her cheeks flushed,
waving her arms descriptively. Sunlight caught on the spar-
kling sequined leaves on the shoulders of her blouse, throwing little glints of light around the porch. With an odd sense
of detachment, I noticed that it was a nice scene.

Edie's voice was excited. "The path leads up the mountain to a huge bald rock and meadow mountaintop. Tundra.
Alpine flowers. Edelweiss blooming. Some Colorado blue
columbine. We should do a picnic up there, maybe for the
fireworks Sunday. And old mine entrances, mostly boarded
up. I must have seen five or six. This whole mountain has
to be a honeycomb—"

Bill and Amy were passing iced tea. Bill pushed his
glasses up on his nose and waved when he saw me.

Edie paused in her story. "Where've you been? We were
looking all over for you. You and Meredith are the most
disappearing people. We're ready to go."

I wanted to keep Meredith safely out of this. She's not
good at danger. "Meredith left a note. She's wrapped up
in her slot machines. I don't expect to see her for hours."

"I thought I saw you with the sheriff," David said.

I dropped into the wicker chair next to Edie, but I moved
it a bit farther away...out of easy reach. "A few questions." I shrugged, trying to sound casual. "Has he talked
to all of you?"

Jeena snuffled, and all except Edie nodded. She examined a spot on the floor.

"Edie, didn't you talk to the sheriff?" A dull red flush
grew up her neck. Bill handed me a glass of tea, which I
passed to Jeena.

"I'd be glad to, of course. I s'pose I should call him."
Then she changed the subject. "You should see the relics
of the miners up there. You can almost feel the presence
of those old men, eating their meals, tossing the trash out

on the mountainside. Look—'' She stood and pulled a wad of tissue from her pants pocket.

"See?" She unwrapped the wad gingerly. "This is an old, old sardine can. It must've been left fifty or a hundred years ago by a miner."

"—or last year by somebody on a picnic," Amy added.

"Oh no," Edie protested. "It takes *forever* for things to deteriorate up here. This has to be ancient—look at all the rust. I don't care what you all think, I'm sure it's really old."

"If it really is old, then you shouldn't have picked it up. You're not supposed to take things out of their habitat," David said.

"Then we should've left you under your rock," Edie said. There was a hint of a smile on her lips. She seemed glad to fight with David, relieved to move the conversation away from the sheriff.

"So, where is it you're going?" I asked.

"We're talking about touring the mine down below Silverado. You can ride in the ore cars."

It sounded dark and claustrophobic to me. "You're kind of into this mine thing."

Edie shrugged. "*We* thought it would be a great afternoon thing."

It wasn't my idea of a great afternoon *thing*, but Bill grinned pinkly at Amy, gently massaging her hand. He flushed and looked shyly at me. "You can't imagine how beautiful it is inside a mine. You can feel the history, the hopes of the men, see the marks of people who lived fifty, a hundred years ago. You've got to come. It will be so special." I think he really meant it.

Edie frowned. "Stella, are you sure Meredith wouldn't like to go to the mine?"

David laughed. "She's already in her mine. Trouble is, instead of a gold train, it's a gold drain for her. If you ask me—"

"Nobody did, David. Stuff it." Edie stood.

"Whose idea was it, anyway?" I asked.

"Bill's," Amy said softly, patting his hand. "He's just full of wonderful ideas." She smiled at him, her face suddenly soft and vulnerable with love. For once she didn't search her teeth anxiously.

"Oh no. Amy, dear, it was really your idea. Isn't she wonderful?" he asked the group in general. Amy's tongue darted over her teeth.

David rolled his eyes.

Edie snorted. And Jeena sipped her tea and smiled slowly, seeming to explore some internal place the rest of us couldn't see.

I wondered about the picture of Edie and David, and what had happened to break up that romance. I was pretty sure it wasn't Edie, since she kept the picture.

I decided to go. With the exception of Yvonne, it seemed like people get murdered alone most of the time. Odds on, I was safe as long as I didn't eat or drink anything. Or get too close to anyone in the dark.

TWELVE

WE WALKED THE STEADY downhill mile and a half to the Last Chance Mine below Silverado.

Jeena motioned me to lag behind with her. Worry lines criss-crossed her forehead. Edie dropped back too.

"Sometimes I have a little trouble with enclosed places," Jeena said.

"But you said you wanted to come."

"I know," Jeena murmured. "I do." She swayed and bumped against me, then straightened up.

"This is well lit," Edie said. "You don't have anything to worry about."

I fished in my purse. "I've got a mini-flashlight on my key ring. You can carry that," I said. "Then you don't have to worry about the dark." That seemed to relieve her, and she perked up a little, but she walked slowly, as though she wasn't sure of her step.

The tour entrance was duded up like a corral with a rustic wooden rail fence enclosing a tiny parking area; a quaint wagon wheel, petunias, and an antique ore car stood before the rustic old mine building that housed a small gift shop and ticket sales booth. There were benches strategically placed for people wanting to sit.

The entrance to the mine itself was imposing, with a heavy open gate of rusting iron and lighting that cast shadows on the rough-hewn rock walls. The sheer massiveness of the mountain rock was awesome.

"It's bigger and darker than I thought," muttered Jeena. Her gaze darted nervously about.

"You can always wait out here for us," I suggested.

Jeena considered the idea, then shook her head. "I don't

feel that great, you know, but I think I'd rather be with you than by myself.''

We headed over to the tour cart. It was a hybrid cart modeled after an ore car, somewhat elongated, with three bench seats that held two people each behind the driver. The wheels had iron rims fitted to rail tracks leading into the mouth of the mine. It wouldn't be able to turn around. Once started, it had to finish.

It was pulled by a flop-eared mule whose head hung to his knees with enthusiasm.

''Come on, Jeena,'' Edie called. She had put herself in the very middle bench seat. ''I've saved you a seat.'' She thumped the bench seat in front of her. ''Hurry up!''

I clambered aboard and hauled Jeena up. She hesitated, undecided where to sit, with me or Edie. Finally she huddled on the seat next to me, gripping the mini-flashlight.

''Looks like the maws of hell,'' David said as he climbed up.

''Shut up, David,'' Edie said. She patted Jeena on the shoulder. ''He's just trying to be clever, Jeena.''

I looked at the looming dark and felt a dank breeze on my arms.

David sat down next to Edie directly behind Jeena, his long legs so cramped in the space that his knees bumped her back. Bill and Amy sat in the backseat, their shoulders and hips melded. Bill slipped an arm around her. She giggled.

Right at a quarter to two, the tour guide began his spiel. ''Now, while we're in the mine, you must keep your hands and feet inside the cart. The tunnels are narrow, and you could be hurt if you are careless. Above all, stay in the cart at all times. No one is allowed to leave the cart at any time, since you could be lost or worse if you enter an unsecured tunnel.'' He pointed to a battered cage that hung from a pipe bracketed to the corner of the cart. Inside, a sleepy pale yellow canary clung to a narrow perch, bored to death. ''You'll notice our canary. In the old days these mines frequently had bad air. This was sometimes just the absence of oxygen, and sometimes it was actually noxious gases, seeping through the rock layers. So the miners carried caged canaries into the mines to test the air. If the air was good the birds survived. If the bird dropped to the cage floor, it meant bad air.''

Nothing like mentioning suffocation just as you're entering a small, dark hole. It seemed to me a bad plan to raise everyone's anxiety before we were even in the damn place. I felt Jeena tense up. Even I was a little anxious.

"The mines in those days had no lights," he droned. "Because, of course, there was no electricity, the miners used candles. Inside on either side you can still see the streaks of carbon from torches they pushed into the rock walls. Farther on you'll see the rusty iron candleholders still in the rock crevices.''

The mule pulled forward.

A naked lightbulb glowed overhead on the scalloped granite ceiling of the mine. The walls of the mine were rough and black with white quartzlike rock streaks. Layered in places, it branched into intricate rock webs, then reformed in jagged layers. I hadn't expected to be fascinated with rock walls.

Behind us the circle of the opening receded, then abruptly disappeared as we turned the corner, the cart slanting downward. We were somewhere around twenty yards into the mine when I sniffed the first whiff of cold mine air. We left the lightbulb behind, joggling forward out of its circle of light.

Our guide spoke again. "There's light up ahead, but this will give you an idea of what the miners faced.''

"It's pitch-black in here!"

I was pretty sure Jeena said that.

"We'll only be without light for a short while.'' He struck a match and lit a candle, holding it high over his head. "*This* is the amount of light the miners had to find their way in the mines. It wasn't until later that they had lanterns and helmets with battery lights.'' His voice was deep, muted, as though he were far away.

I felt something brush the back of my head and started. Jeena clutched my arm. All the stories I'd ever heard about bats in caves flashed to mind. I was glad David was tall. If the bats swarmed they'd smack into his head first.

"There's a lightbulb ahead. It isn't completely dark," I whispered into Jeena's ear.

Dark shapes passed on the left. She gripped my forearm. "What if we get lost? There are hundreds of tunnels in here."

"That's right," continued the guide. "There *are* hundreds of miles of tunnels in this one mountain alone. It was a particularly rich source of gold and was an active mine until as recently as the forties." His voice seemed distant, smothered.

Bill asked, "Is there a chance they'll reopen it if there's a rise in the price of gold?" He, too, was muted, blanketed by the darkness.

"Too many tunnels, too much rock," Jeena muttered. She was peering from side to side, running her hand over the rough wood of the side panel for reassurance. "I'm never going to get out of here."

"Of course you are." Edie reassured her. We joggled around another corner. Overhead a lightbulb glowed, very dimly. "Look!" Edie said. "You can see the veins of gold ore, and the glitter...it's beautiful!"

David spoke up. "Not gold! Mica. All the gold's gone."

"When I was walking up the mountain behind the inn this noon, I saw lots of mine entrances," Edie said.

The guide raised a warning hand. "You gotta be careful. Some of those entrances you were talking about, they may be all to the same mine, because there was one big one on that mountain. But some of them may actually be cave-ins."

"Amazing," Edie said. "Do people get lost much?"

"Not if you stay on the cart. This place is set for the tour. But if you go up on the hill and mess around you can get into trouble. Specially in the back areas. Some of those places have weathered, and the seals have fallen away. I wouldn't be a bit surprised at anything I'd find in one of these.''

Jeena made a shuddering noise. ''There's water in here. Mold. It smells of…of old, wet rocks. There isn't enough air.'' She began to shake. It dawned on me that we might have more than just a little problem here.

''Of course there is,'' Edie said.

A halo of darkness surrounded Edie's head, as if the tunnel were consuming her. The mine was oppressive, or else Jeena's fright was; I couldn't tell which. I kept thinking about all the tunnels and how easy it would be to get lost. We lurched around another corner.

Jeena began to mutter to herself. ''The mine's closing in. We're in hell. The maws of hell. This is hell. We're all going to die.''

''Nonsense,'' I said. I leaned forward to the guide. ''Is there a shortcut? I think Jeena's having real trouble.''

''Nope, but I can go a little faster,'' he said and urged the mule onward. He raised his voice. ''Everyone hold their arms in, it's narrower here.''

''The walls are getting closer! There's no room. I can touch the walls. They're cold, hard.'' Jeena's voice had an edge of panic to it.

''Well, that's because we're going a little deeper into the mountain,'' Edie explained.

''Edie, shut up,'' David said. Now there was a nasty edge to his voice.

Deeper into the mountain. Wrong thing to say. In the face of panic, reason is a real bad idea. It's never effective. In fact, it usually leads to greater panic. It certainly did this time. I looked at the cage. The canary wasn't on his perch. I imagined him, his little feet straight up in the air, clawing for oxygen. I knew how he felt.

Jeena shifted on the seat. I grasped her arm. ''It's fine. You'll be fine.''

She wasn't fine. Her teeth were chattering. She was shaking.

"Can't you hurry up?" I asked the guide. He clucked and flicked the reins at the mule, sublimely unconcerned.

The lights were timed; as we moved forward, the ones ahead of us turned on and those behind us turned off. We were a bubble of feeble light drifting through the darkness. It was not a helpful image. I decided not to share it.

My fingers were stiff with cold, frozen. Jeena's fright was catching.

She shook my hand off her arm. "I can't breathe! The oxygen ran out. We've got to leave. There isn't enough oxygen."

Jeena leaped up. I reached for her and felt my fingers grasp the cloth of her shirt, then felt it slip through my fingers.

"Jeena," I shouted. "Stop! Wait!" All I could think of was to catch her before she became hopelessly lost. A hand clamped down on my shoulder. It felt like a grip of iron. I shook myself and it released.

I flipped my legs over the side of the cart, slid from the seat to the ground, and ran up the tunnel after her.

My feet seemed to move beneath me without urging. The voices behind me dwindled into echoes. I stumbled blindly, groping along the tunnel walls. Where were the lightbulbs? How could I turn them on?

"Come back!" the guide shouted. "You're not allowed out of the cart. Stop!"

The guide seemed very slow to react. "Jeena!" I shouted, then listened for the sounds of her feet on the tunnel floor. It was rough, uneven. I heard her just ahead, stumbling. "Jeena, turn on the flashlight."

I ran, dragging my fingers along the surface of the rock wall for contact and direction, my eyes burning, my ears ringing.

My foot slipped.

My toe caught on the rail. I stumbled, nearly fell.

Something whizzed by my head, big enough to stir the air. I heard something soft fall ahead of me, little stones clattering on the floor of the tunnel.

A muffled groan. Jeena.

Suddenly my fingers lost the wall on my left. It disappeared. I must've come to one of the dark tunnels that had branched off from the sides. Where was Jeena?

I raced on, my hand ahead of me, groping in the pitch-dark, completely blind. Every ounce of energy I had went into finding my way as fast as I could. Hurry.

If she stumbled into one of the old tunnels she could be lost forever. For that matter, so could I.

Then, with no warning, I smashed into a rock wall.

My hand, then my forehead and knee, crashed into hard, cold rock. I bounced back from the impact, stumbled, twisted my ankle, and fell to the ground. I landed on a soft body.

She moaned. At least she was still alive.

I rolled to the floor, waiting for the starbursts before my eyes to cease. Shook my head carefully. It hurt.

I felt for Jeena with my hands. Found her. Sought a pulse in her neck.

It was strong and regular. Her breath was fast. I patted her down, groped in her pockets for the flashlight but couldn't find it.

Then I heard footsteps behind me.

"Who's there?" I called. No one answered. I held my breath and put my hand over Jeena's mouth to quiet her breathing.

"Who's there?" I called louder. No one answered.

Jeena moved and moaned. Her hands gripped mine.

"Shh."

I reached out, feeling for the rock wall, for the tracks, for all those things that would orient me. Someone stood nearby. I couldn't tell where.

I whispered in Jeena's ear to lie still and quiet. The darkness was our ally. Our protection. I couldn't risk movement. Even the tiny bits of rock beneath me would give away my location if I tried to stand.

I heard Jeena's breath getting more ragged. I put a finger across Jeena's lips. She nodded, and I could tell she was trying to control her breathing. I opened my mouth wide so that the tiny breath I drew wouldn't whistle against my teeth.

I heard a soft footfall. The sound ricocheted off the walls so I couldn't tell where it came from, only that it was too close.

Voices echoed in the distance. Then a light flickered far away, down the tunnel in the direction from which I'd come.

I could sense hesitation of the person in the shadows. Then a tiny penlight flashed on, not enough to show who it was, only to give away location. The circle of light moved away, the soft footfalls growing more distant. Ahead, far down the tunnel, a very dim flickering light seemed to be moving toward us.

In front of me, maybe twenty feet, a human shape materialized, outlined and backlit by a yellow stain of distant lights. I couldn't tell whether it was tall or short, thin or stout. Then it disappeared, swallowed by the inky black of the mine.

THIRTEEN

GRADUALLY LIGHT SEEPED into the tunnel, and I could see the vague outlines of two passages, one to the left and one to the right, branching off from the one in which we were. I felt the weight of the glare of the person I'd seen, lurking in the dark. Light was suddenly an enemy, leaving me even more vulnerable. Then the figure melted into the darkness of another tunnel.

Muffled calls echoed toward us.

At first I was afraid to reply, for fear the lurker would return, but when the voices began to fade and sound farther away I called out at intervals. What if they missed us? I shuddered.

"Stella, who was he?"

"Stay down," I whispered. "He could still be there." I'd called the figure "he" too. Out of habit, I think. Yet it occurred to me that "he" could just as easily be a woman. Either way, it had to be someone who knew the mine.

Far down the tunnel, light flickered dimly, but grew stronger. Voices murmured and echoed in the tunnel, the distortions making it impossible to guess where they were. One moment they sounded closer, the next they were far away. The echoes, the flickering lights, the smell. Hell must smell like an old mine. Except we were cold. Stone-cold.

"Stella! Jeena! Where are you?" I didn't recognize the voice.

I hesitated, then shouted. "We're here!" I might as well. Whoever lurked in the shadows already knew we were there. And now he or she could see us.

"Stella!"

"Don't move. Stay put. We'll find you." That was the

guide's voice. "There's a switchbox here, there'll be light soon."

Suddenly the overhead lights flickered, then came on. However dim they were, the light dazzled me. I blinked and was forced to look at the darkness of the floor until my eyes adjusted.

To either side were tunnels, left and right of the main tunnel. I had run into a Y-shape in the tunnel. Thank God.

If I hadn't, would I have known Jeena was there, crumpled on the floor of the tunnel. Would I have tripped over her and found her? Or would I have missed her and raced on, turning into one tunnel or another until I was hopelessly lost?

My gaze fell on a large rock, black, like a lump of coal, in the middle of the tunnel, about three feet from Jeena's body. It must have been the rock that whizzed by me in the dark.

"Stella! Jeena!"

A rush of feet, then the group pounded around the corner.

The guide was in the lead, still holding a candle, even though the lights overhead shone. He was visibly shaken.

The rest came in a bunch. I tried to grin and act overjoyed they had found us, but I couldn't. My face wouldn't cooperate. My cheeks were stiff with suspicion and I scrutinized each one for signs of guilt. Every face was the picture of innocent concern.

Amy wasn't in the group, but Bill was, just behind Edie and making little clucking noises.

Jeena moaned. Her eyes were wide, her pupils dilated, her face pale. I put a hand on her forehead, searched her face and hairline for blood, but there wasn't any. Only a soft lump on her forehead, about the same place I had one from running into the tunnel wall.

Edie knelt beside me. "Are you all right?" I glanced down at her hand, warm and rough on my arm. It was dirty, her fingers smeared with carbon. I looked into her eyes, and her gaze faltered and dropped to Jeena. Suspicion made me shiver and pull my arm away from her.

My gaze fell on my own hand, the left one, which I'd dragged along the wall of the tunnel. It also had smears of carbon.

David and the guide supported Jeena, nearly carrying her. Edie clamped a surprisingly strong hand on me, but I shrugged it off. It seemed to take forever to reach the cart.

The lights were on all the way back. Jeena and I had not really run as far as I'd thought.

As we walked back, I noticed that with all the lights on, you could see how the tunnels intersected. It accounted for the sound effects, the rising and falling of the echoes of voices, the tricks of the flickering light from the candle.

And it explained how the figure reached us so fast.

Jeena and I had run in a circle. So as long as they knew the tunnels, any one of them could have done it. They had all protested they'd never been here before. At least one of them was lying.

When we reached the last bend in the tunnel, Amy was waiting for us, twisting her hands, wiping her sweaty palms with a tissue, the picture of concern. "I couldn't believe it when you jumped off the cart, Stella. I mean, I thought you'd be dead."

Amy seemed almost cheered by the thought. "Of course, as soon as you jumped off, everyone jumped off and raced after you. In the dark and everything." She brushed her hair back from her forehead.

"But you didn't," I said.

"Oh no. I'd just have gotten lost," she said. "I'm not good at finding my way in the dark. I figure getting lost is the really big danger."

Jeena lay on the floor of the cart between the seats, and I climbed up to sit where I could watch her. I stretched my legs out on the bench over her. Tiny goosebumps covered my arms. There was no way to turn around or back up. The guide urged the mule to go as fast as he could. It wasn't swift.

When we returned to the entrance and the cart came to a stop, we walked Jeena to a warm spot in the sun while

David volunteered to go to the inn and get a car to take her back. She didn't look like she'd be able to walk that far, and her pupils were still curiously dilated. I glanced at my watch. Not even three yet.

Edie sat down on the other side of Jeena, stretched her arm along the back of the bench, and fanned herself with her other hand. "Lord! I've never known anyone with claustrophobia. Are you okay?" Edie still had a nimbus of darkness around her head, as though the tunnel clung to her. My heart was skipping a little in my chest, and my tongue seemed glued to the roof of my mouth. I shook my head, blinking several times. The aura disappeared.

Even though Edie looked almost as wholesome, down to earth, and warm as ever, there was a certain reserve in her eyes. I wanted to pierce it.

"Edie, thanks so much for being there in the tunnel when we were waiting for the light. It meant a lot."

She startled. "But I wasn't there."

"Sure you were."

Jeena stirred. "I thought I saw you, too."

Twin furrows deepened between Edie's eyebrows. "Honest to God, Stella. I wasn't there." Her voice cracked with emotion. "But I'll tell you this. You better leave things alone, or someone really will get hurt." She marched off in a righteous huff.

I called after her, "Somebody already has been hurt, Edie. Hurt to death."

IT WAS JUST AFTER THREE, and Jeena and I were sipping, or in my case guzzling, ice-cold soda from cans that I had personally opened.

For most people there are two primary reactions to danger—fight and flight. But for me there is a third: feast. Many cultures have curative foods—soul food, health food, and chicken soup, to remedy and nurture all kinds of ills. For me it's chocolate, cola, and corn curls. I munched my way through two chocolate bars, a diet cola, and two little bags of corn curls. Basic junk food is hard to poison, so it was safe.

We sat wrapped in deep chairs in the library of the inn, somewhat recovered. I contemplated the books, scanning the titles behind the leaded-glass doors of the oak bookcases.

"Jeena, have you ever had those claustrophobic attacks before?"

She closed her eyes, refusing to answer.

I changed tactics. "What are the odds anyone has ever opened these cases to select a book?"

Jeena faced me, her hand across her brow like the heroine in one of those endless dying-aria operas. She didn't answer.

I got up and opened the bookcases. The books were genuine; some were dog-eared. The smell of old, dry paper rolled out over a thin film of dust on the shelves. The titles were dim, and I had to bend close to read them: *Hardy Boys, Treasure Island, Swiss Family Robinson, Magnificent Obsession*. My gaze traveled along the shelf over titles that brought up warm, fuzzy feelings. On the shelf below I found old textbooks, Samuelson's economics text.

I looked closer.

The dust was scraped off at that place, and the books were loose, as if one had been pulled out and the others repositioned so it would go unnoticed. At least one book had been borrowed recently. Beyond was a large, ancient, well-worn tome. I pulled it out: *A History of the Last Chance Mine*. I opened it carefully. At the back, between the last page and the cover, was a yellowed map of the mine.

When I turned around, Jeena was watching me from beneath her eyelashes.

"Jeena, how're you feeling?"

She grimaced and stretched. "I'll make it." She sounded as though she'd just climbed from death's bed, but her cheeks were pinked up and her eyes watchful. Except for the little round egg on her forehead and the one on mine,

we were pretty close to normal. Which of course isn't saying much, since the weekend so far included a murder, an
invasion of my room, an inquisition by the sheriff, and
nearly losing our way and perhaps our lives in the old gold
mine.

"Who knows about your claustrophobia?" I asked.

She looked a little dismayed at the subject and chewed
on her lip before she answered. "I've always had a little
fear of dark, close places. I guess you could call it claustrophobia. I got locked in a closet once, when I was a child.
I guess that's when it started. I don't want to talk about it
anymore." Jeena's cheeks paled slightly, and she pushed
damp curls back in an abrupt movement. Two strands
caught on her still-sweaty forehead.

"But who knew about it?"

"I don't make it a secret. At the same time, I don't
advertise it." She shrugged. "I really don't."

"I didn't know it was this bad."

"I didn't know it, either. I wouldn't have gone if I had."

"If someone knew you were claustrophobic, and knew
you'd be anxious going into the mine, could they scare you
enough to make this happen?"

Jeena plucked nervously at the cane ribs in the arm of
the wicker chair, intensely interested in the click of her
fingernail against the wood.

"What do you know about this?"

"Nothing."

"Jeena, I can tell when someone's working on 'truth
avoidances.' These are different from outright lies, because
they avoid...and different yet again from 'truth omissions.'
When you've spent as much time as I have listening to
people recount their tax liability, you become very well
versed in the fine art of splitting hairs and avoiding the
truth."

Jeena bowed her head, lower lip caught between her
teeth. When she finally raised her face, her eyes were
clouded and tense. "It's my punishment. I'll never be able
to get away from it."

"What was it that you did?"

"I can't talk about that. It's over now. They said it wasn't my fault. Not my fault. That's what they said."

She plucked rhythmically at a loose cane on the chair and began to rock—short, nervous little jerks in her chair—refusing to meet my gaze. Even her breathing changed to short, panicky breaths. Jeena was definitely a piece of work.

"Did you know Edie when you were, uh, in the hospital in Kansas?"

Jeena's cheeks washed to an unhealthy gray. "It was suicide. They said so."

I kept my expression vanilla-pudding bland. Jeena seemed to have entered some altered state. "When did you meet her?"

Her gaze shifted about the room, then caught on some invisible magic blackboard with answers inscribed on it. "Hemlock. Couple years ago. In the garden."

"Do you know anything about Yvonne's death?"

Jeena didn't answer and made no effort to get up. She looked at a ragged cuticle on her right first finger, then chewed on it as though she couldn't make up her mind what to say next.

"Jeena, none of this makes any sense. Either you know there's something wrong, or you don't. Now tell me."

She waved her finger in the air, a little drop of blood oozing out of the corner where she'd torn the cuticle away. She wiped it with a crumpled tissue.

"Jeena, how did Yvonne's mother die?"

Jeena stopped waving her finger and looked at me. Her eyes had a faraway look in them. I couldn't tell whether she was actually floating in her memories or if she occupied some other environmental bubble.

Finally she roused and focused on me. "Poison. Maggie had a series of heart attacks, then just dropped dead one day, like Yvonne. Her stepfather tried to cover it up, but when Yvonne accused him of poisoning her mother, he said it was her."

"I thought you didn't know him."

"I heard about it from the papers and from Yvonne." Jeena lowered her voice and leaned toward me conspiratorially. "Yvonne was nuts, you know."

She lifted my drink in a loose grip on the glass and began to sip — slowly, holding little mirth in her eyes — refusing to meet my gaze. Even her drink, so demure, so shut, pained her. She drank it so delicately a piece of water — "Did you know her, when you were all in the hospital in K there?"

Jeena's cheeks mottled to an unhealthy gray. "It was sinking. They met —"

I kept my expression vanilla, putting nand. I ve wanted to have earned some ahead stay. "When did you meet her?"

Her face shifted up on the room, face caught on some glitter and, I reckoned with shower fixed just to a dimwit. Couple years ago in the smash —

"Did you know anything about Yvonne's death?"

Jeena didn't answer and spoke no edge to act up. She looked at imagery course to her chair and fingers then showed on it although she couldn't argue on her arm, with cramp act.

Jeena, none of this makes any sense. Either you knew the's something wrong, or you can't somehow out.

She waved her finger in the air, a little drop of blood coming out the corner where she'd hurt the prickle drew. She wiped it with a crumpled tissue.

"Jeena, how did Yvonne's mother die?"

Jeena stopped waving her finger and looked over at me. Her eyes held no way into un them. I couldn't tell whether she was actually floating in her memories or if she channeled some other environmental input.

Finally she took a hard fought on the to room. Maybe had a series of hard breaks, such the dragged that one day, like Yvonne. The courtier, I had to scare it up, but when Yvonne accused him of poisoning her mother, he said it was her.

"I thought you didn't know that."

FOURTEEN

I NEEDED TO BE BY MYSELF for a while. Somewhere in that word salad there were kernels of truth, but it would take time to identify them.

At three-thirty I told Jeena I was going to my room for a nap and suggested that she take one too. It wasn't all that long since she'd been a flattened, fainting person on the floor of the mine shaft. I climbed the stairs rapidly and passed the door to Edie's room. Music was booming from inside. Country-and-western, not the sort I'd have thought Edie would choose.

I let myself into my room slowly, looking around with suspicion. I stepped over the doorsill, closed the door behind me, and slowly, deliberately, measured what was different.

The bedcovers were slightly wrinkled, as though someone had lain there recently. The pillow bore the imprint of a head. There was a distinct scent in the room that was familiar. Only one person I knew wore that particular scent.

Jason.

Good!... Terrible.... Wonderful!... Shit!

"Jason?"

The water ran in the bathroom. I knocked on the door. "Jason! Are you in there?"

"Do you want to come in?"

"It sounds like water in the basin."

"Desert shower."

"How'd you get in here?"

"I used your key." He reached a wet arm out and waggled a ragged credit card at me.

"Jason! Now what am I going to do?" Now that he was here, I could get irritated with him, too. Alienate another basically warm and generous human being in my dwindling circle of friends. But he was company. And I was pretty sure he hadn't killed anyone lately, which was more than I could say about some of the rest of them up here.

I threw myself on the bed, enjoyed the resonant bouncing. One of those things from childhood I've never gotten over.

That's when I saw it. His gear. The camera bag, the suitcase, the cooler with a six-pack inside. The bag of corn curls. He'd piled it on the floor on the far side of the bed. Where I wouldn't see it until he'd talked me into letting him stay. Hah!

"Jason!"

I heard the squeak of the cold water spigot in the bathroom as he turned it off. The door swung open. Jason emerged toweling his head, his jeans hanging from his slim hips, beads of water on his lean chest, shoulders, and arms. He tilted his head inquiringly at me. Just like my old, wonderful golden retriever, Caesar, used to do when he thought I might have a cookie in my pocket. "If you keep shouting, you'll ruin your reputation."

I sat up. It's much too difficult to be a hardnose lying down. "Jason, what are you doing here?"

He looked injured. "There aren't any available rooms in the whole Silverado area."

"It's the Fourth of July weekend, that's why."

"I know. So here I am. All yours." He sat down beside me on the bed, toweling his back and chest.

"You're not mine, Jason. And you're not staying here. You can't stay here. Do you hear me?" It's pretty hard to concentrate on refusals when someone is toweling muscles in front of you.

"Of course I can. There's plenty of room, babe."

I recognized Humphrey Bogart in there somewhere. Jason reached into a suitcase, drew out a bottle of Bay Rum aftershave lotion, sprinkled it on his hands, and slapped his cheeks and chest.

"I'm clean, tidy, and suave. You can't ask for more."

"Did Humphrey Bogart wear Bay Rum?"

"He should have. My grandfather did."

It was the first time I'd heard him mention, even in passing, any of his family. I'd worked and pried for weeks trying to learn more about them. I scrutinized the half of his face that I could see. He'd said it on purpose to pique my curiosity. It worked.

"Your grandfather?"

"But you wouldn't want to hear all about that. And I don't have time...if I can't stay here." He turned his melt-your-heart brown eyes on me. I hesitated.

He stood, walked to the armoire, opened it, and took out a shirt from inside. He started to pull it on.

"You already unpacked!" I leaped up. "How damn dare you? You figured you could just wander in here and throw down your bags, hang up your clothes, like some lion throwing his spoor around, and then I'd beg you to stay. Well forget it. Take your stuff and your grandfather and get out. You can't take me for granted just like that. Who do you think you are? And leave the corn curls."

"I brought them just for you."

"Then take them with you."

"I'll tell you about Granddad if you let me stay."

"Out. Where you stay is your problem."

"You know what the difference is between an enraged pit bull and an enraged woman?"

"No."

"You can reason with the pit bull."

The plaster swirls in the ceiling seemed to meet and melt into each other so that there was no beginning and no end, only a series of soothing, hypnotizing intertwined grooves and lines. The wallpaper was mauvy-brown sprigs of thyme against a cream background, all calculated to soothe the troubled spirit. It didn't help.

I looked at Jason, his crooked grin and lazy eyelids. He was half amused, half annoyed, and he had no idea of the confusion he stirred up in me. And I had no intention of letting him know.

He moved toward me, his arms outstretched. "Stella, I'm at least a solid friend. I can be useful. As I see it, you can use some help here."

He pulled me into him, wound his arms around me, his hands on my back. I couldn't think straight. His lips lowered to mine, hot, soft, searching, caressing. For a moment I didn't care that I couldn't think straight.

Desire welled up in me, followed by a flash of painful memories that brought me right back to earth with a thump.

"Jason, let go of me."

"I can't." He murmured and nibbled on my neck, sending ripples of warm pleasure through my body.

An alarm went off deep in my brain. "Yes, you can. Now let me go." The alarm was still sounding. "I said, let go."

"I did. *You* are holding on to *me*."

I was.

I dropped my arms to my sides and walked to the windows. My stomach and belly ached. I cooled my forehead against the glass windowpane. I didn't need any confusion, any complications. And especially not with young men of unknown gene pool.

My head hurt, my thoughts were in disarray. It was worse than a really bad shoulder-pad day—one of those no-win situations when just as I get up in front of someone, a pad slips to my chest to make a third bulge.

"So does this mean we can...work together?" he asked.

"*Work* together, yes. That's all." I glanced over my shoulder at him. I recognized the expression in his eyes. It belonged to a much wiser, more knowledgeable man.

"Okay. For now." He grinned and tucked his shirttails into his jeans. "Now, tell me what's been happening and what I can do to help...solve the murder and keep you out of trouble."

"First, let me place a call."

I called Mr. Gerster at his home and spoke to him briefly. He gave me the name and number of a friend of his with the *Wichita Daily Observer* and said he would let him know to expect my call. Next I placed a call to the *Observer*, but I had to leave a message on voice mail.

I summed up for Jason what had happened so far and went into what I suspected: one of the group—Edie, David, Jeena, Amy or Bill—had poisoned Yvonne to keep her from talking. And Edie was looking like the guilty one.

Then I summed up my nighttime activities, Edie's peculiar skulking, and finally seeing Angie, who I suspected was ensconced in unit five. "And if that isn't enough, I've checked with each of them to see if they keep the same story about why Angie isn't here. They all say they don't know, but Jeena lies constantly about everything, so I can't tell whether she even knows what she's telling me. Edie lies sometimes, David lies about bridge—otherwise he only snarls—and Amy and Bill speak only in love-sickened euphemisms."

"I don't see the connection," Jason said. "I mean, what's Edie's motive?"

"I don't know for sure, but I'm betting it has to do with the mental hospital and Yvonne's mother's murder. Now, in addition to needing to know a lot more about Yvonne and her mother's death, we need to know more about each of these other people.

"First there's David. He's moody, attractive, and reserved. He's a pharmacist and owns a drugstore on East Colfax. Check on him—license, store, reputation, former wives and girlfriends still living—that sort of thing. And there's Jeena, who is excessively jealous of him and has a mental health history in Kansas." I padded around the room; it seemed safer than sitting anywhere near Jason at the moment.

"And then there's Amy and Bill. They handed out iced tea that I think was laced, and Jeena lost her senses in the mine and went claustrophobic."

"So based on that you think they laced her tea?"

"Maybe. Of course, David was sitting next to Jeena on the porch, and he could have slipped something into it."

"In front of everyone?"

"It worked on Yvonne."

Jason frowned. "I think you should get the hell out of here."

I explained why that wouldn't work well. "We just have to be careful not to eat or drink anything we don't personally fix."

"Stella, anyone can read up on poisons and figure out how to dose someone. But you can't buy poisons without registering for them."

"The police will check those registers. I want you to check with the people at the tour mine and find out if they know any of the bridge group. Also find out which of these people have been in Mexico in the last two years."

"How in the world am I going to find that out?"

"You're an investigative reporter. Investigate."

"You're just trying to get rid of me."

Fortunately, the phone rang.

It was the *Observer*. The editor said the reporter who had followed the story would be in later today or tomorrow, Saturday. I arranged to call back in the morning.

The sun was beaming outside; it was four-twenty, if I could believe my alarm clock. Jason packed his things. "I'm going out for a while. I'll check into the sheriff's office. By the way, where's Meredith?"

"Oh, Lord. I don't know. She was at the slots earlier." A gnawing worry started to grow.

"Well, while I'm out I'll look for her."

"I'm going to the Golden Eagle. I'd like to see who registered for unit five."

Jason stopped at the door and turned toward me. "Stella?"

"What?"

"Please be careful."

It was sort of nice to have someone worried about me. Of course, my mother worries about me, but it isn't the same.

I watched out the window as he walked down the path from the inn to where his car was parked. Evidently he'd left his bags at the desk, because he didn't have them with him, only his camera pack. He got in the car and pulled out. I could still smell his Bay Rum aftershave.

FIFTEEN

WHEN I WORKED at the accounting firm, Edie and I had been friends. We had shared lunch, shopped together occasionally, gone to movies. She'd been one of the first to suggest that I needed to get out of my disgusting long-term relationship with Rick, and she'd still been supportive when I dragged my feet. It's surprising how many people lose patience with you if you don't follow their suggestions right away. Edie wasn't one of those.

To think of her as a killer was almost impossible, except in the most abstract, unreal way. Even then it was so painful, I felt a terrible weight in my chest and a kind of searing numbness where my heart was.

But Edie was the one who visited Yvonne's motel room, put jewelry on the counter, and told me I'd get hurt. And I suspected she was the one near us in the mine. She had changed. There was a sharper definition to her, an edge in her voice and hardness in her manner that had not been there before. It could come from a bitter love disappointment, or it could come from the desperation that drives a person to kill.

I could see her killing to protect a child or to avenge some heinous wrong, like a torturer-murderer she thought would continue to victimize people, but other motives eluded me. I thought about that one for a while. She had sheltered Angie from her husband, had warned me this morning...could she have killed to protect Angie?

I puzzled over the kind of relationship that would extend to killing, but didn't come up with anything that made sense, except that if she was the killer, she would have a damn good reason. And she was so smart, she'd be damned hard to catch. In that case I was the fall guy, since the sheriff saw me as his most promising suspect.

Music thumped through the wall from Edie's room.

I sprang from the chair and strode to the door, unlocked it, and stepped to Edie's door. The thump of music came straight through, just as loud in the hall as it was in my room. I knocked.

Then knocked again, and a third time. Then I tried the doorknob. It was locked. I didn't want to enter alone, if Edie was there.

Puzzled, I went back to my room, picked up my key, and decided to try to locate the room maid. Fluffy darted off his twig and blinked at me, begging to come along. I relented.

All the doors along the hallway were closed, although I imagined Edie's door pulsing. On a whim, I tried each one of them to see if they were all locked. They were, all but Jeena's. She was asleep on her bed. I reclosed the door quietly, so I wouldn't wake her.

Downstairs at the front desk I found only the little card announcing emergency numbers and breakfast time and the green blinking light of the telephone console. I went back along the back hallway to the Johnsons' door and knocked. Mrs. Johnson answered.

It was only ten to five, but nice warm smells of her supper wafted out the door. I realized I was hungry—for *her* dinner. I told her I'd like to speak to the room maid, and she looked surprised.

"I did all the rooms. Is there a problem?"

"No, no. Well, maybe. You see, someone was in my room other than you, and took a key I had. I wondered if you saw anyone upstairs while you were cleaning?"

She frowned. Tiny lines of concern creased the skin between her brows. She looked worried and tired. She could have been a member of the bridge group. "Someone in your room? No, no one. Everyone was downstairs playing cards. Until Mr. McClintock came upstairs, then there were some others upstairs, but I don't remember anyone in your room. You mean the key to the inn, or the key to your room?''

"Neither of those. It was a different key. Did you make up Edie Lorton's room today?''

She looked puzzled, but she answered readily. "Lorton? No, she said not to. She didn't explain, just said to leave it, she'd see to it.''

"Did she register anyone else in the room? Like, say, Angie Sayers?''

"She registered herself. That's all I can say.'' Her gaze dropped to the side.

"Did anyone else, not with our group, come into the inn today?''

She hesitated, thinking. "Only the young man, Mr. Paul. He said he had your key.''

I didn't explain that the key was missing before he showed up; I was concentrating on the subtle shift in her expression. "Were you able to find a room for him?''

"Yes.'' She didn't volunteer any more information. I considered pursuing it, but her stubborn jaw convinced me to shift to a new topic. "Did Angie Sayers come to the inn?''

"Angie Sayers did *not* come to the inn. She's not welcome here.'' She stepped back and started to close the door.

So Mrs. Johnson knew Angie Sayers. "Wait!'' I stepped into the room. "Why isn't she welcome?''

Mrs. Johnson hesitated for a moment, then spoke. "Things are always missing after she's been here. Now I must go.''

"Would your husband have seen anyone else in the inn?''

"My husband died—years ago.''

"And you're sure no one else came upstairs when you were up there?''

"Only Mr. McClintock, when he was dripping coffee from his crotch. He seemed to have had an accident.'' She smiled briefly. "He was the only one. And Miss Lorton. She came up once and went into her room.''

"Did you see her come back out?"

"Oh yes, right away."

"Was her radio playing?"

Mrs. Johnson shook her head.

"I wonder if you could unlock her door for me now. She doesn't seem to be in there, but her radio is playing very loud."

"I couldn't possibly. That's against the rules. You'll have to talk to Miss Lorton."

"But it's Edie that I'm worried about. She's usually so quiet, never plays loud music, and she doesn't answer, no one has seen her, and the radio *is* very loud. I'm afraid for her health." And I was, too, but it was company I wanted.

Mrs. Johnson hesitated. "Well, I guess it won't hurt. Just a minute." She disappeared into her apartment—to turn down the stove under her dinner, I thought—and returned. I followed her to the front desk where she checked for messages, then upstairs. She pulled a set of master keys from her pocket.

"Do you keep those with you all the time?"

"Always." She hesitated as though she might refuse to open the door, but the radio was blaring so loudly that she unlocked the room and stepped inside.

The radio, on the far side of the bed, pulsed with sound. Both single beds were made, but the one on the left was rumpled as though someone had lain on top of the bed-spread, and an apple core, brown and withering, stood on the bedside table. I drifted to the radio. It was a clock radio, set to turn on at two p.m., apparently to create the illusion she was there. But why, since we were all at the mine? I turned it off.

There was a note on the dresser, tented and placed over two twenty-dollar bills. I moved back around the beds, with a wide detour to the dresser.

"You shouldn't touch that," Mrs. Johnson said. "I should never have let you in here."

I touched it anyway. With one fingernail I lifted the note open and read the few words scrawled inside.

E...
My share. See you soon.
A

The *A* had to stand for Angie. Could Angie have left the clock radio on?

I let the note drop, turned, flashed empty hands at Mrs. Johnson, and glanced around one more time, then zipped into the bathroom. I wanted to make a quick recheck of the pharmaceuticals she had.

It was all the same as this morning. If Edie had left she'd have taken her toothbrush.

"Miss Stargazer, you shouldn't be in here."

"Just wanted to make sure she wasn't in the tub passed out."

"Please come along."

I remembered the glowing green numerals on the telephone console at the front desk. The clerk had told someone there was no room service. Two to one it was Angie. But why had she left the motel? Why weren't they staying together, and why had Edie told her to stay inside last night? Everything seemed to shift like sand in a windstorm. I needed some firm facts.

"Mrs. Johnson, I'm worried about Edie's safety." I put as much angst into my voice as I knew how. "When was the last time you saw her?"

Her chin was still set stubbornly, but her gaze flickered and she looked uncertainly at me. Finally, she spoke. "This afternoon. She came in after the mine trip and left right away again. It must have been just after three."

"And where did she go?"

"I don't know. I don't keep track of my guests. She just went out the back door and up the path."

"One last question. I noticed that one of the books in the library had been taken from the shelf. Could you tell me what it was?"

"What!" She relocked Edie's room and stormed down the stairs into the library. I pointed to the bookcase on the right side of the fireplace, and she opened the door. She scanned the shelves. "I don't see what you're talking—" She ran her hand over the books on the second shelf. Past Samuelson to the loose spot. When she turned around, her lower lip was caught between her teeth, and she was slow to meet my gaze.

"There used to be a book on common poisons and their antidotes."

"You don't know how long it's been gone?"

She shook her head, worry deep in her eyes. She must have been thinking ahead to news stories: KILLER LURKS IN B&B.

"I haven't opened this cabinet in over a year." Her lips settled into a thin, worried line.

FROM MY ROOM, the meadow behind the inn had looked grassy, almost verdant. Up close, as I marched up the path, I saw that the grass was sparse. The green color I'd seen from a distance came from low-growing alpine plants cling- ing to the thin soil, which barely covered the underlying rock. No wonder the deer nibbled the leaves of the bushes.

Opposite the Golden Eagle Motel, puffing heavily, I looked back at unit five again. I thought I saw the curtain move ever so slightly, as though Angie had been watching the trail and had dropped it back into place when I looked that way. I slowed, then stopped. Now that I was here I wasn't quite sure how I'd approach her.

I circled the parking lot beneath the hill, where I couldn't be seen from the motel, then climbed up and approached the motel lobby, pushing in through the door. The husky- voiced innkeeper bustled to the desk. I smiled at her, in- fusing into my eyes the absolute maximum warmth I could muster.

"I'm supposed to meet my friend, Angie Sayers, I think in unit five, but I'm not sure it's correct. Could you tell me if she's there?"

The woman flipped quickly through a card file at the

desk, frowned, and then went through it again. "No, I don't find her here anywhere. You sure you got the right place?"

I shrugged. "Oh, I think so. I wonder if she's going under her new name, she just got remarried a month ago." I leaned over the counter, friendly to the nth degree.

She returned my gaze, her eyes narrow and crafty. I rounded mine innocently and smiled wider, trying to look as much like a cherub as possible. "What's her married name?" she asked.

I looked stumped. I twisted my lips, rolled my eyes as though I was searching a computer brain. "I don't remember for sure. I think it might have been..." I shrugged and leaned over the counter. "Oh dear, she'll be so upset if I don't find her." I tried to look like Jason when he wants something from me. "Maybe A. Lorton?"

She sighed and ruffled through the cards. "No A. Lortons. Just an Edie Lorton."

So Edie was registered here as well as at the inn. It explained why she was walking up the mountain all the time. She'd been coming up here. The rusty sardine can must have been her idea of a cover-up. She was hiding Angie, for some reason.

I heard a gasp from the other side of the counter. The atmosphere in the motel lobby turned strange, and the innkeeper was wide-eyed.

She would never have remembered me if Fluffy had stayed inside my shirt pocket.

She was staring intensely at my chest, her mouth open and rounded. I thought she needed help. I wasn't going to let another hapless woman slip away from her mortal coil while I stood helplessly by.

I bounded around the end of the counter, raced to her side to pound her on the back. With the excitement I forgot how to do the Heimlich maneuver, but it didn't matter.

"You've got a...lizard on your chest," she said. "Hold still, I'll get it!" Then she lunged at me, arm raised, arcing downward toward poor little Fluffy clinging to my breast.

I bolted.

Halfway back to the inn I lost my breath but regained most of my senses and slowed to a walk. Fluffy was an excited bright green, his little eyelids bright turquoise, his eyes beady black, and his ribs pumping. I stroked him under his chin to reassure him. He dropped nose-first to the bottom of my shirt pocket. He's a sensitive little guy. It would probably take another two days of reassurance before he would be back to his staunch self.

I was a block away from the inn, on a fairly steep stretch of road, toenails jammed painfully into the toes of my shoes. It was half past five, and the afternoon heat was beginning to fade.

I stopped short and then went straight back up the path, past the empty motel lobby, and on to unit five. I rapped on the door and waited. Then I stepped to the side and tried to peer into the room. The door opened slowly.

"Angie…?"

"Wrong, sister."

Angry dark eyes glared out from under dark, tousled hair. Two days worth of beard stubble covered his cheeks and chin. He was six feet tall and built like a Mack truck.

"Oh, excuse me. I was looking for…"

"Edie?" He grinned suggestively and leaned heavily against the doorjamb. "Edie, eh? Well, she'd like to meet you, too, I suppose. She likes young women, you know." He waited for me to say something, but my mouth was too dry to speak. I wanted to hit him for the insinuation, but he looked like the sort who would enjoy hitting me back.

"You wanna come in?" He gestured to the inside of his motel room. The air rolling out was acrid with stale body odor and cigarette smoke. His invitation made me feel instantly covered in slime.

"No, thanks, Mr.—?"

"Sayers. Andrew S. Sayers. I'll find Angie if it takes forever. She's mine, and that two ton-bitch Edie can't keep her from me. And you can tell Edie when you see her that I'm pissed off and ready to kill."

PORK.

A lot of things fell into place now. Angie's angina. Edie's nervousness. Probably the others also knew about Angie...and had been covering.

I'd have been relieved if he'd slammed the door in my face. I don't even remember what I said, just that I oozed away from the door and lit out for the inn. His laugh followed me, raising the hair on my neck.

SIXTEEN

THE PHONE WAS RINGING when I got to my room. I lifted the receiver to my ear expecting to hear Jason's voice. But it wasn't him.

It was Jerry Blake of the *Wichita Daily Observer*. He had a deep, easy-to-listen-to voice with just a hint of sinus congestion. He wanted to know why I was calling before he would talk to me, and after I told him, his sinus congestion seemed to get worse. It made me feel a bit better for Yvonne that someone felt bad enough to choke up about her death. Once he started talking, Jerry had a lot to say.

"Did you know Yvonne well?"

There was a hesitation before he answered. "I got acquainted with Yvonne while I was on the story. She's a real decent kid who had a hard time. You want to know the truth, I believed her. I think she got a bum rap.

"There never was an autopsy because her mother had been sick for some time, a recurrent heart condition that would make her collapse every so often. She died at home, and Yvonne found her. Took it real hard, and then accused her stepfather of killing her..."

"Was there another woman?"

"Rumors. Nothing ever came to light."

"Yvonne's biological father in the picture?"

"Died about ten years ago. She never accepted her mother's remarriage to this Stephen Douglas Prescott. She didn't get along with him. Yvonne tried several times to get the police to investigate, then she got sick, too, but...not the same way as her mother. Yvonne ended up with some pretty serious mental problems, hallucinations, threatened him with a knife, left a long slice cut on his left arm—"

"Scar?"

"I'd guess so. Anyway, she was taken to the local psych emergency room and hospitalized for a couple of weeks or so. They thought she'd been on some drugs, and that may have caused her hallucinations. Prescott never pressed charges, but there were rumors that he suspected that Yvonne poisoned her mother and he covered up for her because he felt sorry for her."

"And what did you think about her mental status?"

"I don't know. She wasn't nuts. She always said she was drugged. I think she got emotional, lost it with Prescott, and the police didn't believe her after that. Prescott is a very convincing guy. It was one of those cases where you could arrange the facts either way and it looked right. The clincher for the cops was Yvonne's motive—lost inheritance."

"But the murder could more easily have been to get the inheritance than to avenge its loss."

"That's what I figured, too, but it didn't go anywhere."

I thought a minute. "With that kind of history, there isn't a police department in the world that would give Yvonne the benefit of the doubt. It's a blooming wonder that they didn't charge her with murder." A scrap of paper on the floor caught my attention.

"Jerry, can you hold a minute?"

I picked it up. It was a note from Meredith.

Stella,
    Am having time of my life at casino. Don't worry about me.
    Found a hilarious man, too. See you later.
                                                Meredith

With a niggle of concern, I reread the line about the man. Meredith and men are a sometimes hazard. I yanked open the door, but there was no one in the hall, no footsteps on the stairs. She must have slipped it under the door earlier, while I was out.

I picked up the receiver again. "I'm back."

"Well, the police considered charging her, but dropped the idea because there wasn't enough evidence, just suspicions. And it seems the stepfather spoke up for our Yvonne, defending her—which made him look like a prince."

"What about the will? Was there a lot of money involved?"

"Lots. Her mother was loaded and left it all to her husband. That was a big surprise, since she had always been close to Yvonne, but they had argued and were distant after that. Anyway, Prescott packed up and left the area about two years ago—"

"Two years!"

"Apparently he was just sick of all the disruption from Yvonne and left."

"And went where? And looked like what?"

"Dallas, Texas. He was about six feet tall, lean, brown hair, in his mid-forties. Tended to look younger. Sound like anyone you know?"

It did. David. I did some rapid calculations. "He must've been quite a bit younger that Yvonne's mother."

"Yes. That may have been part of the trouble in the home with Yvonne. But her mother was pretty youthful."

I thought of the picture I'd seen. She had been very attractive.

We talked a little longer, then he rang off. I had started to make notes when the phone rang again.

Jason's voice boomed over the wires into my ear. I rolled over to the edge of the bed and sat up to organize my thinking.

"Stel, I'm at the sheriff's office. They did an autopsy, and the preliminary results are in. You were right. She was poisoned. Some solution of cyanide." Jason's voice was low and excited.

"Cyanide...cyanide. So that's why she looked so pink." I remembered from some college biology or chemistry class, or maybe from a blood-and-thunder novel, that cyanide poisoning causes the skin to flush. It has something to do with the action of the poison in the blood stream.

Instead of feeling great, vindicated, I felt lousy. I got up from the bed and, still holding the phone to my ear, strolled to the windows.

"She looked pink? I don't know about that, but say, listen, Stel. This is a great story. Gotta thank you for it. And Bob's great." I listened for a note of sarcasm, but it wasn't there. It never was. Jason was the most straightforward, open character I knew.

"Jason, while you're there try to find out if the keys to Yvonne's car were in her purse. Oh, and before you called, I was talking to a reporter from Wichita who knew Yvonne. He said that her stepfather, Stephen Douglas Prescott, left Wichita about two years ago and went to Dallas, Texas. He was in his forties, and looked younger."

"*Some* women are attracted to younger men."

"And look what happened to *her.*"

"Stella, don't you think you're a little overinvolved here?"

I peered into the travel cage. Fluffy's beautiful little black, beady lizard eye blinked back at me. He smacked his lizard lips. It's his special I-love-you-too gesture. He does it when I'm especially lonely. Jason claims Fluffy does it from boredom, but Jason doesn't really understand him.

"Possibly, but let's not discuss that now. You just check out Prescott. I have to get going. I've got to find Meredith."

"Wait!" he shouted. "You've got to hear this. One of your group—Jeena Gay? Her husband died only a year ago. And under very peculiar circumstances." The way he drew out the last two words set my teeth on edge.

"How peculiar?"

"Very. I'll tell you all about it. *And* I found Meredith. It's six-thirty. Put on a sweater and be ready in ten minutes."

"For what?"

"Me." He hung up, and I was left listening to the dial tone.

JASON WAS PROMPT, and ten minutes later I was climbing into his sporty little red Miata.

"I didn't think cub reporters could afford new cars. Or any cars, for that matter."

Jason settled himself behind the wheel. "Nice, isn't it?"

I nodded. "Very bachelor."

"What do you mean?"

"There's barely enough room in it for you *and* your ego."

"Cranky, aren't you?"

"Where's Meredith?" I had no intention of going into my psyche tonight.

"She's in the middle of her biggest win. She's had a couple of mini-jackpots—up about twelve hundred dollars, as we speak."

"You're kidding!"

He shook his head. "Nope."

"She said she'd met a hilarious man—"

He laughed. "You don't have to worry. She's okay. Now, if it were Zelda, we'd have a major problem. She'd be sucked into his smarm, but Meredith is fine."

"So what was all that about Jeena?"

He started the car. "I'll tell you over dinner." The car rolled forward. "Put on your seat belt. You're going out with me tonight."

SEVENTEEN

WE HAD A GREAT TIME. Jason drove west farther into the mountains on I-70 to Frisco and a restaurant called the Blue Spruce. Inside, the decor was what I think of as mountain elegant. Set in a home, small intimate rooms, totally comfortable, with food so good you almost weep.

We disagreed, we argued, we agreed, we laughed. Jason outlined all he had learned about Jeena and her late, not too lamented husband. The time flew by. It was closing time at the casinos, two a.m., when we got back to Silverado, and we were sitting in Jason's car, still talking, when Meredith came by, accompanied by a tall, muscular man in the kind of shirt you see on the covers of romance novels where the hero is a pirate. I called out to her, and he left her at the car.

"How's the luck going?" I asked. Meredith's face was bleary with fatigue. "Not so hot, at the end." She leaned against the car. "What are you two doing out here?"

"Just talking. Who's the bodyguard?"

She straightened, suddenly defensive. "Do you always have to denigrate men?" she replied.

"Do you remember Ted Bundy?" I asked.

"Yes."

"If those girls had known him better, they'd never have been killed, because they wouldn't have gone out with him."

"You don't need to spy on me."

"I'm not."

"Just take care of your own love life."

"I don't have a love life."

"Well, you might. If you'd talk nice and look around you once in a while." She stomped up the steps.

"Hormonal, I'd say." She had caught me by surprise. Meredith is usually placid, if a little flaky.

Jason shifted in the car seat. "Maybe. Stella, look at me." He put a hand gently on either side of my face. "Stella, LOOK at me."

"I am. If you get any closer I'll be cross-eyed."

"Don't joke, for once."

"I have to. I have to leave. See you tomorrow." I ran from the car. Later, alone in my bed and lonely, I wished I hadn't, but I stayed put. I already had enough complications in my life.

I DIDN'T SLEEP very well that night, even though I had a chair jammed under the doorknob to prevent intruders. I had to burrow under the covers to keep warm in the cold mountain night air. The inn wasn't wasting any money on heating.

Images of Jason's warm brown eyes were interspersed with Edie and Angie and hovered in my dreams until I finally woke at dawn, tangled in the sheets, tired and cranky—but with a much clearer mind and a burning question.

Where was Yvonne's car?

I didn't have an answer to that question, but I had figured out that if Angie had come to Silverado with Edie, she wouldn't have a car to leave in...unless she'd also filched Yvonne's car keys when she'd liberated her pearls. It would be child's play to park the car in the municipal lot right after she'd followed me back to the inn, hiding it in plain sight. That way she'd have a ready escape route, her own personal plan B, whenever she needed it.

It was Saturday morning about six a.m., and the sun was barely peeking over the rim of the mountains. I pulled on my jeans, a T-shirt, and tennies and left the inn. Edie's car was parked sedately at the end of the row.

Silverado is a small town with very limited parking space. If Yvonne's car was here unnoticed, the most likely place was the municipal lot. This early in the morning I

figured there would be only a few cars parked there, cars
of those people who had stayed overnight. Far fewer than
during daytime. Yvonne's car ought to stand out.

I power-walked up and down the ranks of cars. There
were more than I'd thought, and the sun was warming the
early-morning chill off my back by the time I reached the
end. It was so dry there was barely any dew on the wind-
shields. Her car wasn't there. I went to the parking booth
and talked to the caretaker who had just come on shift.

"There coulda been one with a stuffed cat in it. Hell, I
don't know. There's hundreds in here all day long. Can't
remember any of them, 'less it's got something really unusual." He scowled at me. "And there's nothing unusual
about having a Kansas license plate. I come from Kansas."
He retreated to his hut, closed the door, and poured himself
a coffee from his thermos with a shaking hand.

I knocked on the glass window. "Hey! It's really important." He rubbed the back of his neck with a work-
reddened, knobby-knuckled hand and refused to look away
from his coffee.

I was halfway across the parking lot when I heard him
call after me. When I turned back he was standing in the
doorway of the booth, coffee mug in hand.

"Try my son. He was on yesterday." He gave me his
address. "Might catch him now. He works the mine when
he isn't here."

His son lived in a tiny old house, one of the original
miner's homes, high on the breast of the mountain at the
end of a lane no wider than a four-wheel-drive track. He
was a younger version of his father—slow to warm up, and
sullen beyond cautious at first—but more solidly built.

"Yeah, I seen it. She left like a bat out a hell. Stiffed
me."

"You work at the Last Chance Mine?"

"Yeah, why?"

"So were you there yesterday afternoon?"

"Yeah." His eyes grew wary.

"Did someone pay you to turn off some lights and give a party a scare?"

He froze for an instant. "Don't know what you're talking about."

"I think you do. Someone paid you to turn off the lights. And then when one of the women freaked and ran, you followed. You're the figure I saw."

"It was a joke."

"Who paid you to do it?"

"No name. It came in the mail. I didn't know it would cause a problem."

"What else would you do for money?"

"Get outta here. I don't need this." He slammed the door in my face.

I WAS STILL UPSET with myself when I returned to the inn. If I'd handled him differently, he might have told me more. Now it was too late. The sheriff might get him to talk, but I sure wouldn't. Unless I could come up with something mighty creative.

And until I came up with it, I'd concentrate on Edie.

I stepped inside the back door of the inn and into the kitchen, fragrant with the smell of spicy freshly baked muffins, and the dining room, where several of the bridge players were gathered around the table, munching on breakfast.

"Anyone seen Edie?"

Murmurs of "no" came from all in the room.

I ran up the back stairs to the second floor. I knocked at the door to her room, but there was no answer. I tried the doorknob. It was still locked.

A nasty, uneasy feeling grew in the pit of my stomach, and it wasn't my appetite. Edie hadn't been seen in a very long time...not since we'd returned from the mine around three. There were dozens of explanations, of course. Dozens. I just couldn't find a single one that felt logical and good.

Inside my own room everything looked unchanged, nothing out of place. I checked on Fluffy, pushed his cage to

the safety of the back and middle of the dresser top, and
gave him a wax worm with an apology. He hates them and
only eats them when he's starving. They're little, fat, white,
and disgusting. I couldn't blame him, so I promised to try
to find a fly soon, explaining that there aren't all that many
in Colorado anyway and very few in the mountains. He
blinked and turned away. The wax worm flopped and wrig-
gled, then lay dead still—a bad image, given the worries I
had about Edie.

I soaped and rinsed off in the shower quickly, shaking
my hair upside down till it was damp dry and as puffy as
my hair gets. I slipped into my good-luck teddy, purple
with gold splashes, and was pulling on a deep purple silk
blouse over a pair of green-gold trousers when I heard
someone at Edie's bedroom door. I settled the blouse into
place as I crossed the floor. Noiselessly, I twisted the doorknob and drew open the door, adrenaline flooding my
bloodstream.

David was bent over Edie's doorknob, credit card in his
right hand, his left hand on the doorknob. He could be
trying to get into her room to eliminate evidence.

"Charging her room?" I asked. I noticed two tiny parallel scratches on the inside of his arm.

"Stella!" He straightened, shoved the credit card into
his pants pocket. "I was trying to wake Edie."

"With a credit card?"

"I couldn't get her to answer the door."

"Silly me. I'd have thought if she didn't answer she
wasn't there." A little guilt muscle in his jaw pulsed.

"But maybe Angie's there," I offered. He was the only
one I hadn't asked yet.

The muscle jumped, but his eyes didn't flicker. He was
good at acting innocent; he was probably good at poker.
"And, of course, you didn't know about the motel room."

"I don't know what you're talking about."

"Oh, I think you know that Angie was here with Edie.
You've done something to Edie, and now you're trying to
get to Angie."

This time his eyes flickered slightly. "What do you know about all this?" he asked, his voice quiet with menace.

"I know that Angie's hiding from some slime, about your size, who says his name is Andrew Sayers, and Edie hasn't been seen since yesterday at least."

David's face froze. "Did you see him?"

"Yesterday afternoon, half past five. Unit five, the Golden Eagle. He's registered under the name of Edie Lorton."

"Oh, my God."

David's expression grew hostile, and for a moment as we stood in the hallway in the midst of all that civilized, polished oak, I wondered if he'd strike me.

His eyes turned to bleak blue ice. "He'll kill Edie. You led him here. You screwed it all up. I knew you would." He swore and turned his attention back to the lock, trying to stuff his credit card into the doorjamb.

He was almost frantic to get into Edie's room. For what—for the note? Because he didn't believe that she was gone? I was vaguely pleased he wasn't an accomplished burglar, but it didn't prove he wasn't an accomplished killer. "That isn't the way it's done," I said.

He stopped sawing with the card and glared at me. "I suppose you know how to break and enter?"

"I know how to get the manager to open the door when it's locked." It's the little things in life that give me pleasure, like the flush of disgust that rolled over his face. "There was only a note in there from Angie, saying she'd meet Edie soon. Presumably that's where they are now."

David looked baffled, then frustrated. "Maybe the cabin. I don't know. I *don't* know. They must have discovered he was here—"

"Edie *knew* he was here. She went up the hill to meet him."

David looked surprised, then shook his head. "She wouldn't do that. She hates Andrew."

"Why?"

"For what he's done to Angie."

David was using the present tense for Edie. If he had killed Edie, would he be clever enough to use the present tense about Edie? Probably.

"She was there. I'm positive. Mrs. Johnson said she saw Edie climbing up the path after we came back from the mine. That would have been somewhat after three p.m. *yesterday*."

David frowned and tapped his credit card against his fisted left hand. "Maybe...she's there now?"

We had the same thought. We pelted down the hallway to the back stairs and up the path behind the inn. At that altitude I was out of breath before we could even see the parking lot of the motel. My feet and shoes were gritty from the dust of the path through the sparse grass of the meadow.

When we reached the Golden Eagle, the dirty-linen bin and a cleaning supplies cart stood in front of unit five. I had a sinking feeling I knew what we'd find.

I looked at David, my heart at the back of my throat, and stepped up to the side of the dirty-linen bin. Then I sidestepped around it, safely away from David, but keeping him in my peripheral vision field.

There was a sudden silence in the air, so quiet that I could hear the low murmur of the cleaning woman humming as she tidied the unit. Even the breeze in the trees had dropped.

My hand trembled as I plunged it into the soiled linens, gingerly probing. I lifted the sheets and damp towels. At last David reached in and stirred around as well. I figured he only pitched in after he was comfortably certain he wouldn't find a body.

I never knew sheets were so heavy, but there was nothing in there but bedsheets and damp, dirty towels. It was only then that I wondered what the cleaning person would have thought had she found us heads down, rear ends up, searching through her dirty linens.

David went to the lobby to inquire about who had checked out. Given my last interaction with the manager, I thought David would be the best one to handle that. I stayed to talk to the cleaning person in unit five.

"Excuse me," I said, sliding around the bin and into the unit, stepping over a huge wad of sheets. The queen-size bed was stripped, and a small woman of middle age with efficient hands was tucking in a fresh bottom sheet. Dust rags poked out of the pockets of her smock like big white lizards. I was glad Fluffy was safe in his cage.

The woman stopped stretching the sheet and looked quizzically at me. "Yeah?"

"Is Mr. Sayers still here?"

She looked briefly around the room. "No, don't see him." These days everyone was a comic.

"I mean, has he checked out?"

"It's no wonder I'm tired. You think I got the energy to go dancing after changing sheets all day? Damn sure I don't. I got a life like everything else, but no, I gotta change the sheets again. What d'you want?"

I wasn't sure how to ask delicately, if she'd found blood anywhere. "Uh, were the sheets dirty?"

She looked at me, new suspicion dawning in her eyes. "Dirty? You think I change *clean* sheets now?"

"I mean, was there any, you know, blood?" I tilted my head, trying to look harmless, and moved around the end of the bed, trying to see if there were blood spatters on the far wall. She stopped tucking the sheet and edged away from me.

"What is this? You have a thing for dirty sheets?"

It wasn't going well. "No, I'm looking for...I'm wondering...if...you, if there...was something weird that happened here."

She pursed her lips and backed over to the telephone, her hand reaching for the receiver. "I'll tell you, something very weird is going on here right now. You better leave, missy." She started to pick up the receiver. She looked at me with the kind of gleam in her eyes that says, *I'm dealing with a real loon, I'd better bring in the troops.*

"No, no, don't call. I'm just not making myself clear. I mean, did you find anything here, like blood?"

She shook her head, her hand moving the receiver slowly toward her head.

"—or a body?"

She put the receiver to her ear.

"—when you came in, did it look like a fight had happened here? I'm not nuts. But this guy was tracking his wife, threatening her. I want to see if he left any notes or clues about where he was going next."

She stopped looking quite so alarmed. "So who are you?"

"I'm looking for my friend, Edie. I think she might have been here, and he might have hurt her, or forced her to go with him."

She pursed her lips and raised her chin as though she could picture the kind of trouble I was talking about all too well. She hung up the phone. I'd won her over.

"You look where you want, girlie. Just let me get on with my cleaning."

She hadn't emptied the wastebasket yet, so I started there. Several sheets of paper were crumpled into balls, and I pulled them out, careful to touch them as little as possible. One after another they were attempts to write to Angie, begging her to come back, apologizing for all that went wrong, promising to reform, and then threatening to kill her and Stella the Stargazer and Edie. Especially Edie. He seemed convinced that Edie was the root of their misunderstandings, the origin of their problems. Without Edie, theirs would be a marriage made in heaven.

I smoothed the papers out, reread the last one because it mentioned me. This was Pissed Off and Ready to Kill. And I'd been face to face with him.

If he'd found Edie, had Edie survived?

His handwriting was abysmally hard to read: ponderous, double-looped, and leaning in both directions, as though it deliberately reflected his conflicted thoughts. He was a very disturbed person. I had no trouble seeing him as villain, but what connection did he have, if any, to Yvonne?

I looked for the pad of paper he was writing on, but it wasn't there. He must have kept it. I pictured him seated at the table in front of the double window, looking down toward town.

The inn was over to the right and below, just out of sight of the motel, but he must have known Angie was there. It would eat away at him. I shuddered and wondered how close I'd come to being attacked by him yesterday.

Edie and Angie had been at the Golden Eagle the night Yvonne was killed. Edie had put the pearls in Yvonne's room, only she said she didn't know it was Yvonne's room, then she told Angie to stay there and left.

But Angie followed me back to the inn, then returned to the motel and moved Yvonne's car. The request for room service at the inn yesterday morning had to have been Angie. She could have left the Golden Eagle and come to the inn because she'd seen Andrew, or heard me in Yvonne's unit, or perhaps the sheriff searching Yvonne's room had frightened her. So, she'd been at the inn by nine o'clock yesterday morning. It was my guess that Angie set the alarm for two, then left the note and drove off in Yvonne's car.

Edie, then, would have gone to the Golden Eagle about three to check out, and pick up anything Angie had left behind, then gone to meet Angie. It felt like some of the puzzle was in place, but it still didn't make sense.

Outside beyond the laundry cart the branches of the pine trees waved in a gentle, mournful exhalation, as if lost souls had just flown through the needles. I glanced at the cleaning woman. She must have sensed the same thing. She made a hurried sign of the cross.

On a hunch I undid the wad of sheets lying on the floor, looking for signs of lovemaking, or rape, but they were merely wrinkled.

The cleaning woman heaved a sigh of obvious relief and

went to the bathroom. I watched her gather all the soiled linens and return to dump them in the cart.

I tried to picture Edie coming alone to talk to Andrew, maybe begging him to leave, explaining that Angie just wanted to be alone. How had he responded then? Had he lashed out at her, clubbing her with his hand? Had she fallen and hit her head? I closed my eyes and tried to conjure up some vision of what had happened in here, but nothing came to me.

A rough male voice interrupted my thoughts. I opened my eyes and saw David standing at the door, his arms dangling loosely at his sides, his long fingers useless. A man defeated—and angry.

"He checked out about half an hour ago. By himself. The manager didn't see anyone with him. But she said she didn't really notice, since she was still upset from a woman who had been in there yesterday, wearing a lizard."

I avoided eye contact. My friend who is a park ranger swears that an enraged wild animal is less likely to attack if you don't make eye contact.

"You guys gonna move out now? I gotta finish up this room."

EIGHTEEN

I MOVED TOWARD THE DOOR as David walked stiffly across the parking area. I followed behind, thinking. I felt safer walking behind where I could see him.

We walked single-file down the path through the meadow, like cows heading for the barn, only there wasn't going to be any nice dinner of hay for us when we got there.

Food is one of my personal favorite comforts, but when I thought of the table at the inn laden with food, all I could see was tuna à la strychnine and hemlock salad with ipecac dressing. My appetite wilted on the spot.

"David, where is the cabin Angie and Edie use?"

There was a minute hesitation. "I don't know. I was never privileged to go there."

"David, dammit. Do you know how important this could be?"

He stopped walking abruptly and faced me, lips pressed together. "Yes. I do. And you can stop worrying. He'll never find them, and it's better you don't try to either."

"He could have both of them captive. God knows what has happened. And it could all be tied to Yvonne's death. Now where is it?"

There was a flicker of something in his shadowed, deep-set eyes, but I couldn't tell what, only that he seemed to be hiding something. "David?" I prodded.

"She may have mentioned a Miller's Valley, I think. But Edie'll call later today. When she does, I'll find out," he said, and turned on his heel, starting down the mountain. His long legs covered the uneven path in giant steps.

I had to almost run to keep up. "When she does call, *if* she calls, let me know. And David, if Andrew Sayers was somehow connected to Yvonne, then he's dangerous enough to be her killer.''

He didn't answer.

"How did Angie know Edie?" I asked.

"Met in college, I think."

"And kept in touch all these years?"

"Angie showed up one night on her doorstep and has been here ever since. Edie took her under her wing, protected her. Angie seems to need that, she looks to others to shelter her."

"So Andrew could have figured out that Angie would come to Edie, so all he had to do was locate Edie. How come you know about Angie, and the others don't?"

He was silent for a while. We were almost halfway to the inn. He stopped and faced me, a disquieting stance. "I had a...a relationship with Edie a while back. Before Angie came to town. Edie trusts me."

"It's very hard to imagine."

He grinned sardonically and stepped toward me. "Some women think I'm exciting."

"There's a sucker born every minute."

IT WAS ALMOST TEN. David stomped into the inn and disappeared up the stairs. I checked the inn's parking area; Edie's car was gone. It had been there when I left around six that morning.

Edie hadn't been seen since yesterday, Friday afternoon, after the mine trip. Mrs. Johnson had been the last one to see her, going up the mountain, probably to check out of the Golden Eagle. The note from Angie indicated that they planned to meet, and it seemed logical they'd go to Edie's cabin. I needed to know where it was.

The county clerk could tell me, but the office was closed until Tuesday because of the Fourth of July weekend. I could burglarize the courthouse, a charming idea. Or I could try to find the clerk of the court. Or I could ask the one person who probably knew everyone in town: the sheriff's dispatcher.

Saturday morning at the sheriff's office was pretty much like Friday morning, except that I wasn't being led into the inner sanctum as a major suspect to explain my nefarious doings.

The dispatcher today had a sour mouth and a sullen expression. She looked like the kind of person who would rather pick up a dead mouse than give you the time of day, much less directions to someone else's cabin.

I strolled up to the counter and explained that I was looking for a mountain property I understood Edie Lorton would be selling. And I apologized for inconveniencing her, blah blah, and finally she interrupted.

"I don't know why you're here on Saturday. It's a holiday weekend."

"That's why I can come. I don't have to work, I got a sitter, you know how it is—"

She frowned. "Talk to Minnie. She's in the back at the dispatch board."

Minnie was a jewel. She didn't know where Edie's cabin was, but she knew the clerk of the court, an old friend of hers. She told me where she lived.

The clerk and her husband lived in a rambling log house built into the side of the mountain at the end of a winding road at the very farthest edge of Silverado. They had a wonderful view down onto town. I knocked on the screen door.

A petite woman in her early fifties answered. She wore jeans, sweater, and a sweatband around her forehead.

She stood back and pointed to the back of the house. A light, soapy ammonia smell permeated the house. "I was just mopping the floor. Come in."

I followed her to the living room, which was dominated by a massive rock fireplace and an elephant-ear vine that twined up the side of the fireplace and across the ceiling to the windows. A Navajo rug hung on the wall, and a pair of worn but polished cowboy boots stood next to the entrance to the hallway. She motioned for me to sit and lowered herself to the leather chair.

I explained what I wanted.

"Minnie called to say you might be coming. I don't know where this place is exactly. But I think it might be one of those miner's cabins over in Walker's Valley. There's several of them that have been bought by people for summer homes. Pretty nice. But I couldn't tell you for sure until Tuesday. If you want to call me, I could tell you then."

"Do you have a map here of the county?"

"Oh, sure. Just a minute." She left the room and returned in a minute, carrying a rolled paper that she spread on the dining table. "I can show you a couple of places where it's most likely."

She pointed out Walker's Valley. "It's real pretty here. A couple of streams, lots of wildlife. Only problem is, when it rains hard, it can flood. See right here? These two streams converge in heavy runoff. Just be sure you get one of the cabins on high ground."

She ran a finger along the highway. "Here's the other valley where there's cabins for sale that I know about. Nice place. More expensive, though. Most of them here are on higher ground, real beautiful. Farther from the stream, which would be safer for the kids."

She looked at me with kindly eyes. "You have to be real careful with the kids around these mountain streams. Every year some kid falls in and drowns. The water runs real swift here."

I felt like a colossal creep. "Yeah. Good point." I thanked her and left.

When I returned to the inn after lunch it was almost four o'clock. It was quiet, no bridge players on the porch. Jeena seemed like the only prospect left for finding out exactly where the cabin was...if she was reliable.

I checked on Fluffy, who was snoozing on a twig, a comfortable, contented brown. Next I scrawled a brief note to Jason, saying that I was going to Jeena's room to talk to her and adding the time, so there would be a clue if I didn't return.

I propped it on the mirror, blew a kiss to Fluffy, and locked my room, although it seemed a singularly ineffective thing to do at this point, since everyone had already been in there, and credit cards seemed to work for keys around here.

Jeena's room was on the third floor, along with David's and Bill's. I was too tired to race up the stairs, but I whipped along at a fair clip, rounded the corner, and rammed smack into Jeena, emerging from David's room. She stumbled backward with a little shriek, and I had to grab the bannister to keep from falling over and down the stairs. She was a surprisingly solid woman.

"Lord! Don't you watch where you're going?" she asked. Her face was flushed, and there was a sheen of perspiration on her upper lip, accentuating a shadow of a mustache. It might have been sexy in a hirsute way, but she was frowning.

She was an unhappy camper, although the image I had of her as a perky Girl Scout leader was beginning to tarnish. I think it was the story Jason told me at dinner about how she had laced her husband's pink lemonade with syrup of ipecac and then locked him in the garage. It seems he died three weeks later of a burst aneurysm, not related to the lemonade incident but peculiar enough for the newspaper reporter to remember it. I should say.

"I want to talk to you a minute," I said. "Did David tell you that we found Andrew Sayers?"

She drew in a deep breath and pulled herself off the wall. "I'm not speaking to David."

I wondered if the tremor in her hand and voice was all due to running into me, or if she'd had a row with David. "You just came from his room."

"So?"

"Well, when you *were* speaking to him, did he tell you?" I regretted the sarcasm as soon as it was past my lips, fearful she'd refuse to speak to me next. I tried to make up for it by softening my tone of voice while appealing to her sense of danger. "Andrew is threatening to kill both Angie and Edie. So, if you know anything that would be helpful, like where Angie would go, then tell me,'' I blurted out. ''And as soon as possible.''

''Good,'' she said. Then she opened the door to her room and went in, leaving me to follow.

Nothing about Jeena so far had prepared me for the state of her room. But then nothing was as it seemed at first glance.

The overall effect was early Halloween. The blinds were pulled so there was only dim half-light, but it was enough to see the chaos.

The bed was rumpled like it had been jumped on. I recognized the look; I'm a recovering child bed-jumper myself. Clothes were everywhere. There was barely any floor that wasn't covered with clothing. She must have brought her entire wardrobe with her for the weekend, and tried it all on. She had to have risen at the crack of dawn to try on all these things. It was too much to relate to. I decided to ignore it for now.

''Jeena, where is Edie's cabin?''

''That slut!'' she shouted and threw herself into the chair by the window.

''Slut'' wasn't a description I would ever have used for Edie. My skin got a creepy-crawly feeling.

''You need to know, Stella, that I don't give a shit what happens to Edie.'' Jeena plucked a pair of shorts from the floor and heaved them at the lamp on the dresser.

From the looks of things the safest spot was just barely inside the door—so I could leave in a hurry if necessary. I stood with my feet close together so I wouldn't tread on anything.

''When did you meet David?''

She stopped pacing and looked at me, her eyes narrow. ''About two years ago, back in Kansas. Why?''

''I thought it was a year ago.''

''Trust me. I know when he came to Denver. It was two years ago. Two womanizing years ago.''

I felt my pulse quicken. That was how long ago

Yvonne's stepfather had left Kansas, supposedly for Texas. What if he'd come to Denver...

"He's the worst thing ever happened to me," Jeena said. The expression on her face was ugly. She paced from the window to the bed and back, her movements jerky and surprisingly uncoordinated, a reflection of her emotional upset.

I decided to steer the subject in a different direction. I turned the doorknob quietly, ready for a quick escape if necessary. "Jeena, did David ever mention a stepdaughter?"

"*And* a wife." Jeena snatched a blouse from the floor, drew it like a rope between her fingers, and snapped it in the air, like kids do in the locker room.

In spite of all my suspicions about David, I was surprised to hear Jeena say he had a wife. "Do you know any more about them? Like how old they are?"

She shook her head. "Isn't that enough?" She snapped the blouse again, harder, and came toward me.

A nearby door shut. Jeena leaped across the room, shoved me out of the way, yanked open the door, and called out, her voice completely different, honey-coated.

"Are you on your way to the opera?"

David's voice rang out. "I'm going to look for Edie."

"But you'll miss the opera."

"Damn the opera." His footsteps clattered down the stairs.

Jeena remained at the door, leaning into the hall, her back rigid. She turned slowly, her face a mask of jealousy. "Dammit! Dammit!"

She closed the door. "Dammit! He goes after that slut while I'm just supposed to go to the opera by myself. He goes after Edie, the turkey-butt, mole-faced, fat-necked old cow."

"I thought the two of you were friends."

Her voice wasn't loud, but she was enraged. "Like hell! Now he's going after her again. She started it. He loved me first. They're dead. They're history."

Jeena wasn't pretty. And she didn't make sense. The term "decompensating" came to mind.

I slithered out the door and closed it behind me. Just before it latched, I peeked in one last time.

Jeena marched across the floor, picking up pieces of clothing, snapping them back and forth. Then she flung them down again. It was a regular clothing storm. At this rate she wasn't going to have anything left to wear. The door to Jeena's madness clicked shut.

NINETEEN

JEENA SAID David had had a stepdaughter and wife. If David was Yvonne's stepfather, then I was willing to bet that he killed Yvonne's mother and Yvonne. He'd said he was looking for Edie, but more than likely he knew exactly where she was. He wouldn't stop at killing again... whatever he once felt for Edie.

I went down those stairs after David so fast they were a blur under my feet, but I heard the front door slam before I even reached the first-floor landing. I whizzed through the foyer to the front door in time to see David cross the road at the corner and disappear down the hill toward town.

I expected him to get in his car, which was parked at the side of the inn, right next to Jason's little red one. I stopped midflight. What if David came back to his car? If it were disabled, or at least slowed down, I would have a chance of following him. A car mechanic I'm not, but even I know that cars have to have all their wires connected. Without them, they don't go far. I felt along the underside of the hood. It didn't open from the outside. The car, of course, was locked.

And then I saw his tires. I unscrewed the cap to the air valve on the right front tire and wedged a pebble into it so the air would leak out. It wouldn't stop him, but it would slow him down. As soon as the tire was hissing loudly, I ran down the steps to the sidewalk in front of the sheriff's office and then past the Opera House.

I passed the Beaufort Hotel and then the Golden Fleece Casino, walking real close to a large man in a bright plaid shirt and white jacket. He was a large, big-bellied man who moved in a wreath of cigar smoke, the sort of guy who you'd picture at a poker table. I figured I wouldn't be seen in his wake so I walked up close behind him, peering in each door, increasingly discouraged. Every so often I'd peek out from behind him and scan for David's head.

David could so easily be the elusive Mr. Stephen Douglas Prescott. He was in his forties, and he was tall, lean, and smart enough to be a successful murderer. It would be easy for him to lighten his hair to a rich auburn color. He wouldn't have planned to kill Edie and Angie, but if they found out…if Edie remembered something about the casino and confronted him…

My step slowed as I pictured the casino that night. If Yvonne had seen him, it would explain why she had drifted away after they all came over to see me. And the murderer had very cleverly chosen the casino as the place to kill Yvonne because it was crowded. Alone in a crowd. There were so many people around at the time, who would notice if a glass of cola was poisoned? Or replaced by a doctored one.

Suddenly I rammed into a soft backside, my face buried in voluminous white jacket, my hand at an unfortunate height.

"Wahh!" he bellowed, and turned on me.

I jerked back, stumbling.

"You assaulted me," he accused. He was huge, getting huger by the moment as he loomed over me.

"My prosthetic knee buckled," I said, flapping my hand at my leg. Then I spotted David's head bobbing among the throng, coming toward me. I was in deep trouble. I glanced side to side. The door to Porcupine Pete's Casino was immediately to my right.

"I don't believe you have—"

"Sorry," I called and ducked into the casino, dodging behind a portly man intent on a slot machine.

David didn't break stride. He entered the casino and went straight to the broad stairs leading to the second floor. He took them two at a time, passing an elderly woman so fast she teetered and nearly fell. He raced on by without looking to see if she was all right.

I climbed the stairs far enough behind him that he wouldn't immediately see me. At the top of the stairs I caught sight of him barely twenty feet away.

He stopped abruptly and turned, scanning the crowd.

I threw myself against a slot machine and draped myself across a stool. Unfortunately, someone was already sitting on it.

"What the hell!" The voice came from a tiny old woman with an umbrella cane and a plastic bowl full of nickels.

"Please, I just needed to—"

"This is my slot machine, go find your own." She jabbed at my foot with her cane.

I jumped back. "I don't want your slot machine. I just need to use the stool."

"Not here, you don't. This is my stool. You go find your own." She jabbed fiercely at my shin, her scrawny arm pumping up and down. "There are places for people like you! You get away from my machine and my stool. I'll call the bouncer if you don't get away from me." She jabbed me straight on the shin.

Pain swept through my leg, and tears sprang to my eyes. I grabbed hold of her cane to keep her from hitting me again. A hand clamped down on my right shoulder.

It was David.

His face was pale, his brows a dark line covering his eyes. "What are you trying to do?"

My tongue was glued to the roof of my mouth. I stared at his fingers digging holes in my arm. The pain finally loosened my tongue. "Let go of me."

"Answer me." Then he shook my arm hard and thrust his face close to mine. "What do you think you're doing?"

I yanked my arm away from him, his fingers leaving trenches of pain. "And just where are you going, David?"

"You don't get it, do you?" He reared back, glaring at me.

"What is it that I don't get, David?"

He didn't answer. His gaze swept the room. He looked like he was calculating the odds of getting away with killing me in front of everyone. I didn't suggest it, for fear he'd act on it.

The old woman who had been so fierce moved to my side. "You get out of here," she said and jabbed at David's shin.

He glanced at her, then looked back at me, his eyes narrow and mean. "You leave me alone, or you'll be sorry."

He stalked off, weaving between the gamblers to a door in the far wall. He knocked, spoke to the heavyset man answering the door, and entered. The door slammed behind him.

"Hey, thanks," I said, turning to the woman.

She glared at me. "I didn't do it for you. Fighting's a jinx...and this is the last of my pension check. Now go away."

"You're putting your pension into that machine?"

"This is my machine. Get away."

I touched the machine. It was cold and hard. I touched the machine next to it. It felt warm, encouraging. "Try this one. It's going to pay off."

She sniffed, shoved five nickels into her machine, and pulled the handle. Nothing. She glared again at me. I pointed at the warm machine.

Reluctantly she put five nickels into it, pulled the arm, and watched the figures spin. The wheels clunked to a stop, cherries all in a row. Nickels poured into the trough.

I was halfway across the room when I heard my name called. It was Jason. His normally happy brows were drawn into a tight, angry line across his face. "Have you lost your mind? He was threatening you."

"If you heard all that, why didn't you intervene?"

"You were holding your own. What do you think you're doing?"

"I'm following David because I think he knows where Edie is. And you're screwing it up. Now move!"

"David? Why David?"

"He fits the description of Yvonne's stepfather. Yvonne

acted afraid of him when she saw him in the casino. And he has a scar on his forearm.''

He looked as if he was going to say something, but just then he glanced over his shoulder and tensed. ''He's coming.''

I drew back, hoping to melt into the wallpaper.

Jason moved in close and put a hand on either side of my head, neatly hiding my face from the advancing David. He ducked his head toward me. ''Look at me,'' he said, then pressed his lips against mine.

No one saw my face. It was the longest, hottest kiss I could remember. Of course it had been so long since I'd been kissed I didn't have much to compare. When I looked again, David had opened a door on the far side of the room and was entering it.

Intimacy definitely wasn't in my plans for now. I wiggled to get away from him. It probably wasn't the best idea. He misunderstood and kissed me again. Of course I protested.

''What are you—'' I was a little out of breath.

''Just hiding you from him, that's all.''

''That's all?''

''Of course.''

''Could have fooled me.''

He grinned. ''I did fool you.''

''Take your hands away.''

''He's coming again.'' Jason leaned in.

''He is not. You're not taking this seriously.''

''I've been taking this seriously from the start. You're the one who's avoiding things.''

''This is the stupidest conversation I've ever had.''

''I doubt it. I met Rick. Remember Rick the Ick? Your old flame?''

There are times when I'm elegant. This was not one of them. ''You arrogant, sneaking... What are you doing rooting in my past? Of all the tiny-minded...''

''Don't you want to know where I met him?''

''No.''

Across the room David emerged, followed by Meredith. I used Jason as a shield.

David and Meredith were followed by a tall, handsome god who could have featured in *Muscle Magazine.* My eyes caught on leather pants stretched across his flat belly. Then on the lean, sleeveless leather shirt, not buttoned but laced with a thong, no less. Then I traced the biceps, the triceps...exceptional ceps.

"Blink, dammit, your eyes are going to dry out."

"I'm blinded by his steroids. He's beautiful," I said. "Exactly the sort of man Meredith always finds...a little on the too-good-to-be-true side."

"He's sleazy. God knows how dangerous, Stella."

"Is *this* the guy Meredith was with last night? I don't remember him."

"The same."

We watched the little procession pause at a slot machine, then Meredith ran a hand up the god's bronze arm muscles. We couldn't hear what she said, but the god leaned over, kissed the top of her head, and watched her stroll away. Jason started to follow her, but I put out a restraining hand.

"Wait. Let's see what happens next."

As soon as Meredith was out of sight, Pecs turned to David and said something we couldn't hear, stared hard into his eyes, then clapped him on the shoulder.

David stood rigidly to one side, his cheekbones suddenly outlined by a dull flush as though he'd been slapped.

"I think I'll check out this muscle man's record," Jason said, slowly. "He looks a little slick, if you ask me."

JASON AND I FOLLOWED David when he left, but lost him in the surge of people at the foot of the stairs. Jason agreed to go to the inn to watch for him; I planned to skulk through the streets, looking for David and avoiding the man in the white jacket.

It was eight-thirty, and as I passed the Opera House people poured out into the cool night air for intermission. My luck—I saw Amy and Bill immediately. Worse luck—they saw me. She yoohooed at me, flapping her left hand. It was no mistake that it was her ring-finger hand.

"Stella! Mrs. Johnson heard from Edie! She says she's fine."

Relief rolled over me like a tidal wave. "When did she call?"

"Around six. She says she's fine."

"That's wonderful," I breathed, and I meant it. "Where did she call from?"

"She didn't say."

The feeling of dread returned. "Hey, you're missing the best opera," Amy warbled. "I just love it. Opera always makes me feel so special. My father always made me feel special, too. He used to call me his princess. Just like Bill. Too bad Bill had such a stomachache. He had to leave for a while."

"It's that hemlock salad, no doubt."

"Hemlock? Oh, I don't think so. Oh, you're making a joke, aren't you?"

With Amy, there's less there than meets the eye.

I went on toward the inn. I dawdled, smelling the alpine city scents, pine and auto exhaust, delaying the time when I climbed the shortcut stairs. The unevenness of the steps, the awkward height, the slippery pine needles, made me uneasy. Along with an increasing sense of gloom.

Halfway up I peered over the side of the steps at the twenty-foot drop to the cement storage patios of the houses that stand on either side of the steps. The pine branches in the night breeze cast unusual, elongated shadows that shifted in the moonlight like a kaleidoscope.

I climbed slowly, wondering if Jason had found David, my hand sliding along the railing, lightly scraping on the rusty chill of the iron. I was near the top of the steps when the shadows flickered in the strengthening breeze and my toe caught on the uneven stone step.

I fell forward. My left hand flew out and broke the fall, sliding painfully on pine needles and rough stone. My shin cracked down on the edge of a step.

I rubbed my shin, hauled myself up, and brushed my stinging palm where a pine needle stuck painfully. I peered ever so casually around to see if this had been embarrassingly witnessed. I didn't see anyone.

Then the shadows shifted again, and I caught a flash of something on the ground. I bent down to see it better. It was a sequin leaf, like the ones on Edie's top.

"Oh, Lord." The decoration slipped from my fingers.

I opened my mouth to call out when a light flicked on in the house below. I had to look.

Faint rays illuminated the storage patio and the outlines of a body in the far, dark corner.

TWENTY

FOR A LONG MOMENT I could only hang over the railing, my breath and heartbeat suspended. I couldn't seem to call out, to mobilize, or anything. Vague, happy sounds of people chattering, the casinos' jangle, a barking dog, floated into my consciousness from some other place.

A white-tennis-shoe-clad foot projected awkwardly. I knew the body was Edie's.

But only moments before, a smiling Amy had said Edie had called two and a half hours ago. And I had sensed Edie was in danger, even sensed on some level that she might be dead, but I hadn't wanted to believe it.

Suddenly I thought, what if she's still alive? Or it's one of my visions? Was I truly seeing a body, and was it really Edie?

Disbelief set in. I'd seen it before in others, but never experienced it myself—initial acceptance, then disbelief. I had to make sure that what I saw was really there. I've learned to double-check.

I raced down the steps to the narrow walkway leading between the steps and the house. A terrible chill filled the pine-scented air and left me feeling hollow inside. I tiptoed to the shadowed corner.

It was a real body. The tennies had one blue and one orange lace. It was Edie.

My eyes filled with tears of loss, anger, and frustration. If I'd done something more or sooner Edie might still be alive.

I knelt and touched her hand for a temperature, her wrist for a pulse or a thready beat, anything that would tell me she was miraculously alive. She was cool and had that awful, too-solid feeling of death.

A sweet-pungent smell filled my nose, an alcohol odor. A soaked brown paper bag lay the other side of her. The killer's first big mistake. Edie didn't drink, not a drop.

I looked up to the top of the steps where she must have fallen over. It didn't seem far enough to kill for certain. I asked Edie's pardon and gingerly felt her head, then the base of her neck. I thought I felt a small wound and a crust of blood.

A spotlight flashed on, illuminating the tiny patio. I heard the door to the house open. A light footstep, a clang of metal, and a shriek.

"Oh, my God." A woman wearing the uniform of a cocktail waitress framed in the light of her back door, advanced slowly, then stopped. "Oh, my God. Oh, my God. Did you...?" The woman's mouth opened to scream.

"No, I didn't," I protested inanely. "You've got to understand."

She stumbled backward, on the verge of hysteria. I knew if I so much as took a step toward her, she might panic. I shouted to her, "Call an ambulance."

"Ambulance? Is she still alive?"

"Hurry! And call the police, too." That mobilized her.

JASON GOT THERE before either the police or the ambulance, and he was much more comfort to that woman than I could be.

"I just got home...," she said, wringing Jason's hand "—not feeling well. And I heard this noise in the back and opened the door and there she was!"

"I didn't hurt her," I protested. Every time I made a gesture toward her, she'd inch toward Jason, so I gave up and went back outside to sit beside Edie. I snagged a handful of paper towels from her kitchen counter on the way out and sat snuffling into them until Samson arrived.

I knew it would be ugly. I was again at the death scene. But I had no idea how bad it would be. I had run nervously through several scenarios, trying them out for pitiful content, before I actually heard Samson's approach. If he had been alone I'm sure I'd have done fine.

He arrived with a quiet competence that was far more frightening than if he'd been blustering and threatening. As soon as he saw me, his jaw muscles worked. "I'll talk to you in a minute. Stay over there, be quiet, and don't mess with anything."

He was joined by the large, cigar-chewing man zipping his white jacket. "Gawd dammit Samson, this young gal in a wild purple shirt was goosin' me, right in the damn main street."

I shrank into the shadows, such as they are at nine o'clock, and that's not much. Samson glanced briefly my way then turned back to Edie. "What do you think, Dolan?"

I dug in my purse for a rubber band to bunch up my hair. Maybe Dolan wouldn't recognize me. Using slow movements that wouldn't attract attention, I pulled my hair up on top and wound it into a knot.

Dolan stooped over Edie's body, feeling her wrist and neck, just as I had. He bent her fingers, then straightened up, with a little backward overstretch, as though his back was sore.

Then he cleared his throat. He still hadn't seen me. "Rigor is just beginning to set in, probably been dead a couple hours, probably four." He rocked back on his heels, sucking his teeth, his fingers jammed into his jeans pockets.

He craned his neck to see the railing above better. "Not much of a drop. Neck's broken, judging from the angle and the way she's lying. Probably had too much to drink, missed her step, and just fell over that railing. Things like that can happen," he said, and looked to Samson for confirmation.

Of course. The killer had counted on that kind of simplistic thinking. But, surely Samson would see beyond it.

Samson pulled a roll of yellow police crime scene tape out of a pack, began roping off the steps, squinting at them, trying to reconstruct her death, considering possibilities.

Dolan ran a hand through his hair. "So, Samson, you want me to sign off on this?"

Samson was slow to answer and continued roping off the area.

I couldn't keep my mouth shut. "Edie was proud of being dry for three years. She had a nearly photographic memory. And she was supposed to meet Angie Sayers." I figured they would soon discover the wound at the base of her neck, and if I mentioned it Samson would hold me for hours.

"I know you," Dolan roared. "You're the one in the street. I was telling you, Samson. She assaulted me."

"I did not. He can only hope..."

Samson glared at me, his jaw grinding. "You be quiet. I said I'd deal with you later." He turned to Dolan. "Check her for another injury."

Dolan knelt beside her. This time he found it. "Damn. There's something here at the base of her skull. Looks like a puncture, maybe by an ice pick or a knife or something."

Samson turned to me, eloquent in his silent and suspicious gaze. I knew that if I got into it with Samson, he'd probably decide I was the one who killed her, but I had to speak up. "Edie's not a small woman, Sheriff, but the railing isn't standard height either. It wouldn't be too hard to push her over. The killer comes down and stabs her, to make sure she's dead, and plants the bottle thinking a cursory exam might not find the other injury. If nothing else, it gains time."

"In plain daylight?"

"Not as visible as you think. How many people watch anyone climbing stairs? You can't see from above. And from below, the pine branches get in the way. If it was dinnertime, everyone would be inside eating or gambling. Not outside staring at the steps."

Samson finished tying off the top of the shortcut stairs and went to Edie, squatting at her side. He flashed a tiny, powerful penlight at her neck, the front and then the back. He grunted and rose, pocketing the flashlight.

Samson squinted at Dolan. "Looks like someone slipped something into the base of her brain." He sounded extra-polite, and his jaw had the especially stubborn look that some people get when they're irritated. "Dolan, don't sign any certificates yet, till you hear from me. And watch for the rest of the crew while I talk to her."

He nodded at me when he said "her" and made the word sound like the Black Death.

Dolan nodded and walked away stiffly, like he'd swallowed a yard of straight iron rod.

Samson pulled a pad from his breast pocket. He spoke with icy deliberation. "Why is it you're always finding the body?"

He waited for me to answer, his eyes little slits of suspicion. The expression didn't go well with his Marlboro good looks. "You refusing to answer?"

"No, not at all," I assured him. "Yvonne was next to me when she died because she was afraid of someone there in the casino and she thought I could help her. Edie, well, I just happened to find her. By chance. I tripped up there on the step and when I tripped, I saw a glint of light from the sequins on the leaf from her blouse."

"I don't see how you saw all that from way up there."

"I found the sequins when I fell. Then I just looked over the edge and saw her."

"Damn good eyesight, if you ask me." He looked at me suspiciously.

He made me go over it three more times, using different questions, asking me to expand each time on what I'd said.

"That's all I know."

"Tell me about the telephone call again."

"Amy told me Mrs. Johnson got the call two hours ago. You can ask her."

"I will."

I felt a hand on my shoulder, long fingers gripping so hard they pinched my collarbone. It was Jason. "Stella, I think you should get back to the inn. Come on, I'll walk you there."

Sheriff Samson considered it, then dismissed me. "Don't plan to leave town in the near future."

Jason took my elbow like I was suddenly ninety-eight years old. "Jason, let go. You make me feel ancient. Besides, you want to stay here, I can tell."

"It'll only take a minute. I'll come back once you're safe in your room."

"Safe? My room? It's Grand Central Station." I didn't want to be there at all tonight, not alone. And that made me think of Angie, who was all alone somewhere waiting for Edie. I knew exactly what to do next.

I needed to see the faces of the group when they heard that Edie was dead. And then I had to find Angie, as fast as possible.

When we got to the inn a few minutes later at quarter to ten, Amy and Bill were in the parlor. Amy latched onto me as soon as I entered the room. "Where are David and Jeena?" I asked.

"Oh, in the kitchen making snacks. Jeena was hungry," Amy replied, and waved in the direction of the kitchen. "They'll be in here in a minute."

"I thought they weren't speaking."

"They got over it."

I felt a movement behind me. The back of my neck felt vulnerable and exposed. I backed up, sheltering myself against Jason. I was reasonably sure I could trust him not to kill me, and I wasn't at all sure about the others. I caught sight of David easing into the room. Jeena was right behind him. I waited for them to get all the way in so I could see them, too.

"When was the last time you saw Edie?"

They looked puzzled. All agreed they'd seen her late Friday afternoon. David glowered. "She told me she was going to run into Denver this morning. But the last time I saw her was yesterday."

"Are you worried about Edie?" Bill asked and wrapped a protective arm around Amy. There was a perturbed wrinkle across his forehead. Beams from the lamp behind him shone through his hair, highlighting it like a halo around his face and slanting across Amy's cheekbones. Her eyes were deep, hidden in the shadow. I wanted to be able to see into them, see what she knew and how she knew it. The room was absolutely still.

"Did you come home by way of the steps?" I asked.

"Oh, no. We walked up by the road," Jeena answered.

"Then you missed Edie."

David's face clouded in question, uncomprehending. I glanced at Amy, then Bill. Both faces puzzled, innocent. I looked around for Jeena and felt the hairs on my arms rise.

Jeena was leaning against the doorjamb, her arms folded across her chest so I could see a long scratch on her forearm that I hadn't noticed before. She was smiling.

TWENTY-ONE

"EDIE'S DEAD."

The front parlor, with its refined Victoriana velvet, warm and solid, with a soft golden glow of lighting, was suddenly like the lining of a coffin, too plush and cushy.

Laughter died on Amy's lips.

Jeena's bizarre smile crumpled, and she slumped against the oak doorjamb, her eyes glazed. For a moment the only sound came from the grandfather clock in the hallway...life seconds ticking away.

"No, no. That can't be," Jeena whispered. Then she turned and buried her head in David's chest, her arms encircling him.

I couldn't tell whether she was seeking comfort from David or hiding her eyes from me. I glanced at each one in the room and wondered which was faking, which of us had lured Edie to the railing and shoved her over.

David's arms hung empty at his sides, unresponsive, his expression bleak, angry. "How did she die?" His words hung in the air.

I answered carefully, deciding to withhold the knife wound. "She fell, or was pushed, over the railing of the steps to the lower street."

Tense, his hands clenched, he seemed genuinely shocked. "She was solid as a rock and athletic. She'd never fall. You're saying she was—" he hesitated, groping for words "—killed. Murdered. Right?"

Amy whimpered, breaking the tension.

David glared at her. "Look at you, pretending to be grief-stricken. Where were you? You never liked her. You were jealous of her." He tried to take a step toward Amy, but Jeena's clinging arms hindered him.

"I wasn't jealous of her," Amy whispered.

I wondered why Amy would be jealous of Edie. Surely David hadn't had a fling with Amy, too. How could anyone as arrogant as David have so much success with women? Then it occurred to me. Arrogance can look a whole lot like strength, if you view it from a one-down position.

Finally Bill spoke up, his voice mellow and instantly calming. "David, all of us feel terrible. This whole thing is awful. But we mustn't jump to conclusions. Those stairs are treacherous. Uneven, steep, and completely unsafe. Why, I tripped on them myself tonight. So let's not blame each other. We need to stand together and be there for each other. What we really need is God's strength right now."

He bowed his head. Amy bowed hers, too, but only slightly. She had her eyes open and glued on David. A tic pulsed in the corner of her eye.

God's strength was all right as far as it went, but I believed in prevention...so He could save His strength for bigger needs. Apparently so did the others. No one else bowed their heads.

"Stop it! Stop it!" Jeena blurted out. "I did it. I killed her, I'm the guilty one. She's dead because of me." Jeena threw her arms around David's neck. "I killed her for you, David. Do you understand? I love you. I love you, I love you..." Her last words dissolved into sobs.

For several seconds, David stood ramrod-still, his face masklike; then his shoulders drooped, and he gently wound one arm around Jeena.

Jason whispered into my ear that he would call the police and left the room. I continued to watch David trying to calm Jeena.

"Oh, David. She was evil. She was always taking you away from me. She wasn't true to you, she loved other men. She wasn't a nice person. Angie's not a nice person either. They're not good for you. I'm..."

It went on and on, painfully. She escalated, driven to rid herself of endless guilt, sobbing. I'd seen children do that,

sobbing ever more pitifully to gain sympathy and under-
standing, maybe to avoid punishment.

Quietly, Bill rose from the sofa, pulling an ashen-faced
Amy to her feet. "I'm going to take Amy to her room, she
doesn't feel well. Too much for her. Let me know..." He
mouthed the words "when the police come," and they
went out, unnoticed by Jeena, who continued to babble.

"Where were you this afternoon, Jeena?"

"In my room."

"I saw you coming from David's room."

"Just for five minutes."

"But David was with me, earlier. Where were you
then?"

"Sleeping in my room."

"What woke you?"

"Nothing. I don't have to talk to you." She buried her
head in David's chest.

That was when I realized that I didn't fully believe Jeena's confession. It was just too, too convenient. It fit too
nicely with her bizarre behavior in the mine. She was the
perfect scapegoat. "Jeena, tell me. How did you kill Edie?"

Jeena raised her head and turned her mascara-streaked
face to me. "She was so damn proud. She thought she
could fix anything. I hated her. And David loved her—still
does. Look at him."

"But just exactly what did you do, Jeena, to kill her?"

"I can't tell you!"

I touched Jeena's arm. It galvanized her. "This is too
much. I can't stand it another minute." She ran from the
room.

I followed her. Upstairs in her room, she threw herself
onto her bed, grabbed a pillow, and curled up, clutching it
to her chest. I put an arm around her shoulders and held
her, waiting until her crying storm passed. I was too sad
myself, and angry, to talk around the ache in my throat.

Finally, her sobs subsided. "Stella, I should never have
done it. Oh, God. She might be alive now."

"Jeena, tell me what it was that you did." I put a hand

on her shoulder, felt her shudder under my touch, then felt her grow more calm, as though she had finally come to resolution.

Her words were hesitant and muffled, spoken around little hiccups and sobs. "I betrayed her. I wrote him. Andrew. Told him Angie was with Edie. I knew he'd come get Angie. I didn't think he'd kill Edie. Just beat her, the way he beat Angie." She looked at me, her eyes brimming with tears. "So I killed her, didn't I? Just as surely as if I pulled the trigger. What'll I do now?"

In a sense, she had. Responsibility is a terrible burden. I knew, because I was living with it, too. I only hoped Jeena would have her sanity and the strength to live with it.

Jeena's mention of Angie brought up the fact that we were missing a very important piece of the puzzle here— Angie. She had known Edie long and well, she was also from Kansas, and she probably had known Jeena. The more I thought about it, the more I knew I needed to talk to Angie. And as fast as possible, before the killer found her. "How can we reach Angie?"

The lamplight emphasized Jeena's swollen eyes and tear-streaked cheeks. She shook her head.

I looked at the bedside clock. It's digital numbers glowed 10:34. "Jeena, we need to get hold of Angie. What's the telephone number?"

"There isn't one," came the muffled reply. "They don't have a phone."

"So Edie never could have called in the message!"

"Only if she stopped to call."

"Where is their cabin? You've got to tell me now. Angie will be frantic."

Jeena raised her head. Her eyelids were red and shiny, swollen. "He knows. He always loved her. Ask David."

David was still a very viable suspect. He had had time to dump Edie over the railing and return to her room, where I'd found him trying to break in. I wasn't going to rely on him to give me directions. "No. You know where it is.

You tell me. You do it. You can start doing things the right way, right now."

Jeena hiccupped, then picked up the notepad lying on the bedside stand and began writing slowly. "It's kind of a deserted drive. The roads are well maintained until the last turnoff. Then it's dirt. At night it's tricky because of the ruts. And if there's been a rain, they can be slick, so be careful. Honk three times at the top of the hill, so Angie will know it's a friend."

I picked up the phone and dialed the sheriff's office. He was still out. My luck—when I finally wanted him he wasn't around. "Look, Jeena. I'll be there and back in under two hours. If there's any delay I'll call you. I will *not* leave a message, so if anyone says they have one, don't believe them. And if you get any funny-sounding calls, check to see who all is in the inn. Got it?" I rose, not feeling as brave as I knew I needed to be. "If I don't come back, Jeena, tell Jason...all about this."

Jeena nodded, but she didn't look as though she remembered any of it. I made her repeat it, then took the keys to her car.

I FOUND A NOTE from Jason at the desk with Mrs. Johnson, who looked wan and tired beyond mere fatigue. Jason had called the sheriff's office and then gone to tell Samson in person. He ordered me to stay at the inn. Fat chance.

I wound through the streets of Silverado, people laughing, strolling, jostling each other. I saw them full of forced holiday happiness, the casino sounds sour, off-key. All canned jollity, jangling my nerves.

It took me longer to get out of Silverado than I had figured. A good runner could leave the inn at the same time I did and reach the outskirts of town before me. By the time I was finally on the road, I'd used up twenty of my sixty minutes.

Edie's cabin was on the backside of a broad ski-country mountain. Jeena had said they'd renovated an old miner's shack into a very rustic summer home. I followed the highway for about fifteen miles, going roughly west, before I saw the sign for the county road and turned off. There was one pass to drive, then down into the next valley. And along there I'd find the dirt turnoff to the cabin. Simple—according to Jeena's note.

As I drove away from the flat of the access road I saw a car with uneven headlights make the same turn behind me, driving slowly. Someone was following me. I pressed the gas pedal and felt a reassuring surge of power.

Clouds were piling up in the western half of the sky, covering its velvety black with a murky gray pall. I looked back for the other car, but it wasn't there. I relaxed.

I thought about Jeena, who was certainly strong enough to pitch Edie over the railing. And her motive? Jealousy. Fury of a woman scorned and all that. Jeena's madness, her scattered sanity, her disorganization, were characteristic of a truly impulsive person. Someone who would lash out in a flash of temper. She couldn't even decide what clothes to wear.

Cyanide doesn't grow on trees—this killer had planned. The road narrowed, and I could hear a mountain stream splashing over rocks. Twice I caught sight of reflecting animal eyes in the beams of my car, then the deer bounded away into the pines.

I slowed to take the curves more safely. At one point where the road jutted out I could see far down the mountainside. There still weren't any other headlights behind me.

I thought about the possibility of being forced off the road, the long fall, the terrible end.

And then I thought of Edie, so quickly bereft of life. What provoked it? An argument? A threat? All it took was a fall, a thrust of a knife, and life was over. It was an impulsive killing, though, not planned like Yvonne's poisoning. Something had happened to make Edie a threat to the killer.

Edie was last seen above the inn, around four Friday afternoon, going up the mountain. But she'd been killed right out in plain sight, pitched over the railing of the short-

cut steps *below* the inn on Saturday probably between five
and seven. About the time everyone at the inn was dressing
or eating dinner. She had to have been meeting someone,
or have been led there. Where had she been during that
twenty-four-hour period?

At the top of the pass, among the baby glaciers of frozen
snow and ice, I shivered from tension and cold, in spite of
the heater. Pebbly debris from the melt-off made the road
slippery and uneven. I felt the cords in my neck like rigid
roots, and I looked in my rearview mirror for signs of headlights but didn't see any. The road angled down steeply
into the next valley and the relative comfort of trees.

Icy, wet-looking patches of pavement flashed in the glare
of my headlights. On the third or fourth switchback the
grade eased slightly, and I stretched my stiff neck, glancing
quickly around and up. Lights flickered in my rearview
mirror.

I swerved briefly across the center line, then straightened.
The car was gaining rapidly...the left headlight more yellow than the right.

I scanned the roadside for a turnoff where I could hide
and let the follower pass me by. But neither side, of the
road offered shelter. One was rock wall, the other was a
drop-off. I pressed on the gas pedal gently, gaining as much
speed as I dared. The lights dropped back, fading in the
distance.

Amy didn't seem to fit anywhere in the puzzle. But that
might only be because I didn't know enough about her. I'd
ignored her most of the time, because she was clearly so
absorbed in getting married to Bill. But what if Amy
thought Edie was interested in him? She'd be furious.
Come to think of it, she'd be lethal.

Every thought I had seemed to lead inevitably back to a
tangle of relationships, love and jealousy and marriage. The
all-important issue of marriage, which for Amy and Jeena
seemed to be the equivalent of ownership, dependency, and
security. I thought of Angie and her marriage. And of Andrew Sayers, PORK, who was in love with her.

I wished I'd reached the sheriff, or at least Jason. I even considered that if Angie had chosen Andrew, maybe she liked that relationship...any number of rationalizations for why I shouldn't go find her. But in the end, I knew I couldn't wait. She had to be found before there was yet another killing.

Descent was rapid, the grade much steeper on this side of the pass than on the other. In minutes I was swaying rhythmically back and forth, taking the hairpin curves in a pattern of left, right, left, right. The car behind me followed steadily, neither gaining nor losing distance.

Once it seemed to swerve dangerously close to the edge above me, but straightened out and proceeded cautiously. I wondered if the driver had been drinking or, just as bad, had fallen asleep with the rhythm of driving the pass.

Or if he'd been checking on me.

At the bottom of the pass the road straightened out, running along the valley floor beside and slightly above a stream that crashed over a boulder-strewn bed. I rolled down my window, smelled rain in the air, and realized I could no longer see any stars.

Lightning streaked across the sky, lighting up the valley in a flash of eerie blue-black and white. The road ahead was a narrow ribbon, winding between lodgepole pines and the stream. A fat raindrop splashed on my windshield.

My fingers were cold on the steering wheel, and I rolled up the window and turned up the heater. This was a narrow valley with steep canyon walls, which would give little or no purchase to climb away from a flash flood. Another raindrop, then another, and another, smacked against the windshield.

I strained my eyes looking for the turnoff. I found it just beyond the opening of the narrow canyon. A barely visible track left the road. I bounced over rocks, scraping the bottom of the car against unseen boulders. It was a track made for four-wheelers and Jeeps. But, I reminded myself, Edie didn't have either of those vehicles. If she could make it, so could I. Logically I knew that. Emotionally, I felt my knees shake and my neck muscles tense with the effort of keeping the car on the trail.

I bumped over a large rock, came to the top of a little hill, and started down the other side. I honked three times for Angie. I had to be close to the cabin, so I decided to honk at every rise, just to make sure I got the right one. I glanced in the rearview mirror. Rain dotted the rear window, streaking it.

Suddenly the steering wheel wrenched to the right, jerking out of my hands. The car whacked rock and slid, then crunched to a stop. I'd hit a rut.

I checked for following headlights; they weren't there. That was good, wasn't it?

I shifted into reverse and pressed the gas pedal. The engine whined. The car didn't move. I pressed harder. Nothing. I twisted the steering wheel, felt the car shift slightly.

The rain seemed to let up, but suddenly I felt uneasy deep inside, like this could get really ugly.

I gunned the engine, let up, and gunned it again. The car rocked slightly. I gunned it again. The undercarriage scraped. Howled. Hesitated. Then rocked backward, slowly backing up to the edge of the hole. At the brink it hovered, teetered briefly, then lurched out and back. I braked. The car shuddered to a stop and stalled.

I put my head on the steering wheel and breathed deeply. I pried my fingers off the wheel, wiped my damp palms on my shirt, and checked the rearview mirror, almost automatically now. Nothing. At least I wasn't being followed.

I drew another breath and started the engine, heard the motor catch and purr, and eased the car forward, avoiding the rut, and around a bend in the road.

Lightning lit the sky. Ahead fifty yards on the uphill side of the road amid overhanging pines, I saw the outlines of a cabin. No glow shone from windows, no warm beams welcomed me. It looked completely deserted.

It was just as deserted-looking when I rolled past it. The rain started again; this time the raindrops came rapid-fire, no hesitant sprinkle. My windshield was streaked with rain.

Was this the place?

Then I saw the sliver of light in the side window. Someone was peering out.

I was on the far side of the cabin. If it hadn't been for the wind picking up and blowing the branches of the overhanging pine, I don't think I would have seen the car, it was so well hidden. But there it was, the gleam of metal. I checked the rearview. Nothing. The rain began to fall in a steady stream.

I pulled in, killed the engine, and buttoned my blouse up to my chin for warmth. Outside, the rain soaked me instantly. I started for the cabin porch, glancing at the other car. It looked vaguely familiar.

I bent and peered into the front passenger seat. A diet soda can and a crumpled candy bar wrapper lay on the floor.

My scalp prickled and shrank. I circled to the back of the car. It bore a Kansas license tag and a crazy grinning cat stuck in the back window.

It was Yvonne's car.

I ran my hand briefly over the metal of the car door, to be sure that what I saw was truly there.

It was. Cold, rain-wet, and very much there.

Angie had driven Yvonne's car here. That was where Yvonne's car had gone...why we hadn't found it. True, Yvonne didn't need it anymore, and Andrew wouldn't recognize it, but how had Angie gotten the keys?

There had to be a connection between Angie and Yvonne, more than some accidental meeting because their rooms were next to each other.

I don't really believe in coincidence. In my lifetime coincidence has turned out to be purposeful 99 percent of the time. You only need to find the key. So to speak.

The wind drove the rain against my cheeks and made a chill river down my face, trickling inside the collar of my blouse. It was surprisingly noisy as it hit the car, even when it fell straight to the ground. I found myself listening to the night sounds as though my life depended upon it. Listening for footsteps, crunch of pine needles, I don't know what, just listening—but there was only the sound of falling rain, the wind in the boughs of the pines, and the smell of newly wet pine needles and dampened granite rock.

I ducked, pulled my head into my neck like a turtle, and started toward the cabin porch and the very thin streak of light that shone from beneath the curtained window. Angie must have darkened the windows to be less noticeable.

I wondered what I was going to say to her, how I would tell her that Edie was dead. In spite of the driving rain, I moved slowly, delaying the moment. My foot was poised for a step when I heard a crunch of twigs and gravel. Then I heard another crunch.

I froze, my foot still mid-air. It was dark enough to hide me, unless I moved. I stared at the scene, watching for motion of any kind. Then the biggest deerlike creature I'd ever seen moved forward beneath its huge rack of antlers. The wind whipped my hair back from my face, driving the rain into my eyes.

Slowly I replaced my foot on the ground and let out my breath. The elk lifted his head, sniffed the wind, then leaped away, crashing through the underbrush. I frowned, squinting into the darkness. He couldn't have caught my scent. I was downwind.

The shadow of a figure moved inside the cabin, came to the window, lifted the curtain, allowing a broad finger of light to pour forth. Angie must have heard the noise of the elk as well, or else she was watching for Edie.

It took me a minute or two to stop shaking. Mostly it was from cold, but some due to surprise. Maybe some from fright.

I crept forward stealthily, so I wouldn't scare the night critters, but also because my footsteps on the carpet of pine needles seemed thunderously loud. I was also afraid that Angie was crouched at the window with a rifle, ready to take me out.

"Hold it."

I stopped, midbreath, my blood roaring in my ears. "Don't move or make a noise..." I recognized the menacing, half-hoarse voice. It was Andrew Sayers.

CHRISTINE ANDREAS

I stopped, trudging my way forward in the city.

"Don't move or make a sound..." I recall that something, but honest, what I have under a layer.

TWENTY-TWO

RAIN PELTED ME, chilling my body. But none of that struck as cold a menace in my heart as the voice of Andrew Sayers.

Fear bound my chest, constricting my breathing. I shivered. "How did you...?" I couldn't finish the question, my throat closed on the words, but he knew what I was asking.

"I've been watching you since you left the Golden Eagle," he answered. "Just followed you over that damn hill, down into town, and back. Once you found Edie, all I had to do was wait. I knew you'd go for Angie. Got on the road right behind you."

"But you weren't there most of the time."

"Turned my headlights off. Now shut up." He was directly behind me, so I couldn't see him. I could only feel the continuous pressure in my back on the lower right side. I lifted my elbow away from my right side slowly, so he wouldn't notice, then turned slightly. I wanted to get a glimpse of whatever he was using to jab me.

"Now don't move, dammit," he said, and jabbed my side again. I remembered the bizarre notes he'd written at the motel. His loosely connected thoughts, his unreasoning fury. He was a dangerous man.

"Now get your ass up to that cabin. Good and quiet." He had his left hand on my left shoulder, leaving little fingerprints of pain. The rain ran in icy rivers down my face and neck. My blouse was plastered to my skin, and I was shaking with cold.

"Now nothing funny."

He used the word "now" as if it were a verbal nervous tic. I wasn't sure whether that was a good sign or bad. His hand on my shoulder kept me facing away from him. He prodded me to encourage my continued good behavior.

I moved toward the cabin, praying that another elk wouldn't pop out of the trees and startle him. Then he nudged me in the back again. It felt more and more like a gun. But it seemed so melodramatic and unreal. And unnecessary.

And if it was a gun, since I'm not faster than a speeding bullet, I wouldn't try out any of my old tae kwon do moves. I stepped up to the porch, where he squeezed my shoulder again, leaving more little round points of pain in my muscle. We were sheltered from the worst of the rain, but the cold was as bad or worse.

"I got a gun here," he croaked, and waved a stubby pistol in the air, where I could see it. It answered my question. I had no desire to find out just how accurate and lethal it was. Bullets of any kind leave very ugly scars and would definitely tear up my teddy.

"Now knock. Three times. Like you honked at the top of the hill back there. And don't do a thing to scare her. Just in case you're wondering, I don't have much to lose."

I nodded, nervous little twitches of my head, and stepped up to the door. I raised my hand and knocked, three sharp raps on the wood. The rain muffled everything, and the sound seemed to begin and end right there.

No answer.

My knuckles stung from the rough wood of the door. I glanced at him. Very little was visible in the darkness, but a sense of barely repressed fury emanated from him. My palms dampened from nervousness. I tried to dry them on my trousers, but my trousers were wet.

"Who's there?" Angie's voice was tight and nervous. I hesitated, until he bruised my side with the gun. I yelped.

"What's the matter?" Angie called out.

The gun barrel left my side. I glanced to the right, over my shoulder. His arm was arcing toward me.

I thrust my right forearm overhead to deflect the blow and lunged at him. Pain flashed through my forearm.

The gun exploded.

The bullet buried itself harmlessly in the porch roof in a shower of wood chips. My right arm was nearly useless.

I twisted. Rammed my left elbow straight into his stomach.

He grunted, stumbled back in pain. I twisted the other way. Aimed my numb right elbow into his side. It had little strength, and I hadn't put my foot behind his. He stepped back, avoiding full impact.

I dodged to the left again, but I wasn't quick enough.

He grabbed my shoulder, yanked me around. I felt his hand on my throat, squeezing. His fingers bit into my skin, pinching off air. He shook me like a dog shakes a bone. My brain rattled in my skull. Little points of light danced before me.

"Angie!" I croaked.

Vaguely, I heard a creak of hinges.

"Andrew! Don't shoot her." Angie's voice seemed a million miles away. I wondered if she meant me or some other unfortunate waif. His grip loosened, and I felt a rush of gratitude. Air burst into my lungs in a raw, stinging gasp. I collapsed against the porch wall.

My throat ached, burned, opened and closed convulsively. Someone was sobbing and gasping. I think it was me.

Angie was outlined against a red glow. Her voice came closer; soft hands tugged at my arm.

"Where's Edie?" she asked.

Andrew's voice cut in roughly, "Who gives a rat's ass! Get inside. Both of you."

I stood shakily. It wasn't a proud moment. I was just plain scared.

With Angie supporting me and Andrew prodding me with the gun, I staggered into the cabin. I had nothing to gain by getting better, so I continued to seem semiconscious. My knees shook, so it was easy to sink to the rough wood floor in a heap.

Andrew flung Angie to the bed and turned to shut the

door against the wind and rain. The grating sound of the lock sent shivers through me.

I shrank into the shadows of the far corner between the wood-burning stove and the kitchen area, where there was heat and where I could hope to find some kind of weapon. My arm throbbed, but I could still move it, so I didn't think it was broken.

The walls of the cabin were rough, unfinished logs. Edie had hung a patchwork quilt on the wall over the puffy double bed. If it weren't for the wild man waving a gun at me, it would have been the perfect rustic hangout.

A distinct odor of liquor, as in cheap, being-drunk-by-someone else alcohol, permeated the room. I spotted a partially empty bottle of Scotch on the tiny breakfast table. Unless I missed my guess, Angie had been relieving her anxiety.

Lightning flashed, and thunder cracked right behind it this time. Noisy sheets of rain hit the roof, drumming against the shingles.

I huddled closer to the stove, as close as I could without being burned. It was an old iron wood-burning stove with a griddle on top. Most importantly, it had an iron griddle lifter.

"Andrew, what do you think you're doin'?" Angie's words were slightly slurred, but her voice sounded unbelievably calm—as if she wasn't the least afraid of him, or was so out of it that she couldn't comprehend the problem. I peeked from beneath my eyelids and listened nervously, expecting disaster.

"A'drew, I'm leaving," she said.

"Over my dead body. Now shut up."

I spotted a door at the back of the cabin, on the other side of the stove, but it had a monster lock on it. The only way we were going to get out of there *was* over Andrew's dead body.

He didn't answer, but he seemed to relax when he saw the bottle on the table. He sidled over, reached for it, and took a long series of swallows. He had to have a throat of steel.

Angie tilted her head toward me and murmured in scarcely audible syllables, "What happened to Edie?"

"She's dead," Andrew said.

"Murdered," I added.

"Oh, my god," she said. Her eyes closed briefly, then opened and stared blankly at the far wall. I don't know what she saw, maybe Edie's face smiling with pride as she held up her dahlias, or maybe nothing. The news seemed to suck substance from her, and in the space of a moment she diminished, so that I knew what she would look like in old age, if she lived that long. She looked small and ineffective and remarkably passive, given what I'd heard from Jeena about how scared Angie was of Andrew.

Then I caught a glint of light from her hand.

In the folds of her hip-length granny sweater, she quietly held a knitting needle in her hand. Ready.

I shuddered.

The motion caught Andrew's attention. His head jerked up, eyes alert. He waved his gun at me. "Get over here. Both of you together."

Angie flung herself at him. She struck out viciously, the long metal needle pointed at his heart. Andrew wrenched back. The needle passed harmlessly to his side. He had moved just far enough away so she'd only scratched him. He laughed triumphantly and backhanded her across the face. The force of his blow spun her across the room. She landed next to me on the floor, her hand to her face.

"Asking for it, are you?" He leveled the gun, taunting us, aiming for first Angie, then me.

I waited. Watched. Barely drawing breath.

The barrel of the gun wavered between us. Angie cringed against me, hiding her face behind my shoulder.

He licked his lips. Wiped his mouth with his hand. The nylon cloth of his jacket rustled.

His gaze flickered nervously between Angie and me.

Each move he made became significant, and I stared as if I could save my life if I gazed at him hard enough.

Angie shook.

All I could think was, *Not yet. I'm not ready to die.*

The rain drummed. A spark snapped. Andrew frowned and gazed at the revolver as if surprised to see it in his hand. After a long moment he drew in a deep breath and pointed the gun at the ceiling. I thought I saw him flip the safety on. The tension eased.

Angie pushed her hair back from her face, and I saw his handprint, angry red stripes on her cheek. Curious, I thought, how such a powerful blow will leave just three slender parallel lines on the face—hardly any indication of the awful pain inside the head.

A tear trickled down from the corner of her eye. "I'm sorry," she whined.

"You shouldn't have left me. You're mine. Do you hear? Mine!" He was screaming by the last word and lashed out with his foot, a long roundhouse kick at Angie's head.

She jerked back, avoiding it. I eased away, moving toward the front door. Angie hung her head but kept a wary eye on him. "It won't happen again," she whimpered. "I promise."

"Damn well better not, bitch." He backed up, slumped to the bed, elbows on his knees, his gun dangling from his fingers. I eased another three inches toward the door.

"You!" he shouted. "Get back there with her." I got over there. He seemed to be thinking, planning.

"Angie, when did you leave Silverado for here?" I asked.

"Just after all of you went to the mine. Edie was supposed to meet me here."

"You knew Yvonne Talmadge in Kansas, didn't you?"

She looked at me, her eyes vacant. "No."

"How'd you get the keys to Yvonne's car?"

"She gave them to me."

I shook my head. "No, she didn't."

She scrubbed her forehead with her hand. "I took them.

Her room was right next to mine. She left them on the
dresser. She wouldn't need them anymore. Edie said it'd
be all right. It was her idea." I doubted Edie had told her
any such thing, but this was closer to the truth.

"You knew Jeena, from Kansas, didn't you?"

Angie nodded. "Yes."

I continued. "And Jeena's husband."

Angie nodded again, and her gaze flicked to where Andrew sat on the bed, listening. For whatever reason, he
didn't seem to care now that we talked to each other.

Angie sighed, then spoke in a haze of alcohol. "Jeena's
husband stroked. Died suddenly. She didn't handle it well.
Never was what you'd call strong. Her husband, Richard,
always took care of her. Through all her illnesses."

"Illnesses?"

"Well, breakdowns."

Andrew stirred. "Oh, shit, Angie. Say it out. Jeena's a
complete wingnut. Fuckin' nuts. Always has been. If it
hadn't been for Richard, she'd still be in the loony bin.
Fact, I don't know why she isn't. Hell, she couldn't make
up her mind to kill, she doesn't have a mind. She can't
grab her ass with her hand. If she weren't so crazy she'd
kill, though."

"She wouldn't kill anyone, she's just…you know…"

"You disagreeing with me, bitch?"

"No!" Angie hung her head, again keeping a wary eye
on him. "Andrew, we could just leave Stella here and go
away together."

I wasn't sure now whether Angie was trying to do me a
favor or was joining with him, a kind of captor-
identification.

The rain pelted down on the roof. Wind moaned around
the eaves. I pictured the canyon as I'd driven down it. Narrow, steep, rock-walled. I wondered how much rain had
fallen above on the mountain. The streams would be full
and furious, rushing to the valley floor.

"Andrew, the rain—it may flood. The creeks are already
swollen, this rain will make them worse. This is a narrow

canyon. We're on the valley floor. We've got to get to higher ground. Remember the Big Thompson flood of 1976? That was a summer rainstorm that dumped about seven inches of water on the mountaintop in an hour. The Big Thompson River was already swollen with snow melt runoff. A wall of water poured down the narrow canyon. Wiped out everything in minutes. This could be just like that." I raised my voice cautiously, trying to urge him to listen. Andrew faced me, eyes inscrutable, hidden in the shadow of his frown.

Angie's shoulders tensed. She was listening.

He rubbed his face. "Shut up. The river's too far away."

"Not for a flash flood," I argued, turning full force now on Angie.

"She's right, Andrew. There's a second river, behind the cabin. If that rises, we could be in big trouble."

"You lying slut. Shut up."

"But Andrew, we should get out of here," she persisted.

I had to trust that she knew better how to manipulate him. After all, she'd survived marriage to him.

"Andrew." She moved toward him on her knees, a supplicant. "Andrew, sweetie. You don't want to risk it. Not when we could get out of here. We're not going to stay here anyway. Why don't we just start out now?" She gazed into his face with an expression of slavelike devotion. It was revolting.

And very convincing.

I wondered where Angie's loyalties lay...if even she knew. Edie seemed forgotten in the moment. Angie was almost crooning to Andrew, reminding him of all the good times they used to have.

I glanced around the cabin, looking for anything that I could use if I got the chance. My gaze stopped at the old-fashioned oak coatrack. An umbrella stood in the drip pan. Yvonne's umbrella. I stared at it, then looked back at Angie. She was almost at Andrew's knees, fawning on him. She raked her hair back from her forehead, pulling it to one side, thrusting her face toward him. I gasped.

She was wearing my silver earrings.

"You stole the umbrella and my earrings. Of course! You were in Edie's room the whole morning. You could practically stroll through my room."

Angie twisted around, her eyes wide and solemn. Her hand crept to her ear.

Andrew laughed. "Yeah. You didn't know, did you? Little old Angie here is a klepto. Didn't you wonder *how* she knew Jeena? From the funny farm. They were out there together. The Bonzo sisters." He laughed again.

"I'm s-s-sorry," Angie stammered. "I didn't mean...I don't know what gets into me. You can have them all back. They were just so pretty." Her lower lip trembled. A child, caught with her hand in the cookie jar.

"The umbrella?"

"I thought it might be useful."

"And the key?"

"I needed her car to get away. I was afraid to stay any longer. I kept hearing noises in the next unit. And I knew Yvonne wouldn't be using it."

"Did Edie know it was Yvonne's car?"

"No. Edie didn't know Yvonne."

"Did you take a key out of my room, too?"

"Key? I didn't take a key from you."

"From behind the curtain?"

"I didn't think of it. I'm sorry. Don't be mad. I won't do it again, I promise."

At this rate we might not live for her to have the opportunity. "So, how did you know Edie?"

Angie's face clouded. "College. We roomed together."

Andrew hooted, slapped his knee in exaggerated glee. "Hah! Tell her about Edie and how smart she was. How she took care of you. That's why you're in such good shape now." He leaned forward, his face twisted in derision. "Look at you. You're nothing. You're worse than nothing, you don't even exist. I've got the power, and you've got the fear. That's what we're all about, baby."

Angie shrank into herself, growing smaller with each

word. She stared at the floor, one hand shielding her face from him.

Andrew laughed again. "You thought you were getting stronger when you ran to Edie, didn't you? Well, look at you. You aren't stronger. You just changed places."

I was ready to go for his throat, but he still had the gun.

Lightning and thunder split the sky. The storm was growing.

Andrew got up, irritably yanked the curtain from the window, and peered out. "Fuckin' rain."

I couldn't stand doing nothing. "Andrew, you know it's going to flood, like a flash flood. It'll be bad," I said.

He straightened up, scowling.

"If we leave now, we can get out of here before we're stuck," I urged.

"Yeah," Angie chimed in. "There's no food here."

He hesitated for a minute, then yanked open the door. Wind-driven rain splattered in on the floor. "Well, shit. Get your crap, Angie. You—" he waved the gun at me "—you're staying."

TWENTY-THREE

A LOG SNAPPED in the stove. Andrew closed the door, shutting out the sound and the smell of the storm. All we could hear was the drum of the rain on the roof.

I huddled on the floor, inching toward the kitchen counter, where I'd spotted a knife block in the shadows.

Angie had risen to her feet when Andrew decided to go; now she stood indecisively in the middle of the cabin, looking first at Andrew and then at me.

"We can't just leave her here, Andrew. She could drown."

"Hell we can't."

"Please, Andrew, it'd be the same as murder."

A number of thoughts, all bad, occurred to me at once. I twisted so that my right hand wasn't visible to him, reached into my pocket, and silently pulled out the keys to my car. I inched them behind me until they were under the edge of the counter, and prayed they would be hidden in the shadows.

"But you've already killed twice—haven't you, Andrew?" I said. I rose slowly, my back against the counter.

Andrew reached for the bottle of Scotch and took another long draw. I fumbled behind with my right for the knife block. It was a long shot, but worth the try.

He lowered the bottle and belched. "Hell, someone else killed that stupid bitch for me." He laughed, a long, drawn-out, nasty chortle.

"Someone you know," I said.

His eyes screwed up in his face; thinking was a chore for him. "Never saw her in my life before. 'Course, she was real careful not to say her name. One of those pansy broads who thinks she's something special." He slammed the bottle down on the table. "She came up to the motel looking for Edie and some guy. Talking so nice, her lips folded together like the air I breathe is gonna poison her."

"Wasn't Jeena?" I felt the knife block, but I couldn't reach a knife.

"Sheeit. If I'd seen Jeena I'da died laughing."

"Hell of a loss to humanity," I said. I lounged against the counter, pulling the knife block closer. It scraped on the surface.

His face stiffened, and he lurched toward me. "Get away from there. I see what you're doing. Think you can fool me, heh? Well, you can't." His hand grazed my cheek and left it stinging.

"So you haven't killed anyone?" asked Angie. Hope crossed her face. She was grasping at straws.

"Hell, no. I don't need to kill anybody—yet, thanks to the little bitch who took care of Edie." I pictured a woman, talking so nice, her lips folded together. He could be lying, and it could have been Jeena. But why would he cover for her? Then I pictured it again. Amy.

"Little? Mousy?"

"White-faced and sheeplike. Now shut up."

It occurred to me that he was having to screw up the nerve to leave me behind. For a multitude of reasons, that wasn't particularly comforting, but Angie seemed much relieved.

"Let's just take our car and go." She grabbed his elbow and tugged on him. He shook her off.

And came toward me. I felt my stomach churn.

"We gotta fix the big mouth, here."

"Leave her alone, Andrew."

He ignored her, glancing around the cabin. "Come here." He motioned to me. I didn't move.

"Come here, dammit." He pulled the gun from his jacket pocket. "Hold out your hands. Angie! Get over here. Use your scarf. Tie her wrists. Tight."

She hesitated. "Drew, she won't follow us. Leave her alone."

"Tie her, I said."

"It's my best scarf," Angie whimpered and tipped her head down apologetically. Even I wanted to smack her.

"Hell, you probably stole it. Now tie her up, dammit."

Angie made a wrinkled mess of her face, pouting, and wrapped the scarf limply around my wrists.

"Behind her back, stupid. Tie her hands behind her back."

"I'm sorry, Stella, really I am. But you know how it is—" Angie rewrapped my wrists, this time competently.

I did my best to bow my wrists so that it appeared tight, but he checked the scarf, snorted, and shoved his gun in his belt. Then he retied it, tighter. "Where's the keys to your car?"

"I dropped them. Outside." I glared at him. "When you stuck your damn gun in my back." He glared back. He didn't believe it. He patted me down. "Angie! Dump her purse out!"

"She didn't have a purse."

"It's on the porch. Not a woman alive who goes out without a purse."

"Stella, I'm sorry. Really, I am. I'm terribly sorry." She'd said "I'm sorry" so many times the words were meaningless. She retrieved the purse, wet and bedraggled, and dumped it upside down on the floor.

Coins rolled, pens clattered, and a square of chocolate with bits of crud stuck to it dropped to the floor. Several empty chocolate-bar wrappers floated out, then a small box of mint dental floss. And one set of keys. He pounced on them.

"These are house keys." He sounded surprised.

"I live in a house. Not under a rock, like some I know."

He tossed them down and snatched the dental floss, tossed it in the air, contemplating, the way a snake contemplates, with his eyelids at half-mast.

"Sit!" he ordered. I sat. He pulled the whole length of dental floss out and bound it around my ankles.

"The nice thing about dental floss is, it's strong, and if

you pull against it, it'll cut you up.'' He grinned. ''Hope you can swim.'' He picked up the knife block and the bottle of whiskey on the way out.

Their car started on the second try. Then all I heard was the rain on the roof.

HE WAS RIGHT about the dental floss. I thought I felt it break my skin on the third big yank. So I worked away at the scarf that held my wrists, without success. Finally, I inched my way over to the wall and pushed myself up until I was standing. The knife block was gone, I couldn't see any scissors, I couldn't see anything that would cut through the scarf or the floss. I sagged against the counter.

A log fell in the stove. At least the cabin was warm.

The stove!

I looked over to the back door. There should be an axe, or a hatchet... My gaze fell to the woodbox. Nothing. My heart stopped.

There was a spreading dark stain on the floor. Water was seeping in beneath the back door. I listened to the rain. It wasn't as loud overhead. It seemed to be letting up. But there was a new sound.

A roar. Of water. From behind the cabin.

I glanced back at the floor.

The water was spreading. Even soaking into the floor, and leaking down into the cracks between the floorboards, it was advancing steadily. Flooding.

I strained against the scarf, desperately pulling against the knots. It only made them tighter, and I still couldn't slip my hands out. The fire in the stove popped. My gaze fell on the stovetop.

The griddle. And the griddle lifter. It would be red-hot. I hopped, wobbling, to the stove, turned, back up to it, and felt for the lifter. I missed at first, scorching my fingertips, before I found and grabbed the handle. I took three deep breaths. Glanced at the spreading water on the floor and held the lifter tight against the scarf on my wrist. I could smell it smolder. The heat burned my skin. Still, I held it hard against my wrist, straining against it.

I felt it weaken. My skin seared. There was a nasty smell in the air. I breathed as deeply as I could. Oxygen diminishes pain, I reminded myself. And hoped that it was true.

The pain was terrific. I couldn't stand it much longer. I checked on the progress of the water. It had spread in a five-foot fan, moving toward the front door.

I counted to five, slowly. That was as long as I could do. I moved the lifter away. Put it on the stovetop. Then, twisting my wrists, I wrenched against the binding. A minuscule loosening. Then a ripping sound, and the scarf fell away.

I grabbed the lifter again, burned away the floss. The pain was nothing compared to my fear of the rising water. It was shimmering beneath the door, welling into the cabin.

I grabbed the keys from under the edge of the cabinet, grabbed Yvonne's umbrella, and pulled a jacket from a peg on the wall by the door.

Outside, the roar of the river behind the cabin was even louder, more threatening. I raced to the car.

The engine started immediately, and I backed out without turning on my headlights, but I had to use the lights to navigate the road. The ruts were full to the brim with water. I wondered if Andrew had had trouble navigating.

At the bend, where I'd slipped into a rut coming in, the rut had become a gully. I steered to the uphill side of the track, struggled to keep the wheels on the solid part of the road.

It seemed to take hours to reach the county road. When I did, I could see by the glare of my headlights that the river was seething over its banks. The water was barely ten feet from the edge of the road, rushing around and over the rocks, moving ever closer.

A wall of water could be on its way. I thought of the Big Thompson flash flood. Most of those who tried to outrun it by running before it perished.

If I turned to the valley, I'd have to find a spot where

the canyon walls were scalable, leave the car, and climb to a safe height. And I'd have to climb far and fast.

On the other hand, if I went toward the pass, I'd be driving straight toward the wall of water. Furthermore, the road passed so close to the river it might be washed out. But it was shorter, and the road climbed steep and fast and high.

It was about a half mile to the base of the pass incline. And all of the intervening road was beneath the seething water. I hesitated. Rolled down the window. There was a faint roar in the wind. I felt my heart pumping, and adrenaline hit my blood stream.

It looked like even odds.

Lightning flashed. Far down the valley road I saw the taillights of a car. They weren't moving. I turned toward the pass.

The road was barely an inch deep in water. But at forty miles an hour the car hydroplaned to the downhill side, closer to the water. The river was visibly advancing to the center line.

I drove as close to the uphill side as I could. I was at least on an incline, but not far enough from the stream to be safe.

My hands shook. I was panting. My eyes ached from straining to see. The rain fell so densely it was opaque, and the headlights reflected back, like they were shining on a black plastic shower curtain.

I pressed the accelerator, plowed through the swirl. With every rise in the road, the car surged ahead.

The windshield wipers were on fast, flapping water furiously. The rain drummed on the car roof, drowning out all other sounds. It was claustrophobic, like riding in a coffin.

The windshield fogged up. I had to roll the window down to let in fresh air, in spite of the spray of rain.

Then I felt the wheels grab pavement more solidly.

I listened out the window again. Now I heard the dull roar, but could see nothing.

I pressed the gas pedal, shot up the incline, racing for higher ground. It was too dark to see. I urged the car forward, climbing. Pressed as hard as I could on the accelerator, felt the steering wheel shudder and the car lose traction, then clutch the road again.

The roar was louder.

The flash flood.

Lightning flickered in the sky. I was up about fifty feet from the streambed and climbing. I raced. Higher, higher still. Lightning flashed almost every second; I could see the advancing blackness.

The roar was deafening.

Blackness obscured the trees along the streambed. A lodgepole pine flashed before my headlights, teetered toward the road, hung over me.

I floored the gas pedal.

The tree toppled. Branches crashed, scraped the back of the car, clawing at it, dragging it down toward the water. The car shuddered, slipped backward.

I crammed the gas pedal to the floor. "Come on—"

Then, slow motion, the last of the tree fell into the darkness, disappeared. Roots and all, ripped away.

The car was still climbing. In seeming slow motion, I kept going, upward. Away from the deadly wash.

The rain lightened. Then stopped, as suddenly as it had begun.

I continued, climbing the pass until I reached the place where the road jutted out. There I pulled to the side and parked. Lightning still lit the sky, to the east now, where the storm was centered.

I walked to the edge of the road, feeling an incredible lightness of body. I waited for a flash of lightning. Two rapid flashes lit the valley. I gazed down.

The road was gone.

The mountain bled from a terrible gash in its side into a lethal ribbon of black, swirling water that dragged it all— mud, rocks, trees like matchsticks—through the canyon. The trees tumbling in the flood wedged against those still standing and ripped them out, carrying them down, until the whole clogged, violent mass fanned out below in foaming madness.

My knees wobbled. I felt sick and giddy. But I was alive. I doubted that Andrew and Angie were.

THE REST OF THE DRIVE was a blur. At the bottom of the pass a patrol car, lights flashing, blocked the access ramp to the highway. When I pulled up and stopped, the officer ran to me, waving his arms. I rolled down the window. He stuck his head in.

"Flash food warning."

I nodded. My teeth chattered in spite of the heat going full blast. It was an effort just to say, "Road's gone."

"What's your name, miss?"

"Stella. It's *all* gone."

"You don't look so good, miss. You better come over here."

I had trouble prying my fingers loose from the steering wheel. I followed meekly. There was no fight left in me.

He put me in the backseat of his patrol car, gave me a cup of cocoa from his thermos, and thrust a blanket in my lap. Then he radioed Silverado.

The next thing that I remember was Jason leaning over me. He scowled. "What in hell were you doing? You could have been killed!"

"How did you know I was here?" I groaned; my head spun.

"I was with Samson when the call came in. You're in big trouble now. I don't know why you do these things. I don't know why you can't just stay put. I don't know why I care." Jason looked at me, just the way Caesar used to when he was trying so hard to understand me.

I laughed giddily and started to pat him on the top of his head, then found myself touching his cheek instead. "Except for the flood, Jason, I was safer with Andrew, who was threatening to shoot Angie and me, than I was at the inn—where everyone looks nice but one of them is a killer.''

He thumped the car in frustration. "Except for the flood! Andrew Sayers safer! Where the hell *is* Angie? You didn't...kill Andrew, did you?''

"Kill him? Me? Jason, who do you think I am?''

"I'm not always sure, Stel—''

"How can you say that? You don't know a thing about what I've been through. I could be dead by now. The bottom line is, I tried to tell Andrew about the flood, but he took Angie and went off down the valley trying to outrace the water.'' A tear of exhaustion leaked out onto my cheek.

"Stella, I keep trying to tell you. You're in such trouble now. I don't think I can bail you out of this one.''

"Bail? What's this 'bail' business? What're you talking about?''

"Samson. He thinks you killed Edie because you ran—''

"I didn't run—''

"—he'd be out here right now to arrest you, but I convinced him that you'd turn yourself in.''

"You shouldn't have told him that, Jason.''

"Stella, what the hell—''

"Jason, I'm not turning myself in. If he wants me, he'll have to come get me.'' I climbed from the car. "Now, it's time I got Jeena's car back to her.'' I walked as steadily as I could.

"Stella, you can't do this. I won't let you.'' He jumped between me and the car door, spread his arms wide. He didn't look like Caesar anymore. He looked like a huffing, puffing, well-intended, indignant, but very attractive male eagle, guarding his nest. Only the nest was Jeena's car. And I was too mad at him to care about anything other than getting around him and into the car.

"Jason, put your arms down. You look like the women in my fitness class when they try to strengthen their bust-lines.''

"You're not going to drive away from here.''

His arms were still up, and it looked like he was going

to wrap them around me, but not with romance in mind. I had to do something. I was not going to jail.

"Jason, I don't know how to talk to you. We barely get to a point where we can trust each other, and something comes up like this. We're talking two different languages. And the fact is, you basically believe I'll do just about anything, don't you? You must think I'd kill someone and just sit there, cool as can be, while their bodies stiffened in death. How can you think I'd sit there all meek and mild after murder?"

"You? Meek? I don't think so. Now Amy, *she's* meek."

"So you agree. Now move, I need to get in the car."

He moved. His mother had trained him well. He was out of the way before it dawned on him.

"Stella, you've done it again. You've changed the subject."

"And *you* are as good as accusing me of murder."

"I'm not! Dammit!"

"Jason, we'll just have to talk about it later. I'll see you in the morning. Now step aside...or I'll run you over."

"You already have. Dammit, Stella, you can't do this. You just can't."

"Swearing is the refuge of the weak mind. And yes, I can. Besides, I'll be safer on my own than in jail. The real murderer thinks I'm still up here in the mountains. And while you're working with Samson, see what background you can get on Amy...quiet little, smart little Amy."

TWENTY-FOUR

JASON STOOD IN THE MIDDLE of the road, flapping his arms in the air, furious with me as I drove away. I wasn't sure whether he was mad because I put him in a difficult spot with Samson or if he was just worried about me.

I hadn't slept long, but my mind was clear and active. All the way to Silverado I thought about what had happened since Thursday night.

David was my all-time favorite suspect. He fit the description of Yvonne's stepfather. He'd talked to Yvonne in the casino, had been there, bumping into people. He'd bought a drugstore in the last year, he was the right age, slender, very intelligent, and obnoxious. He had all the qualifications.

Since the coroner couldn't be completely specific about Edie's time of death, David didn't have an alibi. He could easily have lured Edie down to the steps, pitched her over, finished her with a quick knife thrust, and raced back to the inn. He had claimed he was breaking into her room because he was worried about her, but it was far more believable that he would break into her room (*after* killing her) to search for incriminating evidence. It all made complete sense that David was the killer.

Except that Andrew was convincing when he identified *Amy* as the person looking for Edie.

Amy.

So much of this terrible crime was rooted in jealousy.

Amy was so determined to marry that she wouldn't let anything stand in her way. Amy must have seen Yvonne talk to Bill in the casino. She was easily jealous enough to kill anyone threatening her marriage—an event she'd planned from childhood. She'd been thrilled to snare Bill, and her insecurity must have driven her jealousy to passion. And Amy had the intelligence to plan a murder.

She had reacted to the news of Yvonne's and Edie's deaths with pallor and seeming distress, but not surprise. Both times she left the room quickly, dragging Bill along. They were always leaving the room together, Amy pale, leaning on Bill. Using dependency as a mask for an iron will.

I thought about how Amy played bridge. She was tentative, indecisive, and played her cards with trepidation...when Bill was there to see it. Poor little Amy. But in spite of all the show of ineptitude, she'd played very well and scored highest at the end of the night. Beneath the poor-little-old-me facade lay a deliberate and skillful woman.

What I knew about Amy added up to wealthy, secretive, and smart. She was jealous, she was there at the casino, and she had the opportunity to put something in Yvonne's drink. And she had been glaringly absent on Saturday afternoon.

This sounded the same as the rationale for Jeena being the killer. The major difference was that Jeena was nuts. She was impulsive, but she couldn't carry out long-term plans; she couldn't even decide what clothing to wear.

But Amy could.

Then there was money. Amy was assumed to be wealthy, but was she? This was something Edie would have known. And Edie, with her incredible memory, must have remembered seeing something at the casino, probably the poisoning of the cola.

Bill wore expensive clothes, had a Rolex watch, and drove a Mercedes convertible. In a very tasteful, used-to-having-money way, he'd given the impression of wealth. I had known few ministers with that kind of money, but it sure enhanced his appeal, especially to a husband-hunting woman.

And finally, when it came down to it, I didn't much like Amy. She reminded me of a black widow spider. It was easier to see her as a killer than some appealing apple-dumpling type.

If I couldn't prove the murder directly, I had to prove it by elimination, and there were too many loose ends. I had to start by winding them up.

I needed to gauge the depth of Amy's jealousy and get clear details of her movements on Friday night and all day Saturday. I needed to find out what her Kansas connection was, what it was that Yvonne knew.

And finally, I needed to account for Amy having cyanide poison available.

I thought I knew the answer to that. Amy was a frequent visitor to Mexico. She could have obtained cyanide in any number of forms. Perhaps by explaining that she was an entomologist and needed to kill bugs for her collection, who knows.

It was eight a.m. on Sunday morning.

With any luck, I could tie this up in a package by evening, in time to see the Silverado Fourth of July fireworks display, famous in the area for being loud, garish, and gorgeous.

The inn was closed and slumbering when I stepped quietly out of Jeena's car. Mrs. Johnson would be up, fixing coffee and breakfast muffins. My mouth watered at the thought. I hadn't eaten since the day before, and my stomach roared with the first whiff of cinnamon baking in the oven.

Mrs. Johnson looked up apprehensively when I knocked at the screen. Her expression softened but didn't lose the worry lines beneath her smile when she recognized me. She reluctantly opened the door.

"You have a nice night at the casino, Stella?" She stepped back a cautious distance, like she might be letting in a disease.

"Depends on how you look at it," I answered. I didn't think an account of my adventures would do a thing to reassure her. "Could I get a cup of coffee and a muffin, by any chance?"

She nodded and poured me a steaming mug full. "The muffins won't be out for a few minutes."

"Mind if I sit here with you for a while?"

"Why...sure. Have a seat." She pointed to a stool across the island from where she was working, and smiled with a forlorn stretch of her lips that told me she thought she was accommodating the grim reaper. I tried to pour earthy warmth into my thanks, with little success. I decided on the earnest approach. "Mrs. Johnson, I need your help. I'm worried about the strain of Edie's death on the others. You know some of them from before, right?"

She didn't answer. She dropped her gaze to the bowl of eggs and milk, beating them furiously, thinking. Her reluctance confirmed for me that she knew something.

"It could really be important."

"This is a confidential, discreet place. I don't go telling stories on the guests. All of you have the right to privacy."

"I know. You're very careful. And completely trustworthy. All I want to know is which of this group you've met before."

"I don't know. It's...not right."

Suddenly, I realized that she might be frightened, not of me, but of being a target for the killer.

"Mrs. Johnson, if you know something, you're safer telling. If you keep it secret, it's dangerous for you." I watched her struggle with her dilemma, saw the warring factors cross her face.

She stopped beating the eggs and placed the wire whisk on the counter, droplets of milky egg dripping onto the white countertop. She looked back at me, taking my measure.

"Truly, Mrs. Johnson," I pleaded. "I *am* trying to help, not to make things worse."

She sighed. "I don't know what to think. My mind is a muddle."

"Why don't you start with who actually called to make reservations for this group. That's not confidential at all."

"That would have been Ms. Amy Wilson."

"Do you remember anything special about it?"

"Nothing."

"She'd been here before, she knew what your layout was."

Mrs. Johnson blinked rapidly, and her hands fluttered in alarm. "Well, just to look around. She hasn't stayed here."

I thought for a minute. "But Bill Orloff had."

"Well, perhaps. A time or two."

I leaned forward like a conspirator and grinned, hoping to disarm her. "Ms. Wilson was curious about who Mr. Orloff was with, maybe?"

The corners of her mouth twitched. "Oh, I say that was more than a little possibility."

"And Mr. Orloff was with someone?"

"You know," she said, her scruples forgotten. "He never was with anyone. He'd come, spend a few days, hiking up the mountain, going to the mine, gathering rocks. Just loves it here. Always so nice and complimentary. Interested in how the business was."

She paused. Her eyes had a softened, faraway look that changed just before she spoke again. Her voice lowered, and she looked warily around the room, checking for intruders. "Now that Ms. Wilson is a *case*. You won't believe it, but she accused me of trying to have an affair with Mr. Bill. Me, a respectable widow. Can you imagine that?"

Actually, I could. And it would have been a far better choice for Bill.

She shuddered. "She's a piece of work, I'll tell you."

"So what'd she actually say?"

Mrs. Johnson leaned toward me. "She was right here in this kitchen. Stood next to me. And in a low voice that no one else could possibly hear she said, 'He's mine. And I'll kill anyone who tries to take him away from me. Got it?' And then she smiled and patted my hand. And said, 'Don't ever forget.'"

Mrs. Johnson looked at the back of her hand and rubbed it, as if she could still see a stain where Amy had patted her.

"I'll tell you, Stella, I figure she meant it. My neck shivers whenever she's around. Not that I'm after Bill, not me. I figure I made it this far without my Stan, I'll make it just fine."

There was a wistfulness in her voice that betrayed her. And it certainly would have been apparent to Amy.

"Well, be careful, Mrs. Johnson. Don't let Amy think you've got any designs on old Bill." I sipped the coffee and watched hungrily as she pulled the pan of muffins from the oven. Cinnamon-apple crunch. Wonderful. I tried not to drool on the countertop.

"And Jeena. When was she here last?"

"Jeena?" Mrs. Johnson's forehead wrinkled in thought. "She's never been here before. No, the only other one who has been here overnight is Meredith. She comes for the gambling. I've only ever seen her at the casino with Anthony."

"Anthony?"

"He's one of the men at Porcupine Pete's Casino. If you ever see him, you'll remember him."

I digested this morsel of information along with a muffin. "Spectacular pecs?" A worm of worry crawled in my chest. I didn't want to hear that my friend had a gambling problem, a romance problem, or anything else. "Pecs?" I flexed my muscles.

"Amazing," she laughed. Then her face clouded. "You know, if she's a friend of yours, you might want to warn her. He's got a reputation around here for being more than just a pretty face. He has a use for the muscles..." She watched my face, to see if I got the veiled reference.

"An enforcer? Gambling debts?"

She nodded. "Not a nice guy, really."

An enforcer! Meredith was in over her head. The worry worm chewed away at my soft spot for my friend. I had even encouraged her to gamble on the way, thinking she would be safer if she focused on gambling instead of romance.

She glanced at me, and a knowing look flickered in her eyes. "I'm sorry. I shouldn't have said—"

"No. You should have. I have to sort out all this."

"Please. People's private lives are theirs to know. I shouldn't have told. You probably wouldn't know, but life can be so lonely, and a little 'interlude' can just lift... Well, let's just say it's better by far than Prozac." She busied herself with more muffin batter, spooning it into muffin cups, then sliding the pans into the oven.

"Well, I do know...about the lonely," I said, and chewed a shred of cuticle on my index finger. Too well, I thought. "And David McClintock?"

"Well," she said, and smiled ruefully. "He's been here several times, with Ms. Lorton. I'd say he cared for her a whole lot. He's like my husband used to be. Close with his feelings, doesn't say much, but you can tell. There are all those little signs that he cares."

Yeah, I thought. Like snarling at you when you play the wrong card. Things like that.

"He would touch her on the shoulder, look at her in that certain way. Stan used to do the same thing to me. I had to learn to ignore his mouth, he just couldn't be tender. It wasn't in him. I think because it was too dear to him, you know what I mean? Too threatening to him to admit any tenderness." Mrs. Johnson's voice trailed off, her eyes misted with memories. Her loneliness, almost palpable, struck a chord in me.

The door to the kitchen burst open.

Jeena stuck her head in. "Mrs. Johnson, is coffee ready? Oh, Stella!" she said as she spied me. "Thank God! I thought you'd...I heard about the flood..." Her eyes filled, and she rushed to me and hugged me. "David and I waited for hours. Oh, thank God!"

Mrs. Johnson turned to me and spoke in low tones. "You won't be telling now, will you?"

"Trust me," I answered.

JEENA AND I SLOUCHED at the long table in the dining room, Jeena sucking up the coffee like it was nectar of the gods, which it was, of course.

"I'll tell you everything, but only after *you* tell *me* everything," I said.

Her eyes looked puzzled, and wary. "What d'you mean?"

"I mean, what did Edie know about you that you didn't want her to tell?"

"I don't..." She fell silent, her face miserable, then lowered her gaze to her hands, gripping the cup so tightly that her knuckles were whitened on the tops. Her voice was nearly a whisper. "My depression."

She looked at me from dark pools in her eyes. "I have a problem. If I don't take my medication I get out of bounds." She laid her head on her folded arms on the table.

"Your husband ate the hemlock salad...and Edie knew about it."

"Edie pulled me through it. See, Edie was the one who rescued me. She was always rescuing someone. I met her through Angie. I think Yvonne had already been discharged by then."

I rose and left Jeena staring at the hairs on her forearm.

Meredith answered at my second knock, hair tousled, eyes sleepy and red-rimmed. Mascara smudged the hollows beneath her eyes, and her usually tanned face was sallow. She exclaimed over my return with labored cheer, and I told her the same thing I'd told Jeena—that I'd explain as soon as she explained. She didn't even try to bluff. Her whole body sagged like the wind had been knocked out of her.

"Come on in. I saw you at the casino last night. I knew you'd ask." She waved me to the chair by the window and threw herself onto her rumpled bed. "I don't have an explanation. What you saw there was a flattered fool.

"I started with nickel machines, then quarters. But you win big on the dollar machines. Well, you lose big there, too. But in spite of the odds, where I can lay down the cash is on blackjack. At least, that's where I can bet my life away.''

The room felt hot and stuffy to me. I wanted to open the window for some fresh air. Then Meredith shivered and drew her knees up under her chin, winding the sheet around her shoulders for warmth. I figured the chill was in her heart, but I decided not to open the window.

"It's a stupid little story, really. I gambled, bet more than I had. Borrowed, borrowed some more from the wrong people, then met Anthony. You saw him. A heart-stopper. He paid attention, he consoled, he offered to lend the money to win back what I'd lost.''

She made a dry barking noise that I decided was bitter laughter. "Stella, you won't believe this, but I thought he was really interested in me.''

"When you did find out differently?''

"Last night. I thought Anthony was a straightforward card dealer. I should be old enough to know better. But, oh, never mind.''

"So where do things stand now?''

"Well, I have a little gambling problem. I owe a whole lot more than I can pay back.''

"I never dreamed. Meredith, I'm sorry I told you to gamble instead of romance.''

"It isn't your fault. I started a couple of months ago. After that last awful bust-up.''

I looked at the misery in her face and remembered exactly how I'd suggested she stick to the slot machines. "How much do you owe, all totaled?''

"Four thousand.''

"Oh, Lord. What—?'' Then I thought about the check I'd moved from bra to bra. I pulled it out. "Here, take this. Pay off what you owe and save the rest for me. What's left will pay what I owe on rent, plus a little.''

"I couldn't, Stella. It's too much.''

"Take it.''

The phone rang before she could respond. She picked up

the receiver and held it gingerly to her ear. ''H'llo.'' She listened for a moment then handed it to me.

I expected to hear Jason's voice. ''Hello?''

It was Jeena. ''Stella. Samson is at the front desk, asking for you. I thought you might want to know.'' Her voice changed dramatically. ''Well, dear, I was calling to check on you, I'd better run.''

I tossed the phone and the check on the bed and raced out of the room, down the hall to the back stairs. I could hear heavy footsteps coming up. I took the steps two at a time, lit on the landing, and turned to bolt through the kitchen. A hand grabbed my arm.

''Gotcha!'' Samson smirked at me.

TWENTY-FIVE

SAMSON HELD ME with a no-nonsense grip, and not even the homey scent of Mrs. Johnson's muffins could keep the hallway from shrinking around me. I had a choice, according to Samson. I could go with him to the jail nicely, or in handcuffs. I chose nicely, but I still protested...nicely...all the way there.

He questioned me for nearly an hour in his office, with interruptions for updates from his dispatcher on the progress of the flood search. I'd grown used to the smell of Pine Sol and burned coffee when he finally closed the manila file, shoved it to the corner of his desk, and rubbed his eyes.

"Call Jason. He'll tell you I'm innocent and trustworthy."

"He'd say anything for you."

"That's not true."

"Huh!"

"Call Stokowski. He'll vouch for me."

"I talked to him a little bit ago. He said, 'Whatever you think, Bob, but if I were you, I'd lock her up every time. She's guilty as hell.' Now come along," he said and made a dry, crackling sound that I assumed was a laugh.

"What are the charges? I want a lawyer."

"Settle down. You're charged with obstructing justice, and you'll get a hearing, but of course it's Sunday, the Fourth of July, so it will be Tuesday before its heard. Stokowski told me you were a pain in the ass, and you'd never stop interfering. You've caused enough trouble. If you hadn't interfered, I'd have the killer in here now."

"Who?"

"I have an APB out on Andrew Sayers."

"Andrew's not the killer. Who told you about him?"

"As soon as McClintock told me about Sayers chasing after his wife, Angie, I figured he killed Edie. He'd stop at nothing to get his wife back. It's just pure dumb luck you aren't dead."

"He may have left me to fate, but he didn't kill Edie."

"He didn't, eh? Well, just who did then? Or did she stab the back of her neck and fly over the railing by herself, despondent perhaps because Angie had left?"

"No. Edie loved David. I don't know what went wrong between them, but she loved him. She was helping Angie out—like she helped everyone out. It was her role in life. Her pride. She even tried to warn me to stay out of it, but of course I thought she was threatening me. Actually, it was Amy who killed her."

"Amy? Throw a hundred-and-fifty-pound woman over the railing? Much less stick her? I don't think so."

"It wouldn't take that much if she got the right angle, I nearly fell over myself yesterday. That one-hundred-and-ten-pound puff of lavender could have levered her over. Then she could stab her easily; Edie would be unconscious." I grinned my best wolfish grin. "I'd be glad to demonstrate for you."

"Sure. And you're going to tell me Andrew is a right nice guy. You can just cool out there in jail for a while. By the time you make bond, I'll have everything straight."

"Yeah, you and the tooth fairy," I said.

It was a mistake to say that. But it felt so good...until the door banged shut, and I was left in the cell to contemplate my next move. I shuddered. Where was Jason when I really needed him?

It turned out Jason had been in the next room, working diligently on gathering more information from a nonresponsive Kansas. A couple of hours later when he came in to visit, he had an air of satisfaction about him I didn't like.

I slumped onto the slab bed. The blanket was made of steel wool and scratched my skin. I rubbed the prickles on the back of my neck. "Are there bugs in this place?"

"Not unless you brought them."

"Jason, you could get me out of here if you wanted to," I protested. "All I need is two hundred dollars bond money. Samson won't take my credit card."

"Stella, you pushed him too far. He was really mad."

"Where is he now?"

"He's tied up with the flood. They're searching for more victims. Which is where I'll be in a minute, too."

"You're going to leave me here to rot?"

"No. I'm going to leave you here to be safe. I can't think of a single place you'd be safer."

"Who'll be here?"

"The deputy."

"Jason, please lend me the money. One hundred fifty-seven. I have forty-three."

"What happened to your check?"

"I gave it to Meredith. She got in over her head with the gambling."

He whistled softly. "All of it?"

I nodded. "Nearly. But there should be plenty to repay you."

He looked at me, sorrowfully. "Stella, you're lying through your pretty teeth. Sorry."

"I am not. And I'll never forget this, Jason."

"Well, at least you'll be alive to remember."

There was nothing else to do, so I closed my eyes and slept. When I awoke, I guessed it to be early evening, my eyes were dry and scratchy, and my hair was a limp cap on my head. I rubbed my eyes, wondering what time it really was. It's so hard to tell in summer. Voices filtered through the closed door. Maybe Jason had rethought it. I tugged at my shirt and smoothed my jeans. The door swung open.

Bill stepped in.

My heart did not sing. I sank back onto my slab cot and peered at him through barely open eyelids. Fluffy looks at me like this sometimes when he's thoroughly suspicious.

Bill hustled through the door, his gaze fixed on me, the

expression on his face intently concerned. He planted himself in front of my cell. I suddenly understood what a gorilla at the zoo feels like when she's on exhibit. He had muscular fingers with fine dark hair on the backs of his hands. He gripped the bars, and I noticed his Rolex.

"Stella, this is terrible. I don't know what Samson can be thinking to lock you up in here. I just couldn't stand the thought of it, so I came along to see if I could do anything."

I rose from my pad, interested. "You're a lot more considerate than Jason."

He frowned, a guarded look in his eyes. "Jason?"

"My friend Jason. Big brown eyes, golden retriever looks—"

The puzzled look cleared from his eyes. "Oh, yeah. I saw him the other day with you. He's staying in Mrs. Johnson's back unit."

"Yeah, him. So, do you think you can spring me?" I asked. Bill looked surprised.

"Why, I suppose I can. In fact I know that I can; I just did. I didn't want you languishing in this place with who knows what kind of vermin—"

I scratched a dry patch on my elbow, wondering if I had been chewed on by those same vermin while I slept. "So, Bill, when do I get to leave?"

"Soon, I suppose," Bill said, glancing toward the door.

"I owe you two hundred bucks."

"You can pay me later. I know you're good for the money."

The sergeant came through the door, keys clanging, and opened my cell. I picked up my belongings and followed Bill out of the building.

"Hey, Bill, thanks," I said.

He smiled. "The rest of the group is going up on the mountain to watch the fireworks. If we hurry we can meet them."

"I need to stop at the casino, Bill. Why don't you go on, and I'll meet all of you up above?"

"You don't know where we'll be. I'd better wait. But hurry, Amy will begin to worry."

"Amy? Oh, sure." I stopped myself before I told him that Amy's only worry would be how to kill me without being caught. "I'll only be a minute." I darted into Porcupine Pete's Casino and ran up the stairs to the room where I'd seen Meredith and Pecs. I hoped to find him there. Or at least someone who could verify what she'd said.

I opened the door and stuck my head in. The room was empty, the air stale with cigarette smoke. It was set up for blackjack, but the table was clear—no cards, no sign of recent use.

Turning to leave, I found myself face to face with muscles and a leather shirt, conveniently open down the chest to show off his pecs and his abdominal ripple. My gaze traveled lazily up Anthony's golden, sculpted body to his face, with its cold hazel eyes.

"Can I help you find something?" he asked. He flexed his biceps and took a deep breath, as though that would send me spinning out of control. I realized he was turning his charm on me—and that he expected that it would work wonders.

"You can tell me how much Meredith owes you."

"Meredith?" His manly brow wrinkled in feigned concentration.

"Yeah, Meredith. You know, your current squeeze, the money tree, the lonely windfall."

"What's it to you?" He looked good even when he was pouting, if you like them churlish. I don't.

"Look, I'm with the Department of Health. She's been found to have hepatitis G. You heard of Typhoid Mary? That's Meredith, only she's got something worse."

He was suspicious, but listening.

"It's a very dangerous new form of hepatitis, and it depends on how long you were together whether you are in any danger."

"I never heard of this hepatitis before."

"This is a very contagious strain of the hemococcus bacillus lizardus virus. If you're in the danger zone, then you'll need to report to the health department in Denver for vaccination. Anyone who gets a vaccination quickly enough is safe. Now, how long were you with her?"

"I guess it was about—" He rolled his eyes up to some calendar he kept behind his eyelids while surreptitiously counting on his fingers. I guess he thought that if he couldn't see his fingers, I couldn't either.

"Uh, from about three to about nine. That'd be nine hours." He frowned. "No, six. Six hours."

"Sorry, pal. You're in trouble. Right in the danger period. If you want to stay alive, you need to get down to the Denver health department." I looked at my watch. "You've still got an hour and a half. If you hurry you can make it."

"You don't look like a health department person. What's that virus?" He stepped in front of me and scrutinized my face.

"It's a new strain. Very dangerous. Fatal for most people. That's why the guys call it 'Virus G' for short." I leaned in close to him and lowered my voice. "*G* stands for 'goner.'"

He frowned. "No shit."

"Yeah. It's ugly." I stepped up to him, all sympathetic, and lifted his eyelid with my thumb. "Oh, God. It's started already. Little scales right there."

I looked at him with wide eyes. "You have to go straight to the emergency room at Denver General. Tell them you have this virus. They may tell you it doesn't exist—but don't believe them. Insist that they hold you and treat you. Be sure to say that. Hold and treat. You got as much right to a hold and treat as anyone. You just tell them, you've earned your hold and treat. If you don't convince them, you'll die. Remember, *G* for Goner."

With enormous satisfaction I watched him run down the stairs.

Bill was hunched at the foot of the stairs, worriedly looking at his watch. He broke into a relieved smile when he saw me.

"Bill, was Amy with you all yesterday afternoon?"

He looked at me quizzically. "Well sure, I think so. Why?"

"I'm just trying to understand where everyone was when Edie was killed, which I figure was somewhere around six-thirty last evening."

"How do you figure that?" he asked, leading the way out of the casino.

"Well, that's based on other places where we know she went yesterday, and on Andrew Sayers."

"What an odd and persistent person you are. I can't imagine Amy hurting a fly. She's that kind of loving, gentle woman."

Loving, my ass. "Was she with you all the time?"

He slowed his pace while he thought. "Well! For heavens' sake. Amy was with me all through most of the afternoon. I went for a walk and she joined me, then we were in the inn for supper, and then we got ready for the opera. She wasn't with me for maybe an hour, but you know how long it takes to get ready for the opera, so I don't imagine she could even have had time to go out to the parking lot, much less go to the steps and argue with Edie. Besides, she's much too small to do it."

Amy wasn't too small at all, she just acted small. There's a difference, but Bill was so besotted, he wasn't hearing it.

There were two possible times. The first was when Bill went for a walk and Amy joined him, and the second was suppertime. But suppertime fit the best. Amy could have eaten quickly and excused herself to get ready for the opera. She'd been the one who had arranged the rooms, and hers was near the back stairs. She could have slipped down the back stairs, met Edie, gone behind her on the steps, shoved her against the railing, run the knife into her neck, and tipped her over the railing. Then she could have returned to the inn in time to dress for the opera, no one the wiser.

The size difference wouldn't make it impossible if Edie wasn't on guard.

We walked along the street, winding up the road past the inn.

"The others are...?" I asked. Bill was nice enough, but I didn't want to spend the whole evening alone with him, or any one of them.

"Already up above. There's a perfect meadow where we can picnic and watch the fireworks. We'll be the only ones there." He looked truly delighted, so I didn't say that I'd rather be in a leaky ship in a storm at sea.

We passed the Golden Eagle Motel and wound up the road until it ended in a cul-de-sac. Bill pointed to a footpath. "You won't believe how beautiful it is up there. All the alpine flowers are in bloom, edelweiss, Indian paintbrush, anemones, they're just glorious." He was puffing a bit.

The sun was dropping rapidly toward the mountaintop.

We climbed along the steep path, higher than I'd been before. I guessed the altitude at 10,500 feet. Scrubby-looking trees clumped in the shelter of boulders. I hadn't spotted any alpine flowers yet. Plants aren't a strong point of mine. I can usually spot Indian paintbrush, but anemones sounded like sea creatures.

"So, where is this meadow? If we go much farther, we won't be able to see the fireworks—we'll be on the other side of the mountain soon."

"Not much farther." He pointed to a fork in the path. "We take the left-hand fork."

"Is Jason up here?"

Bill shook his head. "No. He must be with Samson."

I looked over the stark, sunset-washed beauty of the tundra, searching for signs of the group. It occurred to me that anyone with a rifle and a decent telescopic sight could pick us off. I shivered, feeling terribly exposed.

He stopped and gazed around. His face was rosy with the exertion of the climb, and he was out of breath. "Where do you suppose they are?" he asked, bewildered.

"Maybe we should have taken the other fork in the trail."

His face crinkled in concern. "Amy specifically told me to come here."

Amy. Always her fine hand seemed to be manipulating us, placing us in odd, menacing places.

Bill shaded his eyes against the sun's rays slanting from the lower western sky and gazed around, searching for signs of them. His hand trembled. He seemed unusually intense.

"Are you all right, Bill?" I asked.

"Just feeling a little shaky. I think I'll rest a minute on that rock, if you don't mind." He started toward a large boulder about twenty feet away off the path.

"Do you think it's safe? There are old mine shafts around."

Bill waved off the concern. He reached the boulder and shuffled around the end of the looming rock to the other side, waving me forward. "Stella! It's beautiful. Come see it."

I trotted over to him. A bone-white timber lay half-hidden in the alpine flowers, waiting to catch a careless toe. I stepped cautiously over it, reaching to the rock for support. Just downhill was a yawning hole, a mine cave-in.

"Watch your feet there," he called. "Give me your hand."

My feet slipped out from beneath me, and I fell heavily on my hip. Pain burst through my leg. I slid feetfirst, scrabbling desperately, clutching at the dry, hard ground. Dust and pebbles grated through my fingers.

"Help! Bill!"

I plunged suddenly into a cold, dark hole.

My fingers caught a tuft of alpine plant and curled into the root system. I jerked to a stop. For a moment I hung suspended, dangling, my feet searching for a hold, my heart thudding.

"Help!" I could barely croak. My mouth was dry with fear.

"Stella! Hold on."

Clods of dirt and rock fell past me into the hole. The roots of the plant loosened.

"I'm coming," Bill shouted. I heard Bill scramble toward me, heard him puffing, felt his fingers circle my wrist, biting into it.

Then, one by one, his fingers slipped from my arm.

TWENTY-SIX

MY FEET HIT FIRST, then the rest of me smashed down. Pinpoints of light and pain burst behind my eyelids when my head smacked the rock floor.

Stunned, unable to breathe, my first thought was that I was too young to die. My second was that Fluffy wouldn't have anyone to care for him, and my third was that I was still alive. Somehow.

My eyes were dry and full of dust, but gradually they adjusted. I calmed myself and began to see through the dimness around me.

"Stella?" Bill was calling me.

A feeble groan was all that I could do in response. Finally I got enough wind to answer him. "Here."

"Where?"

"On a ledge. I must have fallen, about twenty feet. I'm on a narrow ledge, maybe two and a half feet wide. Three more chocolate bars and my butt would have been too wide." Feebly, I waved an arm to him. His head bobbed as he craned to see me.

"Move out where I can see you."

I rolled forward, still too shaky to sit or stand. The edge of the rock was a bare six inches from my face. "Any farther and I'll be doing a swan dive."

"I see you. Great! Stay put. I'll go for help."

Bill's head disappeared, and desolation descended around me like a cloak. I stared up at the sky, brighter for my despair. A large, round thing appeared on the far upper side of the shaft, teetering on the brink.

A fine shower of dirt rained down. I jerked back against the wall of the shaft. A huge rock landed deafeningly on the edge of the ledge, then bounced off and clattered on…and on. I thought I heard a distant splash at the end of the fall. Chills ran over my neck and arms. My head would now be pudding if I hadn't rolled out of the way.

"Stella, you there?"

I might have answered if my mouth hadn't been stuck shut with fear. That rock hadn't been there when I was sliding into the shaft.

"Stella, are you all right?"

I could see him peering down the shaft. I still couldn't answer. A thought resounded in my brain. If the rock had rolled down *accidentally* from above, it would have entered from the same side of the shaft as I had. But it had entered from the *far* upper lip.

"Stella, I'm going for help. Stay put. These rocks are loose, you could get hurt." Was that a concerned warning, or a threat? Bill's head disappeared.

I thought I'd throw up from fear.

So far, trusting Bill had nearly killed me. He'd grabbed my hand for support, and all of a sudden I was sliding down an abandoned mine shaft. I had called out to him, and a boulder nearly squashed my brains out. Any more help like this, and I'd be dead. Why should I expect him to bring help? Even if he tried, would he manage?

My heart was racing. A thread of light trickled in the top of the shaft, barely enough for me to see my hand in front of my face. A feeling of doom settled over me.

He didn't have to be in cahoots with Amy. He was dangerous just standing in his skin trying to be good. A former Man of God. Maybe God begged him to quit.

Dizzy, I put my cheek back on the gritty rock floor of the ledge, closed my eyes, and pressed my fingertips tightly to my eyelids to make starbursts inside my eyes…almost like July Fourth fireworks…which I wouldn't be seeing this year if things continued the way they were going.

I pressed again. It was more comforting to see the starbursts than to look into nothing. And it helped to contain the spreading panic.

Inconsequential, sad thoughts flitted through my head. I

hadn't talked to my mother before I left for Silverado, nor
had I told her how much I loved her and that I appreciated
all she had done for me. But then, I hadn't planned to die
so young.

I eased over onto my back and lay there, feeling desolate
and sorry for myself, for several moments. Tears of defeat
leaked out of my eyes and rolled down my temples.

The tears ran into my ears and made cold annoying little
pools. I got mad.

I decided that I had two choices. I could die relatively
comfortable, but undiscovered, or I could die trying to find
a way out. I decided on the latter.

The ledge I was on was perhaps thirty inches wide and
about as long as I was, plus a foot—make that roughly six
and a half feet long. I fumbled around on the ledge, found
a good-sized rock, and dropped it into the void. Listening.

This time I definitely heard a splash. Then nothing. I
tried to remember the speed at which objects fall. Thirty-
two feet per second came to mind. I found and dropped
another rock, counting "one, one thousand," etc. The rock
hit on the "two, one thou-" Maybe seventy feet, plus or
minus. I got a D in physics.

Thoughts raced through my mind. Regrets, destroyers of
confidence, ate at the ragged edges of my fading strength.

I took a deep breath.

The air at least was fresh. That gave me hope. And with
the hope came denial, that ever-useful primitive psycholog-
ical tool. "I can do it. I won't die. There's air here."

Air...there must be an air inlet. I sat up. Slowly, tenta-
tively, expecting any minute to plunge to my death. I rose
to my feet, gripping the roughness of the wall with the balls
of my fingers, much the way that Fluffy grips the side of
the cage with his tiny long toes.

I explored the wall with my fingers. It was solid before
me, to my left, and as high as I could reach above me. But
to my right, about a foot and a half over my head, I felt
what seemed to be a large man-made opening. My heart
thumped.

I felt farther along the ledge for about fifteen inches before I felt a drop-off. Rock chunks dropped, clattering against the wall of the shaft, knocking down more rock. Dizzy, I clung to the wall until I was steady again.

I felt for and found a handhold. Then, with my right foot, I felt for a foothold and found it, about two feet up…and beyond the ledge. I put my foot back on the ledge and explored for a left foothold. There wasn't one. I had to go with the right side.

Nervousness greased my hands and feet. I was afraid my feet would slip inside my shoes, not to mention on the rock face.

I tried to picture the rock climbers I'd seen in travelogues. Unfortunately, I'd always looked away at the crucial moment.

With both hands clutching the rock face, I spread-eagled and pressed on my left foot, lifting myself up with my thigh muscles.

The rock snapped. My foot slipped.

Rocks clattered into the shaft, bouncing, knocking off more rock. I slid. Plunged into the darkness. Landed on one foot on a rock outcropping. I twisted and fell backward. Flat on my back.

I saw starbursts again, gasped for air, my heart racing. Sweat chilled my body. I forced myself to take slow, shallow breaths, then deeper ones.

"Just press yourself up," I murmured to myself. My voice was faint but welcome in the silence. "Roll to your side, ease up, and sit. Don't jerk. Don't shake. That's good."

They coach the kids up the wall this way at one of the local sports stores. It definitely helps.

Slowly, painfully, I eased up.

Carefully I fumbled around, feeling my landing place. My feet must have landed on another narrow ledge, and in twisting I had fallen into a tunnel…one where the air rushed through and over me, ruffling my hair, raising goosebumps on my arms.

An air vent.

I laid my head back on my arms, breathed in gulps, and shook with frantic laughter. Some people cry with stress; I giggle. It's an unpleasant reaction, but one I can't change. And at that point I didn't give a damn, I was so glad to be alive.

When I calmed I found I was in a very narrow, dark tunnel.

I rose to my hands and knees and crawled forward, feeling the area ahead of me as I went. No timbers supported the tunnel. It was barely wide enough for a man to work in. The sharp surface wore away the skin on my knees and hands. I rose to my feet. And felt the ceiling of the tunnel.

"They must've hired very short, thin miners." It felt much better to talk to myself. "Watch your step, now. Feel with your feet. You don't want to step into thin air."

I crept by inches along the tunnel. It sloped gently in a downward direction. The tunnel was growing smaller.

Snakes! Rattlers are notorious for liking mines for homes.

"Yoohoo, get out of here, snakes. You don't want to be at this altitude. Not enough oxygen." The thought of snakes was intolerable. I convinced myself that they wouldn't be at the nine and a half thousand feet I figured I was at.

I bumped forward about ten feet, constantly veering to the left, the darkness lightening to a murky gloom. Then abruptly I rounded a corner and saw a beam of light.

The walls of the tunnel were backlit. An opening to the outside! The floor was solid, sloping up to the hole.

"I made it! I beat the grim reaper." I stepped forward and banged my head against the ceiling rock. The grim reaper is a sore loser.

I went to hands and knees, crawling. The tunnel narrowed, catching at my clothes, pressing against my head so that I had to crawl on my elbows, then finally, lie down, combat-crawling.

The hole was a bare twelve inches in diameter. A large

boulder covered most of the vent; the opening I found was the result of erosion.

I clawed at the sides of the hole, enlarged it to maybe fifteen inches. Big enough for a cat, but not big enough for me. My hands were bloody, fingernails torn. But what mattered was getting out of there.

The boulder was stuck tight. I pushed and shoved. Finally, I reached out of the hole and tried to dig away from in front of it. I managed to pull several handfuls of dirt and vegetation from in front, making a little trench, but I couldn't shift the rock.

I shouted, listened for answering voices. There were none. Not even a marmot whistled.

The sun's rays glowed amber in their last dying effort. The hole faced northwest, away from town. So nobody would be there to watch fireworks. I was alone, and soon it would be dark.

I wondered if Bill was trudging up the trail with help, if Jason and Samson had discovered I was no longer in jail and were looking for me. Then I wondered if Amy would return, maybe with a gun. How far would Bill go for Amy?

I backed up the tunnel until I could turn around, then inched my way back into the narrow vent, feetfirst. My legs are much stronger than my arms. I crammed myself in, pressing my feet against the rock until my knees were doubled up against the rock ceiling and I could go no farther.

I drew in several huge breaths to hyperventilate. Then, I pushed. With all my strength, I jammed my feet against the rock and shoved. It wobbled and settled back, but the hole looked a little larger.

I inched a fraction closer and gripped the rough rock wall. After oxygenating, I focused all my strength into my hands and feet and pushed. The rock shifted, then rolled forward into the trench.

It wasn't much, but it looked big enough for my shoulders. My hips would just have to scrape through. If nothing else, in a couple of weeks I'd lose enough weight to slide out.

I scrunched back into the tunnel, turned around, arranged my body parts so that one arm was forward, the other back, and started forward again.

This time I made it to the hole, inching my way forward until I could push my face through. My nose scraped against the rock. But what price life!

My shoulders stuck tight. I tried to ripple my body like a snake, with no success. I don't ripple very well. I twisted to my side, facing the boulder.

Then, doubling up my knees as much as I could in the confines of the vent, I shoved. My shoulder caught, scraped, my blouse tore.

I pushed through.

It was a rebirth. I giggled helplessly, half-in and half-out of the vent.

My hips were the big challenge. I regretted every chocolate bar and candy kiss I'd ever eaten. That's a whole lot of regret.

I pulled, inched, scraped, until I was wedged hopelessly. Then I started digging in front of the boulder again, widening the trench.

I found a stone and used it like a little backhoe, scraping furiously. I pressed forward. The boulder shifted minutely. I pressed again, harder. The rock of the vent cut into my hip. My jeans tore, skin stung. I just pressed harder.

And then the boulder rocked. I pushed. It rolled.

It gathered speed clattering and crashing down the steep side of the mountain. I couldn't see where it went. I didn't care.

I was out. Free. Safe. I felt like dancing, but my legs were too shaky. I sat on the ground, giggling and crying.

For a few moments all I could so was laugh and cry and marvel that I'd actually rescued myself from the mountain. Then I had to get up before my joints congealed.

There was barely another half hour of twilight, not enough to get to town at the rate I was going. But at least I'd get to a place where I'd be able to see the lights of town.

I went southward on the mountainside, angling down. A glow ahead told me that I was going in the general direction of Silverado.

The tear in my jeans flapped as I walked, but it didn't matter. I'd worn them two days in a row, they were filthy, torn and nearly off, but I was alive. Dirty, but alive.

A clump of boulders and low-growing shrubs loomed before me. I circled them and crossed a small boulder field, sending rocks clattering below. I had just moved beyond through another outcropping of rock when I found a narrow path that led downward. I had a bare fifteen minutes left before dark. The air was cold. I shivered.

A patch of white caught my attention. I hesitated, then walked over to it. It was a square of cloth, a picnic cloth, on the ground. The group! I heard a footstep and turned to the path, my heart beating wildly in my chest.

It was Amy. And she was holding a wicked-looking little black gun, pointed right at me.

TWENTY-SEVEN

THE LAST RAYS OF SUN slanted across the mountaintop, casting a flattering golden glow over Amy. If she hadn't been pointing a very lethal gun at my midriff, I'd have thought she was a lovely little afternoon bridge player. My gaze skipped around, reconnoitering, trying to find some cover or escape.

Yvonne and Edie were already dead. It was pretty hard to convince myself that I had fifty-fifty odds of coming out of this alive, but I had beaten death once by getting out of the mine, so *maybe* I could beat Amy. Already most of my aches and pains seemed to have diminished in the face of her gun.

"Amy," I said, too loudly. That was to distract her from the fact that I was easing my way back toward a huge boulder. The others should be around somewhere, unless they'd been sent to the wrong place.

"Just what was it about Yvonne that you didn't like?" I asked. I hoped she'd be less aware of my movement if she was provoked.

"She was chasing him all right! Didn't you see her with him in the casino?" Amy's mouth pursed into a tiny mess of disgust.

"You poisoned her for that?" I moved farther, gambling that she wouldn't shoot me.

"Stop moving. I didn't, *you* did. Bill told me about you. You killed Yvonne and tried to make it look as if he did it." Amy's voice was as tight as her pursed lips. But her body language was that of fear, not guilt.

The gun shook in her hand. Fear made her more dangerous. Frightened, she was more likely to shoot me than if she was in control. I had somehow to reassure her.

"Bill doesn't think I'm a killer. He got me out of jail." I watched Amy closely and eased back again, nearly tripping on a rock in the path.

The gun exploded. I felt the bullet fly by my arm. Amy cried out and staggered with the kick of the gun.

I stood absolutely still. I even tried not to breathe until she relaxed and the gun barrel drooped a fraction.

"You tried to kill him, nearly pushed him into the mine shaft, but he got out of the way and you fell in."

"Amy, I didn't." I took a slow breath. "Amy, let's start at the beginning of this thing. Why would I want to kill Yvonne? Don't you see? I don't have a motive for killing Yvonne. I never even met her before this weekend. She was a complete stranger."

"No, she wasn't. Yvonne wrote to you. You knew she was going to be here. You came here to kill her so she wouldn't tell your secret."

"And what secret is that?"

"I don't know. Bill doesn't know either, but he figured it all out and told me you'd try to kill him, since he knew you're the killer."

"Amy, if he knew I was guilty, why'd he get me out of jail?"

"Be quiet. You're just trying to trick me." She faltered, her gaze dropped, and she drew up her lips again. She had a limited array of facial expressions.

As I spoke, the pieces fell into place. "Amy, he's made this all up, don't you understand? Mrs. Johnson said that Bill had hiked all over the mountains and into the mines. He knows this countryside like the back of his hand. Bill planned the whole thing." I nearly slapped myself. "Amy! Yvonne came here to meet Bill. Don't you see? In one of her letters she said she was to meet someone here. It was Bill." I scrutinized Amy's face, as if I might suddenly be able to see how much of a participant she was in this.

"What an idiot I've been, Amy! I focused so hard on you that I never noticed Bill. He's been there, always supplying answers that pointed the guilty finger at you. And I bought it. The whole thing. As if I were some naive schoolgirl."

I felt sick. I'd been just as blinded, for different reasons, as Amy, who stood before me, gun wavering but pointing straight enough to kill, right at me.

Amy's lips were moving. I realized I hadn't heard what she'd been saying.

"—he didn't. You're the one who's making it all up. All Bill wants is for us to live in love and harmony."

Love and harmony. I nearly threw up.

"Wrong. All he wants is your money. He wants to marry you...of course. And as soon as possible, right? And did you bring up the subject of a prenuptial agreement?"

"That's none of your business," she screamed.

"Colorado is a communal property state, Amy. If you marry without a prenuptial agreement, he inherits fully when you die. Unless you've got some children hidden in a closet somewhere." I was even with the boulder now; two more steps and I could leap behind it, and maybe get away.

"You're so disgusting. And I'm not going to die."

"Amy, you haven't—?"

She nodded, a triumphant smile transforming her face.

"Have you already married him?"

The fading light caught the angles of Amy's face, and I saw her gaze shift to a spot behind me. I spun around in time to see Bill emerge from behind the boulder, blocking my way. My heart sank.

"Tell her, darling." Amy's voice was piercing, hysterical. "We were married by a justice of the peace this afternoon, weren't we? When we said we were just out for a walk. Tell her, Bill."

"Yes, we were married. Now give me the gun, you've done a wonderful job."

He crossed to her, took the weapon, and swung it menacingly in my direction. "So. You made it out." He wasn't congratulating me; he was pissed. And curious. "Just how did you do it?"

I grimaced and shrugged. It's hard to be eloquent with a killer waving a gun at you. "Found an air vent."

Oblivious, Amy beamed at him like a silly cow. I still couldn't tell whether she was in with him, or just bone-stupid.

I shifted my weight to my right foot. It ached the least, so if I could get close enough I could kick him where it would hurt the most.

"Bill, dear, where are the others?" Amy asked.

He ignored her and waved the gun at me again. "March." He pointed up the mountain.

My feet were leaden, and dread closed over my heart.

Amy frowned. "But don't you want to take her to the police?"

"No. She'd only get off. She'd wrap Samson around her little finger, and then she'd come after me. She might kill me this time."

"But Bill..." Amy's voice trailed off as she slowly planted her feet on the path in front of him.

It was totally inconsequential, but I noticed absurd little details, such as that her toes pointed in opposite directions, like a splay-footed hen. And Bill had large blue veins on the back of the hand that held the gun pointed at me. And his eyes kept checking around to make sure no one approached. I was glad that he was nervous. Maybe there was still a chance to get out of this.

"We'll just teach her a little lesson. Now come along." He jerked the gun in the direction of the mine shaft. "Walk. Fast."

"Lesson, hell! He's going to kill me, Amy," I said.

I dawdled the best I could, but it wasn't as far as it should have been. He marched us up the path past the rock outcropping to that same misbegotten mine shaft. I could feel the little hairs on my arms rising in alarm. There was no way I'd be lucky enough to land on the ledge a second time.

He wouldn't want to put bullet holes in me; it would be too suspicious if the rescue squad raised my body later. Most likely he'd knock me unconscious, then pitch me into the shaft. Afterward he'd shove Amy down that same hole and tell everyone she was to blame.

I looked to each side for something I could use as either protection or a weapon. There was nothing. Only little alpine plants, like edelweiss.

My only hope was to enlist Amy's help. It was still hard to see her as guiltless. I had to take it on faith that as much as she wanted to be married, she wasn't a murderess.

"Amy," I said. "Do you wonder why it is that the rest of the group isn't here?"

"No."

"Bill told them to go to the wrong place. He did that so they'd be out of the way."

"She's wrong, isn't she?" Amy asked.

"Of course. Now hurry. It's getting dark."

"Did you know he was once married to Yvonne's mother?" I was guessing, but I heard a little mew from Amy, so I knew she was listening.

"Yvonne knew Bill killed her mother. And she could prove it. And Bill, you wrote to her, didn't you? You arranged to meet her in the casino, planning to poison her there in the midst of all that commotion. You planned this whole weekend."

"Bill!"

"Amy. For God's sake!"

"You knew Amy would be jealous, so if anything went wrong, she would look guilty. The same way you set up Yvonne, when you killed her mother. And I fell right into it, blaming Amy...just because I didn't like her."

And, by God, I *didn't* like her. Even if she wasn't guilty,

I didn't like her, and I'd allowed that to cloud my vision entirely.

"Bill! You...? How could you...?" Amy's voice died in a whisper. She hugged herself and rubbed her arms to warm them. It wouldn't work. The kind of cold she was feeling was the soul-chilling realization that the man of her dreams was the demon of her nightmares.

"It all revolved around Yvonne, her mother, and Yvonne's inheritance, didn't it, Bill? You got her to make a will naming you the beneficiary." I moved as slowly as I could toward the shelter of the boulder.

"Shut up. Get over there." He gestured with the gun, indicating the mine shaft. I could feel the sands of time draining away. I turned to Amy.

"Amy, you're wealthy, too. And you married him. If you die, he won't even need a will naming him beneficiary."

"That's not true, is it, Bill?"

"'Course not. You're not dead. Now hurry up."

"Amy, do you wonder why Bill wanted you to come along? It's so that he can pitch you down that shaft right after me. He'll say we fought and both fell, and he couldn't prevent it. Something on that order."

"No! Tell her, Bill."

"It's not true. Now hurry."

"So how did you kill Edie, Bill? Did you play on her pride? Did you tell her how smart she was when she confronted you? What did you do, agree to go to the sheriff with her? I'll bet you went down the steps ahead of her and then turned around real quick and grabbed her ankles, and she pitched right over the rail onto her head. You used the knife to make sure she was dead."

"You're just like Edie, you know it? Think you're so smart," he said.

"Bill. She's wrong, isn't she?"

He looked at her in sheer disgust. "Of course, dear."

"Amy," I said. "For God's sake, give up the illusions." The last rays of sun sank behind the mountains. There

wasn't a stick or a heftable rock in sight. It was the bleak-
est, most barren tundra I've ever seen. And Amy was about
as much help as a loon.

The shaft opening was dead ahead. My stomach churned.
I didn't have much more time. If I couldn't get Amy's
attention I would be in an altered state soon. "This is where
he pushed me before, Amy. See the skid marks and torn
plants? That's where he'll throw us."

"Don't try anything funny," Bill said, and moved toward me.

"That's a terrible cliché. You're so trite, Bill. I always
thought you'd be more original than murder and a tired old
phrase."

"Yeah, well, death is trite but final."

"You aren't really going to kill her, are you?" Amy
asked.

He paid no attention to her. "Get over here," he ordered
me.

I tensed. I knew he planned to bash me on the head. I
had to think of something.

I put my hand to my forehead. I've never been good at
Victorian swoons, but I remembered Yvonne's seizure and
tried to imitate it. "Oh! I'm going to be sick."

I staggered, stumbling, and swayed back and forth like
a falling leaf until I could land just the right way. It hurt
all the same, and I saw those familiar stars behind my eyelids when my head hit the ground. Down, I jerked around
until I was just where I figured I had to be. I was counting
on Bill to avoid a bullet in my head...just in case my body
was brought up from the mine.

"She fainted!" Amy said, and came to my side. She
started to pat the hand I'd carefully flung out so that he'd
grab it to pull me to the hole.

"Like hell! Get out of the way." Then he kicked me in
the ribs. Hard.

But I didn't move.

"Oh shit," Bill cursed. "Here, hold the damn gun. I'll pull her to the shaft."

"You don't need to do that. She's learned her lesson. Let's just get out of here. She won't try to hurt you."

"Move, Amy, dammit."

She squeaked in surprise, and I felt his hand on my arm. His grip was surprisingly firm, his hand was large, and his fingers dug in painfully.

He started to drag me toward the opening. I rolled my head back, as though unconscious. Through my eyelashes I saw I was only two feet from the hole.

And Bill was between it and me.

"Bill, don't—" Amy said. She was standing uncertainly to the side, the gun dangling from her fingers. "Bill, I said DON'T." She raised the gun, pointing at him.

The moment I saw his gaze dart to Amy, I whipped up my knees and kicked up at his head. And caught him on the elbow. It did little damage, but surprised him.

He staggered, lost his balance, and stumbled backward toward the mine shaft.

At that very moment the first cannon shot announcing the fireworks boomed, followed by a blinding series of giant firecracker flashes.

I rose to my feet, but that's all I could do. I was paralyzed, unable to grab him or to wrench my gaze away. His arms pinwheeled in seeming slow motion, his hands grasping at the air in a vain attempt to pull himself upright.

Overhead was a display of red, white, and blue starbursts, followed by the sharp sounds of explosions.

Bill teetered on the brink of that terrible hole. His lips were twisted in a snarl, and the hatred in his eyes will stay with me for years.

Then he disappeared, just as three gold-and-silver starbursts popped overhead.

His agonized scream followed him for endless moments. The shaft was a lot deeper than I'd calculated while I was on the ledge.

Amy stood in open-mouthed horror, the gun at her feet. I started toward her, but she held up her hand to me, and her words came to me muffled by tears. "I just need to be alone. I do better that way."

Then she turned and started down the mountain.

"Stella!" It was Jason's wonderful voice behind us. I heard his feet pounding over the tundra. Then his warm, strong arms wrapped around me, turned me into his chest, and held me tight. A tremor started in my feet and rose until I was shaking head to foot.

I stood in the shelter of Jason's warm arms and heard the sound of his voice, reassuring me that it was truly all over. He seemed to understand. When my quakes finally subsided I asked Jason, "How did you know to come here?"

"Mrs. Johnson. She found her first-edition book of local mines in Bill's room, with a sweaty glass staining the cover. She was still grumbling about the pencil marks when I got there. He had left a little *a* at this point. He'd marked a *b* farther around—I guess just in case this site didn't work."

"Jason, he killed Yvonne's mother for her money. And he would have gotten away with it, if he hadn't been so greedy and tried to marry Amy."

I lifted my head from his chest. "I don't think he planned to marry Amy, at least not at first. Amy had marriage on the brain. She had decided to marry him, no matter what."

"Marriage isn't all bad, Stella."

"Stop talking while I still like you."

We stood there for a long time. Samson arrived with a deputy, both of them exhausted from searching for flood victims.

"And Angie? Andrew?" I asked.

Samson shook his head. "She made it. Climbed straight up the side of the canyon. She was damned lucky. He never made it. Found him down the valley, caught on a tree." Samson used his high-powered flashlight to see the ledge I described. It seemed to be empty, but he sent the deputy down to town for assistance. "We've got to try. He might be alive."

We all knew better.

Jason wound his arms tighter around me. "It'll be days before they can reach him at the bottom."

And that, absurdly, reminded me of a bizarre little rhyme my mother taught me as a child...

Willy fell down the elevator
    And there they found him ten days later.
    Then up and spake his Auntie Liz,
    "What a spoiled child Willy is."

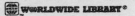

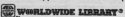

If you enjoyed the humor and mystery
of this story by

CHRISTINE T. JORGENSEN

Don't miss the opportunity to receive this previous
title starring your favorite astrologer/amateur sleuth,
STELLA THE STARGAZER.

#26231-0   A LOVE TO DIE FOR $4.99 U.S.☐ $5.99 CAN.☐

(limited quantities available)

"Stella's quirky humor, human frailties, and sudden
trances will endear her to many." —*Library Journal*

TOTAL AMOUNT	$	
POSTAGE & HANDLING	$	
($1.00 for one book, 50¢ for each additional)		
APPLICABLE TAXES*	$	_____
TOTAL PAYABLE	$	_____
(check or money order—please do not send cash)		

To order, complete this form and send it, along with a check or money order for
the total above, payable to Worldwide Mystery, to: **In the U.S.:** 3010 Walden
Avenue, P.O. Box 9077, Buffalo, NY 14269-9077; **In Canada:** P.O. Box 636,
Fort Erie, Ontario, L2A 5X3.

Name: _____

Address: _____ City: _____

State/Prov.: _____ Zip/Postal Code: _____

*New York residents remit applicable sales taxes.
 Canadian residents remit applicable GST and provincial taxes.

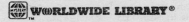
WORLDWIDE LIBRARY®   WCJBL1